T0274436

LIES ON THE SERPENT'S TONGUE

Also by Kate Pearsall

Bittersweet in the Hollow

LIES ON THE SERPENT'S TONGUE

Kate Pearsall

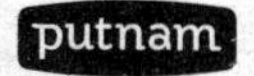

G. P. PUTNAM'S SONS

G. P. PUTNAM'S SONS
An imprint of Penguin Random House LLC
1745 Broadway, New York, New York 10019

First published in the United States of America by G. P. Putnam's Sons,
an imprint of Penguin Random House LLC, 2025

Visit us online at PenguinRandomHouse.com.

Library of Congress Cataloging-in-Publication Data
Names: Pearsall, Kate, author.
Title: Lies on the serpent's tongue / Kate Pearsall.
Description: New York: G. P. Putnam's Sons, 2025. | Series: Bittersweet in the Hollow; book 2 | Summary: "As people in the small Appalachian town of Caball Hollow begin to lose their memories, eighteen-year-old Rowan James, who has the ability to smell lies, investigates the connection between the events and a rupture in the Bone Tree, a gate to the Otherworld"—Provided by publisher.
Identifiers: LCCN 2024016271 (print) | LCCN 2024016272 (ebook)
ISBN 9780593531051 (hardcover) | ISBN 9780593531068 (epub)
Subjects: CYAC: Ability—Fiction. | Memory—Fiction. | Fantasy. | Mystery and detective stories. | LCGFT: Fantasy fiction. | Detective and mystery fiction. | Novels.
Classification: LCC PZ7.1.P4345 Li 2025 (print) | LCC PZ7.1.P4345 (ebook)
DDC [Fic]—dc23
LC record available at https://lccn.loc.gov/2024016271
LC ebook record available at https://lccn.loc.gov/2024016272

ISBN 9780593531051
1 3 5 7 9 10 8 6 4 2

Printed in the United States of America

BVG

Design by Nicole Rheingans
Text set in Perrywood MT Std

For Ellie

And for the girls with fiery tempers and tender hearts.

September

Harvest Moon

A chill in the air marks the full moon in September. As the growing season slows to dormancy, it is time to reap what we've sown. In the midst of wild abundance, do not despair. Heed the urgent stirring of our strength, a rallying cry for courage. Learn to honor the trials that sharpened us into what we are now while we mourn that which is no longer ours and all the paths we didn't choose.

In Season

Garden: arugula, beets, candy roaster and cushaw squash, cantaloupes, grapes, green beans, green tomatoes, mustard and collard greens, pears, peppers, potatoes, radishes, shelling beans, zucchini

Forage: apples, pawpaws, chicken of the woods, wood ear, witch's butter, puffball, lion's mane, milk cap, persimmons, acorns, sassafras, wild carrot, chestnuts, spiceberry, wintergreen, burdock roots, cow parsnip, hackberries, maypops, hawthorn haws, black walnuts, passionflower

Gently shake the pawpaw tree and only take what falls. Fruit plucked from the tree too early will be sour, and it won't ripen further once picked.

Sleep-Easy Tea

When sleep feels an impossible dream, combine lavender, passionflower, chamomile, and lemon balm, gathered and dried under the new moon. Pour fresh, hot water over the tea and let it steep for at least five minutes. Add honey to make it stick and sweeten dreams. Drink one to two cups before bedtime. If it's nightmares keeping you awake, find their shapes in the leaves, then wash them away and cleanse them from your mind.

—*Apollonia James, 1972*

CHAPTER ONE

THE SMELL of a lie is a potent thing, burnt around the edges and foul all the way through. Sometimes it's so strong I imagine it must singe the mouth of the teller like a hot coal. But not even that would stop them. Everybody lies, and that's the honest truth.

Some are chronic liars, almost like they've developed a taste for it, and the stench lingers like smokers' breath, a pungent reminder they're not to be trusted. Others dabble in the practice, a few choice fibs they keep around, like bits of charred meat stuck between their teeth. And then there are the ones who lie like they're doing you a favor. They fill the air with putrescence and expect you to be grateful for the experience. As if the truth could ever be more shameful than their falsehoods.

“I can’t believe I let myself get roped into this,” I mutter as Gran parks the old Bronco in front of Caball Hollow’s town hall, a squat brick box built in the 1980s generic corporate style of so many insurance agencies or orthodontic practices dotted throughout Appalachia.

“It’ll only be an hour,” Gran says. “Two tops. And you know good and well we woulda been here anyhow. At least this way we get paid for it. Now, quit your caterwauling and get a move on.”

“Caterwauling? That was barely whining,” I protest, but she isn’t wrong. The first public meeting of the town council following the sudden death of the mayor last month is likely not the best place for someone with my particular ability. And yet, there’s no way I’d miss it. When we got the call at the diner this morning asking us to cater, I’d agreed despite the late notice. If they’re going to lie about what happened, they can damn well do it to my face.

The first of the maples and poplars have already started to drop their leaves, and they crunch beneath my feet as I make my way to the tailgate, where I collect trays filled with lavender shortbread to ease conversation and squares of chess cake for softening hearts.

For as long as anyone can remember, we James women have been born with certain talents. Sorrel, my older sister, can charm bees to do her bidding, making honey with special properties that enhance any spell. Linden, younger than me by only eleven months, can taste the emotions of others. And my youngest sister, Juniper, sees beyond this world to the next. Yet, since our earliest ancestor, Caorunn James, first stepped out of the Forest and into Caball Hollow more than two hundred years ago, those gifts have meant we've been treated with an air of suspicion, if not downright contempt, by our neighbors. Even when we use them for their benefit, like Gran's healing tinctures. Or the baked goods Linden made for this very meeting. Which is more than I would have done after what this town put her through.

When I reach the wide, heavy door, I press my back against it while balancing the trays in my arms and nearly plow into council member Gayle Anne Gerlach. She casts me an annoyed glance, then puts a perfectly manicured hand on the shoulder of a tired-looking woman I'm pretty sure is the town clerk, leading her away to continue their conversation with a saccharine smile.

My eye catches on the black-and-white photograph of the original town hall, prominently displayed in the fluorescent-lit lobby. The ornate, neoclassical structure was struck by lightning and burned down decades ago, its image a sharp contrast to the yellowed walls and generic industrial carpet of the current building. The only room with any ounce of grandeur now is also the only one filmed by the local public access station—the city council meeting room, with its raised dais for the council members, dark wood-paneled walls, and the large gold medallion with the Caball Hollow town crest, front and center, behind the empty chair reserved for the mayor.

One of the staffers points me to a folding table at the back of the space, and by the time Gran and I have finished laying out the refreshments, the room is thick with too many bodies and too little circulation. The smell of strong coffee wafting from the carafe next to me isn't enough to cover the stench in the air as the council members scramble to impress voters ahead of the election in a couple months. Even local politicians are prone to stretch the truth with empty promises.

Okey Spurgeon, president of the town council, ends a call on his cell phone and steps up to the seat on the dais behind his nameplate before attempting to quiet the crowd and call the meeting to order. Gran eyes me from the other side of the table when I drop down into one of the last remaining chairs. But she holds her tongue for once as I lean forward, propping my elbows against my knees to cover my nose without drawing attention. Not that it helps. I've always been able to sniff out a lie, even when I'd rather not. Beulah Fordham Hayes from the school board cuts me an irritated look anyway, her steely gaze matching the steel-gray hair that ripples in reproach as she turns away.

"All right, y'all, let's get down to our first order of business," Okey begins. His perpetually rosy cheeks are extra sanguine this evening. It's standing room only now. Big entertainment for a small town. "And the reason I'm sure most of you are here. We're only a couple weeks into ginseng season, and already we have some grave concerns.

Preliminary evidence shows the recent car accident near the National Forest that killed one young man may have been related to ginseng poaching."

"Ginseng numbers are dropping every year, and the National Forests in North Carolina and Tennessee aren't allowing any harvesting, which means the licensed dealers are paying more per pound than ever as they struggle to fill orders from their international buyers," Gayle Anne Gerlach chimes in from his right. "It's driving an unsavory crowd straight into Caball Hollow."

"There ain't much ginseng here no more, neither," Hillard Been mutters in that old-man way that means the whole room hears it.

"It sure is getting smaller and harder to find," someone on the other side of the room agrees. "Large root, old 'sang is a thing of the past."

Okey looks annoyed as he brushes a hand over his receding hairline, but ignores the interruption. "As I was saying, in light of recent events, we've asked a representative from the Forest Service to come and address the issue of how we can work together to keep our community safe during ginseng season."

He gestures for someone in the audience to come forward. A woman in a dark green Forest Service uniform stands and makes her way to the lectern stationed in front of the dais. Frances Vernon, known to all and sundry as Vernie, has been a fixture of the National Forest for as long as I've been alive and probably a lot longer.

"We have just the right elevation, rainfall, and mineral-rich soil to produce some of the best wild ginseng in the world," she says, inciting murmurs of agreement. "But wild ginseng is threatened from centuries of overharvesting. Taking the root ends the plant's ability to replace itself for new generations. That's why it's only legal to dig the roots from the end of summer to the first frost, September through November, and only those at least five years old and with seed-bearing, bright red berries. All diggers must have a current permit from the Forest Service to remove ginseng from the National Forest and are required, by law, to plant the seeds where they dug the root."

"And what happens if someone violates those rules?" Gayle Anne demands, her arched eyebrows shooting up over her glasses. "Laws are only as good as their enforcement, and I believe in being tough on crime." She nods decisively, like she's making a campaign promise.

"We've certainly seen an increase in violations over the last decade or so," Vernie admits. "Which is why we now have harsher penalties. A first violation may be a one-thousand-dollar fine, but subsequent offenses can mean much higher fines and jail time. A man over in Mud River just pleaded guilty to five Lacey Act violations for illegally trafficking in ginseng. Each of those could mean up to a hundred-thousand-dollar fine and one year in prison."

A rumble runs through the crowd as this statement sparks dozens of side conversations, and Vernie is forced to raise her hands for silence before she can continue. "We take this very seriously because ginseng is an important part of our culture and heritage, and illegal harvesting puts it at risk of disappearing. But the potential for a big payday means some are willing to take that risk."

"Ranger Vernon, what can we all do to help keep poachers out of Caball Hollow?" Okey asks, gesturing toward the audience.

"If you see signs of possible illegal activity, like vehicles parked in remote areas for long periods of time; possession of sharpened sticks, trowels, or even hoes that have been altered to avoid damaging the skin of the root, which would drop its value; and disturbed soil where ginseng is known or likely to grow, please report it. We'll also be increasing the number of patrols within the National Forest itself," Vernie explains.

"Poachers better stay away from my spot, or the law will be the least of their worries," someone to my left mutters.

"Please do not attempt to confront suspected poachers," Vernie stresses, holding up her hands for emphasis. "There's no need to put yourself in danger. Notify the Forest Service or local law enforcement, and we'll handle it."

"I'm sure we'll all keep a lookout for anything suspicious," Okey says. "Thank you, Vernie." He gestures for the forest ranger to take her seat.

I roll my eyes. The National Forest is nearly a million acres, with the Appalachian mountain range running right through its center. It surrounds Caball Hollow like a massive jaw waiting to snap. With its rocky crevices, deep rivers, murky bogs, dense woods, and laurel hells so dense and twisted that if you wander in you're liable to never make it out, the National Forest is made up of some of the most ecologically diverse land in the nation. The idea that Okey Spurgeon, sitting in a lawn chair inside his open garage with binoculars and a beer, might catch a poacher is so laughable, I have to bite my tongue.

"All right, y'all, let's come to order." Okey tries to get the meeting back on track. "We still have a lot to cover this evening, including the recent uptick in petty theft."

"I'll just say what we're all thinking." Gayle Anne Gerlach taps her ink pen against the notepad on the table in front of her. "I don't think the increase in crime and the increase in unfamiliar faces around town is a coincidence. And I'm not just talking about ginseng hunters coming in and causing problems. We've also got people like those internet folks. They may not be breaking the law, but they've been sticking their noses where they don't belong, stirring up trouble that's better left to lie."

I scoff, earning myself another glare from Beulah Fordham Hayes. No, it's not strangers we need to fear most—they're the ones we keep at a distance. It's the people you trust who are close enough to stab you in the back. Because everybody lies. And in knowing their lies, I become the keeper of their secrets.

Caball Hollow is a one-stoplight town stuck so far out in the middle of nowhere that rarely even does a strong cell signal find its way to us. For generations, our only claim to fame was the folklore of a monster that haunted our Forest. The legend of the Moth-Winged Man, a creature with the body of a man and the wings of a moth said to be a sure sign of impending misfortune, was a tale told by old men to prove their mettle or young mothers to keep their children from wandering too far. Completely fictional. Until it wasn't.

When sightings of the Moth-Winged Man were reported just before Caball Hollow's first official murder a few months ago, it made the news and drew all kinds of morbid curiosity seekers. Most of them gave up once the scandal died down, but the crew of so-called monster hunters with a YouTube channel that rolled into town last week doesn't seem in any hurry to leave and is clearly ruffling a few feathers. I'm certainly no fan, but the idea that crime only happens in Caball Hollow because of outsiders isn't just delusional, it's downright dangerous. The empty chair on the dais is proof enough of that. After all, the murderer was born and bred right here.

"It's true. Crime is becoming a real problem," Beulah informs me. "Just the other day, Roy Bivens couldn't find his keys, and when he went outside, his car was gone. Disappeared right out of his driveway."

"It was in front of the Pub 'n' Grub, where he left it the night before." Hillard Been turns around in his chair. "Fool was probably still so pickled he didn't recognize it. Whoever took his keys did the whole town a favor."

Beulah huffs and picks an invisible piece of lint from her jacket, but Hillard isn't done. "Course, on the other hand, he's not the only one who's lost something lately." He lets the sentence hang, and there's clearly some context I'm missing, but I don't have to wait long for the answer to present itself.

"I already done told you once," Buck Garland growls at Hillard Been from somewhere behind me. He must have come in late, like the others standing in the back of the room. "I got no earthly idea what you're talking about."

"You've got to have it, Buck," Hillard argues, undeterred. "I gave it to you when I retired. It was a family heirloom, and you promised you'd take care of it."

Buck shakes his head in frustration. "You must have me confused with someone else at the post office, old man."

Hillard stares at him, bug-eyed and whompyjawed. "You fall on your head recently, son?"

"I take it y'all lost something?" I interrupt, partly because they're getting louder and drawing attention, and partly just to needle them for my own amusement.

"*We* didn't lose nothing," Hillard insists. "This damn fool claims he never had my granddaddy's pocket watch when the entire Caball Hollow postal service saw me give it to him."

I remember the day he's talking about. The two of them came into the Harvest Moon diner for lunch, like they always do, and Buck was showing the watch off to everybody who'd listen.

"And I told you, you're confused," Buck insists, then turns to me. I brace for the lie I know is coming. "It happens sometimes with the elderly," he says in a voice

Hillard is clearly meant to hear. "But I ain't never had that dang watch."

I know the words are false, but no stench accompanies them. He shows none of the outward signs of dishonesty I've learned to identify over the years. No shifts in the tone or volume of his voice, no fidgeting, no changes in the level of eye contact. And yet I know he's lying, so how can that be?

"I had your name added to the engraving!" Hillard loudly objects.

The rest of the meeting hall goes silent, and those closest to us aren't even trying to pretend they're not watching. I inhale deeply through my nose, trying to catch the scent that should be so strong by now it'd make my eyes water.

"I don't need this." Buck pushes off the back wall. "Call me when you recover your senses," he tells Hillard, pulling his hat down over his eyes as he stomps toward the exit.

Hillard slowly shakes his head. "My apologies, folks," he tells the crowd. "He's not been acting like hisself lately. Buck isn't usually one for confrontation. Most days I'm not even sure he's completely awake."

Slowly, I get to my feet, following the path Buck took. When Gayle Anne Gerlach told the town council clerk that her expenses were work related, a puff of papery smoke wafted through the air. When Okey Spurgeon called his wife to tell her he had to work late tomorrow, a smell like burnt meat slid across the room in a greasy swirl. Or even at home, when my sister Linden says she's fine, despite being bad-mouthed, shunned, then nearly killed less than a month ago, her breath is scented with coal—and it makes me want to burn this whole town to the ground. But now, after Buck had so clearly lied and the air should be thick with the stink of it, there's not so much as a hint of ash. Nothing.

And I have to admit that maybe the only thing worse than knowing every single lie is not knowing.

CHAPTER TWO

LONG AFTER the town council meeting drew to a close, I lie in my bed, staring up at the tongue-and-groove ceiling, counting the whorls in each of the planks. My thoughts are too loud in the silence of the room, mine alone since Sorrel left for college last month, her mattress stripped bare and her favorite honeycomb quilt packed away.

The room seems darker somehow without its familiar pattern, a flower garden of cast-off cotton and a history written in thread. The embroidered remnant of a handkerchief that had once belonged to Gran's younger sister, Zephyrine. Flannel from one of Great-Granny Sudie's old nightgowns. A piece of lacework that once trimmed Gran's wedding dress. Nothing ever wasted, the quilt was warmth created from an economy of repurposed fabrics, much like our home itself.

Nestled in a small valley between shouldering hills, Bittersweet Farm is a sprawling patchwork of flagstone, clapboard, and hand-hewn logs. It tells the tale of the women who have lived here for generations just as well as the words recorded in the James family books, of lean years and those high on the hog, of growth and heartache, of making do or doing without.

A noise downstairs, the muted shuffle of someone trying to be quiet, is all the invitation I need to get out of my own head. Pulling an old blue sweatshirt on over my pajamas, I make my way down the back stairs to the kitchen. Linden stands in the circle of moonlight cast through the small window above the sink, her long, dark hair draped over one shoulder while she fills the kettle. A jar of Gran's sleep-easy tea is open next to a mug on the countertop by the stove.

"Can't sleep?" I ask, and she jumps, splashing water onto the floor.

"You scared the livin' daylights out of me," she whispers fiercely, one hand clutching her chest.

"Bad dream?" I grab the towel from the oven door handle to wipe up the spill. She's had nightmares before, but after she was nearly killed last month by the same person who murdered her friend, it's like she's afraid to even close her eyes.

Linden shakes her head, a low hum in the back of her throat. "Nope," she mumbles, and when the burnt smell of the lie hits me I nearly sag in relief.

"What is it?" Linden asks, because of course she notices, as she sets the copper kettle onto the stovetop and strikes a long kitchen match to light the burner.

"Give me a minute and I'll explain everything." I open the fridge, blinking against the brightness of the interior bulb that floods the kitchen in light.

It takes a moment to locate the apple butter near the back. I dig it out, then grab the loaf of sourdough that Gran was given by the Milton family in exchange for a jar of her diaper rash salve. We sit across from each other at the old wooden table in the middle of the room and I smear two slices of bread with a thick layer of the fragrant spread, rich with apple and just a hint of cinnamon, passing one to Linden before I sink my teeth into the other. While she makes her tea, I fill her in on the meeting and the strange fight between Hillard Been and Buck Garland.

"I've seen Buck with that pocket watch." Linden takes a sip from her favorite old brown mug. "Probably half the town has. Why would he lie about it?"

"That's what's so strange." I shrug, brushing away crumbs. "I thought there might be something wrong with me because it didn't smell like a lie."

She lifts her eyebrows, the concern evident on her face, and I want to take all the words back immediately. The last thing she needs is more to worry about. "Maybe he genuinely forgot about the watch and didn't mean to deceive anyone." I rush to offer a possible explanation.

"If he doesn't remember something like that, we should make sure he sees a doctor," Linden says, and I realize I haven't eased her mind at all, just given her a different reason to fret.

"Hillard did ask if he'd hit his head recently," I admit.

When she finishes her tea and pushes her chair back to stand, I reach out to stop her. Gran is always telling us to search for the shapes of our nightmares at the bottom of the cup so we can wash them from our minds.

"What do you see in the tea leaves, Linden?" I ask. If I know what monsters haunt her dreams, maybe I can help slay them. But after everything she's been through, there are so many possibilities, from moth wings to rocky ridges to river rapids.

Linden clears her throat before she blinks and looks down into the dregs of her mug. "It's a person," she says at last, her eyes wide and shining in the low light when her gaze meets mine. "Falling, and falling, and falling."

I study her face as she seems to get lost in thought for a moment. She gives herself a little shake, smiling gently when she realizes I'm watching.

"I'll be all right," she insists.

I brace for the foul scent of a lie, but it doesn't come. And in the back of my mind, I can't help but wonder whether that means she's telling the truth or my ability is failing me again.

"Let's try to get some sleep." She nods toward the stairs. "We've only got a few more hours until morning chores."

I'm up before the sun, pulling my thick barn jacket tighter against the biting whisper of cold that tries to slide down the collar like a snake in a mouse burrow, seeking hidden warmth to steal away. There's a promise of winter already in the air this early, a crisp freshness beneath the acridity of burning leaves wafting from the next holler over.

I shut the kitchen door behind me, then tuck my hands up into my sleeves and away from the nibbling chill as I make my way to the coop to let out the chickens, too stubborn to break out my gloves in September no matter how cold it is.

Morning chores are among the worst on the farm and often include getting head-butted by impatient goats looking for breakfast, hunting down the eggs our bantam hens like to hide in the rafters, and shoveling shit out of animal pens. All of which should have been the responsibility of our farmhand, Hadrian Fitch, had he not taken off at the end of August, emptying his room over the carriage house without so much as a word and disappearing just as suddenly as he'd arrived the year before.

I warned Gran not to hire him. He showed up in his ripped jeans, untamable dark hair, with tattoos crawling up his neck, and a fiddle case under his arm. Then softened her up with some story about searching for his long-lost brother that wasn't even a fraction of the whole truth. From first glance, I knew he was trouble.

I'm glad to have seen the back of him. Every single word that boy said was untrue. I'd rather clean the barn every day for the rest of my life than catch the lies that fall from his lips like ash.

A memory appears unbidden in my mind: Hadrian leaning against the counter just inside the kitchen, wild curls even darker in the shadows.

I was at the table, eating a breakfast of streaky bacon and fried eggs, focused on soaking up the runny yolks with a hunk of last night's cornbread, when he came in.

"You hungry, son?" Gran asked from the stove, where she was frying up more eggs in bacon grease, scooping a little over the top until they were perfectly cooked. "These are almost ready. Grab a seat."

"I've got to see to the sheep first, ma'am," Hadrian said. "But if it's not too much of an inconvenience, I need to take the truck out to the feed store in Rawbone. We're running low on hay pellets and wood shavings."

The sharp scent of a struck match, sulfur and burning wood, hit me, and my head jerked up. But he wasn't looking at Gran. His eyes were locked on me like a challenge.

"Well, that's just fine," Gran answered, turning her full attention back to the stove. "You know where to find the keys."

A tiny smirk tugged at the corner of his mouth before he turned to grab the truck key from the hook and head back outside. I dropped my fork as the stench of the lie roiled my stomach, pushing up from the table to follow before the door swung shut behind him.

He was nearly to the gate of the sheep pen when I stepped out onto the porch. The flower boxes were right there, and I didn't even think before plunging in my hand and taking aim at the back of his head. The first dirt clod missed, sailing wide and nearly hitting Linden as she wheeled the old red bike out of the barn, but it got his attention. He spun around to face me.

"If you can't be bothered to tell the truth, at least keep your stinking lies from spoiling my breakfast," I yelled. More than anything, I wanted to sink my fingers back into the mud and knock the smug look off his face.

Hadrian lifted a single dark brow, a gleam in his mossy-green eyes. "What are you on about now?" He feigned confusion.

"You told Gran you needed the truck today to go to the feed store." I ground the words between my teeth, giving up any attempt at resistance and chucking another handful of soil at his head. This one only missed by inches, raining dirt into his hair.

I stalked down the steps toward him. "But you and I both know that's not true. So where are you really going?"

"Rowan, stop." Linden dropped the bike and grabbed my arm. "You know what Gran said," she whispered, reminding me of the edict to stop accusing Hadrian of lying or suffer the consequences. Gran had long grown tired of our feud and told me in no uncertain terms that if I had time to distract him from his work, then I had time to take on more work of my own. And they were always the worst jobs, too, like cleaning out the chicken coop or the grease trap at the diner.

But over Linden's shoulder, my gaze met Hadrian's and he winked.

My blood still boils at the memory, and I shove it away, forcing my attention back to the here and now. The sky is just beginning to lighten, the outline of the rolling mountains surrounding Bittersweet Farm sharpening into focus, as I walk the fence line to check for damage. A weak fence is an open invitation to predators, but ours is woven through with the protective bittersweet vines that give the farm its name. Some claim it rose from the earth of its own accord. Though the first known James ancestor, Caorunn, was said to have a special talent for coaxing just about anything to grow.

I spot a frill of orange on the trunk of an old oak near the edge of the pasture and venture closer to investigate. It's a cluster of chicken of the woods mushrooms, *Laetiporus sulphureus*, still fresh. Tender and bright. I flip open the small blade of the foraging knife I keep in my pocket and cut away several of its ruffled shelves. It typically grows on dead or dying oaks, though not always, so I make a note to keep an eye on this one, before it can cause any trouble with the fence.

When I make my way back to the house, I pull off my muck boots on the porch and open the back door. The air smells like Gran's famous cathead biscuits, and the heat of the oven has chased the early autumn bite from the air. Mama and Gran sit at the table, a pot of coffee between them.

"You out there doin' all the chores alone again?" Gran asks as she blows across the top of her mug. "Your sisters are meant to help."

"School starts early enough, let them sleep in a bit," I say, dropping my bounty of mushrooms on the counter as I make my way to the sink to wash up. I'm the only one who doesn't have to worry about getting to class on time anymore or staying up late to do homework.

Mama glances over at me as she surreptitiously rubs her thumb across something shiny, then tucks it back into her pocket. The shadows under her eyes look darker in the glare of the overhead light. Linden isn't the only one who isn't sleeping. I pretend not to see the small circle of the pendant, like I always do. She stopped wearing it after she and Daddy split, but she still carries it with her, reaching for it like a talisman when she thinks no one is watching. I'm not sure if it's love or regret that haunts her.

The story goes that Daddy gave Mama the necklace on their first date. By then, he'd already eaten lunch at the Harvest Moon every single day for a month, trying to work up the courage to ask her out. Until one day, when Mama asked him if he was ever going to. He told her he'd found the necklace at a thrift store for a couple bucks and the swan engraved on the front made him think of her. In truth, he'd been saving a sizeable chunk of his meager pay since the day he met her to buy it from an antiques jeweler up in Charleston. It took a few months for her to realize the pendant was a locket with a hidden catch. When she finally opened it, a piece of paper with the words *I'm already in love with you* scrawled across tumbled out, and by that point, she felt the same way.

They'd been together ever since, until last year, when Mama traded their love to save Linden's life.

I grab a golden biscuit from the pan and try to pull it apart without burning myself or getting scalded on the steam that escapes. After dropping both halves into a bowl, I smother their soft middles with a scoop of thick, peppery sausage gravy from the cast-iron skillet on the stove.

"You should eat something, too, Odette," Gran murmurs across the table.

"I will," Mama promises. It's not really a lie, but it's clear she doesn't mean anytime soon.

Gran and I exchange a look over her head. The loss of appetite, I suspect, is the guilt eating away at her. She hasn't said as much, but I know she blames herself for keeping the secrets that put Linden in danger when all she'd wanted to do was to protect her.

"I don't have to tell you"—Gran starts, settling back into the old wooden chair with both hands wrapped around her mug—"how I blamed myself when my sister took off. Zephyrine was so young when your granny Sudie passed, I think I took to mothering her whether she wanted it or not. I knew something was wrong toward the end. She looked plumb exhausted, and she was barely eating, but she'd already stopped talking to me on account of all my meddling. After she left, I let my own guilt stop me from going after her. When I think of all the time I wasted when I could have been looking for her." Gran pauses, shaking her head.

Decades ago, she and her sister had a falling-out, ostensibly because Gran didn't approve of the man Zephyrine was dating, but the real issue went deeper than that, to differences in how they thought we should use our gifts and our family knowledge. Zephyrine trusted the man she thought loved her with our secrets, and he used them against her to save himself. A sacrifice to an old god he didn't understand. Though maybe a deal with the devil would be more fitting.

"I might have found out a lot sooner that she didn't leave of her own accord. Sitting around stewing in your own juices won't do no good for anybody."

Gran pushes out of her chair and makes her way around the table. "I know what that kind of guilt feels like, but the only choices are accept it or change it. Now that I know where she is, I'm going to do everything in my power to get her back." She pats Mama's shoulder as she moves toward the stove. "So, if biscuits and gravy aren't to your liking, let me fix you up something else."

I slide into Gran's empty chair, and Mama meets my gaze across the table.

"You look so much like your father." Her smile is a heavy thing, weighted with equal parts joy and sadness. Her words aren't strictly true, either. My ink-dark hair and bright blue eyes are James family traits, but she searches out the pieces of him in each of us. His freckles on Sorrel's skin, the exact shape of Linden's smile, the curve of Juniper's jaw, the set of my eyes. They can never quite add up to the whole, no matter how hard she looks.

"Did I ever tell you that I used to sit with him whenever I had a free minute during my shift? And sometimes when I didn't," she admits, lifting her eyebrows. "He listened like every word I spoke was a revelation. We created a whole world, he and I, one that existed only for the two of us. I would never take back the deal I made to save your sister, but I know why the Moth-Winged Man accepted the trade. A life for a life. I killed something that day. Something I can never get back."

I stare into the deep blue of her eyes and realize it's not the regret or the guilt that keeps her up at night. It's grief.

"Your gran has hope now of finding Zephyrine. But I have to abide by my bargain. We don't always get to keep what's most precious. Sometimes we have to let it go." Mama squeezes my hand, then leaves the kitchen while Gran is busy at the stove.

Zephyrine loved the wrong man, and it cost her dearly. Mama loved the right man and still lost. Their stories might be vastly different, but the end result was still the same.

We don't talk about our abilities. As many folks make their way down the garden path to the summer kitchen late at night, careful not to wake wagging tongues as they seek out cures for what ails them, none of them really want to know the truth. It's one thing to believe there might be more to the world than what's known, yet quite another to have it confirmed. People turn dangerous when confronted with something that challenges their worldview. Scorch marks mar the old log cabin wall from where long ago some disgruntled customer decided the best way to deal with a witch was the old-fashioned one. There's a reason we don't trust easy. It's a lesson we've learned well enough over the generations.

CHAPTER THREE

THE HARVEST Moon diner was once a gristmill. The mix of old and new, then and now, from worn, wide-plank floors and thick limestone walls, to stainless steel counters and vinyl booths, is tied together by a menu that works in much the same way. Each meal like a memory that sticks to your ribs.

One of two restaurants in Caball Hollow, the diner is only open until midafternoon, six days a week. The lunch rush is our busiest time, but we have a handful of breakfast regulars, which means work starts early.

When I unlock the back door and step into the kitchen, the scent of diluted bleach from cleanup yesterday is still the strongest smell in the air. Soon it will be filled with the fragrance of fresh-baked biscuits and bacon cooked on sheet pans for fried green tomato BLTs as we begin the day's prep, but now I pause, my hand on the light switch, to take in the way the space looks washed in the gentle glow of the rising sun through the windows. Mornings are the best time at the Harvest Moon, when it's still just ours, before it fills with people all wanting something.

"You gonna just stand there all day, or can we get to work?" Gran chides from behind me.

I roll my eyes and flip the switch, flooding the kitchen with bright light. There's a stack of clean white aprons from the laundry service in the closet, and I grab two, handing one to Gran before pulling on the second. I loop my thick, dark hair around my hand and tie it into a knot.

Gran hums a random tune at the prep counter as she reviews her notes from the previous day. "Pastor Boggs has been asking about my shuck beans, and I've got some ready to cook up, so let's do that for the side today," she tells me without lifting her gaze. "Clean those mushrooms you found, and I'll chicken fry them with some chowchow relish for the lunch special."

I make a disgusted sound in the back of my throat that doesn't escape her attention. Now she does look at me. "You got something you wanna say, child, just say it. No need to hem and haw over it."

"I don't understand how you can keep catering to them after everything that happened." The words burst out of me, loud in the morning quiet. "At the first sign of something strange that they couldn't explain away, this whole town turned against us. Barely more than a month ago someone destroyed the Harvest Moon and nearly drove us out of business." I wave my hands to encompass the entire kitchen, the memory still sharp as a knife.

Giant commercial bags of sugar and flour were shredded, every single surface coated in fine dust. The haze hung in the air like fog. Broken dishes and smashed eggs coated the floor. The freezer hung open, with so many months' worth of work—vegetables from our garden, sauces, broths and stocks, bread dough and piecrusts, and meat—all left to rot. But the dining room was the worst. The words *WITCHES BURN* written in blood and dripping down the wall made the motive clear.

"And now we're supposed to just keep serving them meals here or mixing up diaper rash salves and sleep tonics at the farm like nothing happened?" It's a question, but it's also an accusation, and we both know it.

"You think Pastor Boggs was the one who broke into the Harvest Moon?" Gran asks, her calm all the more infuriating. "Or that we should starve just to spite them all? Need I remind you, this is our livelihood." She clucks her tongue and turns her focus back to the beans.

It's a conversation we've had more than once. An old argument she's weary of that, in truth, changes nothing. And I'm just as tired of it. Maybe she's right, and the only difference is that I have the luxury of holding grudges and Gran has seven mouths to feed.

"But they're not even sorry." And I can't let it go.

"I didn't have two nickels to rub together when I opened this place," Gran says, keeping her eyes on the giant pot as she stirs. "Had to take a loan out against the farm. I was a broke young widow with a toddler. Everyone told me I was a damn fool. Maybe there were easier ways to make money, but I wanted something that was mine."

"And you worked your ass off," I agree. "Which is why I hate that someone nearly destroyed it all out of spite."

"My point is, maybe you wouldn't have to hold so tightly to your anger if you tried reaching for something else. What is it you want that you're willing to risk everything to go after? And if you can't answer that, maybe you should think on it."

Mama and Aunt Salome arrive an hour later with a mess of green tomatoes and peppers, lavender phlox and blue asters from the garden. Gran has the shuck beans boiling away with a smoked ham hock, the bone and marrow of which will create a rich broth, deep with flavor. The grill and cold food stations are set up with everything we'll need during service, and I've just started the coffee brewing at the front counter.

"I wouldn't have planted so many tomatoes if I knew we'd be short-staffed," Mama tells Gran as she takes the produce to the wide dishwashing sink to process. "We're about to be overrun, and we'll need to get them all harvested before the first frost. I don't care what the almanac says, it's coming early this year."

"Help me with these." Sissy nods toward the smaller handwashing sink on the other side of the kitchen as she carries a tray of old jam jars past me.

I grab the floral snips and follow. The fan in the nearby window drowns out any chance I have of listening in on the rest of Mama's concerns, but it's probably for the best. I'm not short on reasons to hold a grudge against Hadrian Fitch anyhow.

"Missing a certain farmhand?" Sissy teases. Her eyes are a swirl of gray, brown, and gold, the depth of color shifting with her moods. Now they're dancing mischievously.

"What would make you think that?" I ask, cutting the stem of an aster a bit more aggressively than necessary. I hated him for the whole year he lived on the farm. I hate him even more now, after he left without so much as a word.

"Oh, I don't know." She gently pulls the flowers away to save the rest from decapitation. "How often do you think about him?"

"Only long enough to curse his name." I turn to face her fully, leaning my hip against the counter. "He showed up looking like trouble the way he does, and Gran trusted him anyway, despite all my warnings. Then, after everything, he just up and disappears in the night like a ghost. He could have at least given us a little notice."

Sissy makes a hum of agreement as she puts the flowers into the makeshift vases. "Maybe some people just aren't made for sticking around."

"Do you resent staying in Caball Hollow?" I ask, determined to steer the conversation away from Hadrian Fitch. These few months may well be the longest Sissy has been home since she moved out when she wasn't much older than I am now. She never stays put for long, here least of all, and I imagine a restless itch growing beneath her skin, like wings desperate to spread out.

"Do *you*?" She lifts her eyebrows pointedly. "You could have gone to college this fall, like Sorrel. And yet here you are."

I shake my head, dismissing the suggestion out of hand. School never came as naturally for me as it did for Sorrel. Hours spent cooped up in a windowless classroom certainly made me feel itchy. "Did you ever want to go?" I ask, suddenly curious. It's easy to picture Sissy in college, with her easy charm and sociable disposition.

"I was interested in learning. Less so, I reckon, in being taught." She pauses in the middle of trimming phlox stems, thoughtful. The mountain twang she'd all but erased emerges more and more the longer she stays. "There's a great big world out there. But if you run long enough and far enough, you'll end up right back where you started. Maybe all along part of my wanderlust was me trying to find my way back. For the first time in a good long while, I'm glad to just be home. But I think maybe that's the difference. Making a choice."

She gives me a wide smile, lips bright as the petal of a fire pink, while she gathers the finished arrangements and takes them out to the dining room.

I quickly down a biscuit and a bowl of shuck beans. Then there's just enough time to trade my kitchen apron for the blue one with my name embroidered on the chest before Mama unlocks the front door to let in the first customers of the day.

All summer long, I was relegated to dish duty, the worst job in the diner. A consequence of Mama's discovery of the snake curled around my hip. It's not that she has any particular objection to tattoos, more that I wasn't quite eighteen when I got it. She lectured me on making permanent decisions when I was too young to fully understand what I was doing. To which I reminded her that she was less than a handful of years older than I am now when she gave birth to me, her second child. Still didn't get me out of washing dishes, though.

I never thought I'd be glad to wait tables, but after a summer of scalding water, half-eaten food scraps, and constant clouds of steam to the face, I have a newfound appreciation for anything that gets me out of the kitchen. I knot the strings of the apron and shove through the swinging door into the dining room.

Hillard Been sits at his usual spot by the front window, permanently reserved for him since his investment in the Harvest Moon last month saved us from closing for good. But after witnessing their falling-out last night, I suspect Buck Garland won't be joining him like he usually does. Before I even take a step, a clicking sound draws my attention.

At our largest table in the corner, the YouTubers are already setting up camp, claiming the only outlet and pulling over extra chairs. They've been coming in for a few days now, barely ordering anything but coffee and drinking endless refills. Their leader, a twentysomething, generically handsome, and personality-devoid walking ego by the name of Sonny Vane, is snapping his fingers to get my attention.

I pointedly ignore him, instead grabbing the coffeepot and heading for Hillard's table. "Morning." I fill the mug in front of him. "How's it going, Hillard?"

"Oh, 'bout the same." He sets aside his newspaper and raises his bushy white brows. "What's good today?"

"Gran has a new recipe for you to try this morning, fried cornmeal hoecakes with sorghum-glazed apples and black walnuts."

"Well, now, I'm not much of one for sweets, but add a side of pork sausage and then we're talking," Hillard, the most notorious sweet tooth in the county, declares, eyes gone glassy in anticipation.

I turn to find Sonny watching me, and my smile drops. He grins and lifts his coffee cup, jiggling it in my direction.

"Good morning, gorgeous," he flirts obnoxiously as I walk over to fill his cup. "Give any more thought to doing an on-camera interview? Your face on an episode thumbnail of my show, and the viewership numbers would be astronomical."

There's truly nothing more annoying than men who hit on their waitresses. I've refused to even hate-watch his channel. Seeing the ridiculous sun logo he has stamped on his laptop already sets my teeth on edge.

"I say this with complete sincerity," I tell him as I move around the table to fill the mugs of the other four crewmembers. "I'd rather share a cocoon with the Moth-Winged Man himself." I say it without thinking and immediately want to bite my tongue.

"Now, that's something I'd like to get on film." Sonny chuckles like it's our silly little inside joke as he stirs sugar into his coffee. "Speaking of, we got a tip this morning that someone spotted a . . ." He shuffles through some papers on the table in front of him, then snaps his fingers at his production assistant, the only woman on the team. She hands him a note, and he glances down at it. "Wampus Cat?"

"Someone's jerking your tail," I tell him.

"What is a Wampus Cat?" the assistant asks. She's even younger than I realized, probably not much older than I am. Her hair is chopped into long, shaggy layers and bleached blond with roots that match the contents of her cup, and she's wearing reading glasses that cover half her face.

"It's a legend. A woman cursed to live as a cat and wander forever." I shift, settling into the story. "Her anguished howl is said to bring bad luck to any who hear it."

"Sounds awful," she says.

"Sounds perfect," Sonny disagrees. "My viewers will eat that up."

"By all means, go chase it," I tell him. "If it were real, it'd be like any other big cat in these mountains. You'll only see it when it wants you to, and then it's liable to be too late."

"Sure you don't want to come?" he asks, and I don't even have the energy to bother rolling my eyes.

"Don't waste your time," a guy in a security uniform chimes in from a nearby table where he's eating breakfast with two similarly dressed men. "She shuts everybody down."

"I'm sorry, do I know you?" I turn to get a better look.

"Kye Hensley?" He gestures to himself, startled. "We went to school together?"

I stare at him blankly.

"Since kindergarten," he insists, incredulous.

"Sorry." I shrug, then spin on my heel and walk away with my jaw clenched.

Kye Hensley was one of a group of boys who would stand at the back of the gym and catcall the girls when the teacher wasn't watching. I can't recall a single actual conversation we had in all those years of attending school together. Any passing interest he might have had was about possessing a pretty ornament to impress his friends. But I refuse to be anyone's trophy.

Linden says I use the way I look to keep people from getting too close, but that's not the truth, or at least not all of it. There are only so many times you can be reduced to nothing but your appearance before you start to wonder if it's really all you have to offer.

As I place the coffeepot back on the hot plate behind the counter, the bell over the door chimes, and Vernie walks in with a folder under her arm. She pulls off the shiny sunglasses that must be standard issue with the Forest Service uniform and smiles, making the lines around her eyes crinkle. She has the look of someone who spends most of her time outdoors—softer and more relaxed somehow, like linens dried on the line.

"Hello," she greets me as she approaches the counter. "I haven't been in since y'all did the remodel. It looks great."

"Can I get you a menu?" I ask, pulling one from the stack beneath the counter.

"Wish I could stay, but I've got to get the rest of these flyers up." Vernie sets her folder down and flips it open. "We're looking for a volunteer to get the lookout cabin up to snuff before the start of fire season. With the uptick in ginseng poachers, we don't have the staff to spare. Mind if I post one of these on your bulletin board?"

"Not at all. I can do that for you." I take the paper from Vernie.

"Thanks." She closes her folder and tucks it back under her arm. "We really need to find someone soon. We've only got a month until fire season and plenty of work to be done."

"You sure I can't get you a grilled pimento cheese to go?" I offer.

"Next time," Vernie says with a wave as she heads out. "Say hello to your gran and them for me."

I take the flyer to the bulletin board near the front door and grab a pushpin. There is a notice for an upcoming school play, offers to babysit and dog walk, someone looking to sell an old car that doesn't appear completely road-worthy, and finally, a call for people to share their encounters with the Moth-Winged Man or any other unknown creature on camera with a fringe of tear-off phone number tabs along the bottom. I tack Vernie's flyer directly overtop of that last one.

It's less than an hour before closing when the dining room finally starts to clear out. I haul a tray full of dirty dishes into the kitchen to find the most beautiful apple stack cake I've ever seen cooling on the stainless steel prep counter. It's six thin layers of rich sorghum, ginger, and buttermilk cake with a filling made of dried winesap apples mixed with cinnamon, cloves, brown sugar, and Gran's apple butter sandwiched between each one.

Linden has taken to stocking the new glass case out front with all manner of delicious treats. An apple stack cake can't be eaten right away. It'll need to be wrapped in plastic and chilled for several hours. But there's no reason not to try a tiny taste of the filling while it's still warm. I grab a fork from the clean tray and slide the pot of apples and spices toward me, my mouth already watering in anticipation.

"I wouldn't eat that if I were you," a voice says from behind me.

I turn to find Juniper cross-legged on the counter under the window with a textbook open in her lap. Sitting on the counter is decidedly against the rules, and she's the only one who could even dream of getting away with it. I stick my tongue out just to get a rise out of her. "Why not?"

"Linden wasn't exactly in the best mood when she baked it."

We've always known Linden could taste the feelings of others. Love, like the first ripe peaches of summer, kissed by the sun. Compassion, like Gran's biscuits, soft and warm from the oven. Grief, like blackstrap molasses, bitter and thick. But only recently did she discover she could use her gift the other way, too, imbuing her baking with specific emotions. Not always on purpose. She's still figuring out the finer points.

"What happened?" I ask.

"That awful woman from the school board, Beulah Fordham Hayes, cornered her after sixth hour today and basically accused her of profiting off the town's recent tragedy because of the scholarship."

"The *town's* tragedy?" I'm stunned by the shameless audacity. After Linden survived an attempt on her life, the estate of the former mayor granted her a sizeable college scholarship. "Ms. Beulah needs to mind her business."

"She thinks it is her business because when the scholarship was first proposed by the Spencer family, she argued it should be merit-based and a worthy student selected by the school board." Juniper drums the end of her pencil against the textbook in her lap.

"And, lemme guess, she doesn't find Linden worthy?"

"She said Linden dating Cole Spencer was an unfair advantage. And that, without specific award criteria, it looked like the Spencers were playing favorites."

"I think the criteria of nearly having your life ended by the family patriarch is pretty specific." I'm madder than fire now, an ember glowing hot in the pit of my stomach.

"Exactly," Juniper agrees. "It's a bad faith argument because the Spencers created the scholarship for victims of violent crime, which is definitely a specific requirement, just not an academic one. And they recused themselves from the selection committee this year, which she also conveniently ignored."

"Where's Linden?" I ask, squeezing the fork in my hand.

Juniper shrugs. "All I know is, she was feeling some type of way when she baked that cake."

I gaze longingly at the pot of apples and spices, weighing whether a taste might be worth a few hours of being miserable. But Linden feels deeply, and imagining the shame, sadness, and hurt that likely flavored her baking after the hateful conversation with Beulah Fordham Hayes is enough to make me back away, sliding the fork into my apron pocket.

"So, are we just going to let it go to waste?" I ask, pained.

"I told her she should gift it to Ol' Beulah." Juniper shrugs.

"Rowan," Gran calls from the other side of the kitchen, where she's cooking up some onion jam for tomorrow's special. "Customer."

She nods toward the dining room without pausing her work, the jingle of the bell above the front door just barely noticeable over the whir of the exhaust fan and the clatter of the high-pressure commercial dishwasher. I puff out an annoyed breath. There's nothing worse than a last-minute table, and I'm already heated.

"Go ahead and sit anywhere," I say as I push through the swinging door. But when I see Bryson Ivers looming over Linden in the empty dining room, that ember catches and sets my blood to boil.

He stands too close to her, his much larger frame making her look even smaller. She's holding a tray against her chest like a shield. I don't even remember crossing the distance. Flames fill my belly, and I see red. The next thing I know, the fork from my pocket is pressed against his throat.

"What the hell do you think you're doing?" I demand.

"Nothing!" Bryson lifts his hands in surrender. He's the kicker for the Caball Hollow High School Devils football team and stands a good head taller than me, yet his eyes go wide with fear.

"Rowan, stop!" Linden grabs my arm and tries to pull me away. "He's here about a school project. We're in the same group."

"There's something not right with your sister," Bryson tells her, and I feel him swallow against the pressure of the fork in my hand before his eyes meet mine. "You're going to regret this."

I step back, breathing harder than the tiny amount of exertion would justify, and hide my shaking hand behind me. That was an extreme reaction, even for me. Four tiny red dots make a line underneath Bryson's jaw from the pressure of the tines, but I'm relieved to see I didn't break the skin. "Yes, why don't you call the sheriff? I'm sure he'd love to ask you about the break-in we had here this summer."

"I don't know anything about that," he mumbles, but there's smoke on his breath. A *lie*. He's always been at the top of my list of suspects. And yet he's too much of a weasel to have acted alone.

"Rowan, that's enough." Linden's voice has gone quiet, a sure sign she's angry.

"Can I get you some ice?" she asks Bryson as he presses a hand to his neck.

"Just finish the project yourself, and don't forget to put my name on it," he tells her before shoving his way out the door hard enough to send the bell clanging against the frame.

Linden takes a deep breath before she turns to the table next to her and starts clearing plates and glasses onto her tray in short, clipped movements. "Bryson Ivers is a damn fool, but I can handle him on my own."

"Juniper told me about your run-in with Beulah Fordham Hayes."

The clinking of silverware and glasses pauses for a moment as Linden takes in my words. "She's an awful woman, but I can handle her, too." Her eyes meet mine across the table. "I appreciate that you always have my back, but I don't need you to fight my battles for me."

"Rowan Persephone," Gran calls from the kitchen doorway before I can formulate a response. She crooks one finger at me without another word, and I know I'm in for it.

"Good luck," Linden whispers under her breath.

I follow as Gran leads me to the storage pantry and closes the door behind us. "Girl, you are trialing me something fierce these days." She rubs her brow in frustration. "I know you're angry and that Ivers boy ain't got a lick of sense, but you didn't do your sister any favors just now."

"I know it," I admit.

"And what if that dining room had been full of customers? Would that have been enough to stay your hand? You keep rushing headfirst into the fire like that, and you're liable to get burnt."

"Well, I can't just sit by—"

"No, you're right, you can't." Gran cuts me off. "It's high time you pick a direction," she says, pointing toward the dining room. "That volunteer position with the Forest Service, you're gonna take it. Use the time away to think about what you really want your life to look like."

"What?" I sputter, stunned by the sudden change in direction from where I thought this conversation was headed. "And why would I go and do a thing like that?"

"Because you can't go on like this. It's not good for anyone, least of all you. You're so angry and you're pushing everyone away."

"Outside of the members of this family," I argue, crossing my arms even though I feel like a petulant child as soon as I do it, "there's not a person in this town I'd trust to so much as spit on us if we were on fire. Lord knows why I should give a flying fig about them."

"You're smart enough to know better than that." Gran sighs, then reaches up to the shelf and pulls out an old book, one that contains knowledge our ancestors have gathered for generations. "We call this the James Family Book of Mountain Wisdom, but it wouldn't exist without community. Because it isn't just what all those who came before us knew or created, it's also what was shared with them. Customs and beliefs loaned by other immigrants and the descendants of enslaved people, the uses of native plants from the Cherokee and the Lenape and other Indigenous people who were here long before we showed up. We've built and grown our wisdom based on what we've learned from all the people of these mountains. And if you turn your back on your community, it's not just them you're hurting. It's yourself."

I shake my head to resist rolling my eyes. "We don't even tell people the whole truth of our abilities. If we can't trust them with who we are, what's the point?"

"Fear is a dangerous thing, Rowan." Gran slides the book back on the shelf, then braces her hands against the wood in frustration.

"I know, we have the remodeling bills to prove it." I unfold my arms, hoping this lecture will be over soon and I can get back to work.

"Not theirs, yours." Gran meets my eyes with a furrow between her brows. "I've been angry with you plenty of times, but this is the first time I recall ever being disappointed." She opens the pantry door and steps out, but not before leaving me with one last parting comment. "You be sure and call Vernie when you get home."

I'm left frozen in place, staring after her.

CHAPTER FOUR

IF I must be banished, I might as well be banished to the mountains. The entrance to the National Forest lies just outside town on a quiet stretch of country road marked by a gateway built of native stone and New Deal craftsmanship.

Yet even now, winding our way up the ridge in the old, dusty green Forest Service truck, Frances Vernon looks me dead in the eye and lies.

"The cabin's not so bad." She shrugs, her curls, threaded through with gray, brushing the wide collar of her uniform shirt as the stink of sulfur like a struck match wafts between us. "The mattress is hard, but the roof doesn't leak . . . too much."

She lifts what must be a very lukewarm cup of coffee to her lips, the Tudor's Biscuit World logo a sure sign she didn't pick it up in Caball Hollow. We're not big enough for chain restaurants, even one as ubiquitous in West Virginia as Tudor's.

I crack the window for a breath of fresh air, watching as the truck tires skirt the edge of the narrow dirt switchback. The higher we climb, the more the colors change, like a temperature gauge beginning at mostly green in the valley and steadily increasing in candescence. The birches and tulip poplars go a bright yellow. The sweetgum, serviceberry, and sassafras turn all manner of oranges. And the sugar maples and the sourwoods blaze a brilliant crimson. It's the sweet trees that burn the brightest, getting ready to run sap in the coldest months.

The condition of the cabin doesn't really matter anyhow. Gran likely expected me to cut a shine about her edict, but I didn't. I'm not one to back down from a challenge. And, if I'm being completely honest, the incident with the fork rattled me a little, too. I get fired up all the time, but not like that.

Vernie pulls into a small turnoff and slows to a stop. I grab my duffel bag from the bed of the truck and follow her toward a small trail, barely noticeable amongst the dense woods. It's farther than I expect, a good half mile uphill. But when we break through the trees at the end of the path, the world drops away.

At my sharp inhale, Vernie smiles. "Quite a view, huh?"

It goes on for miles. A long valley striped by the river far below and layers of tree-covered mountains going on forever, the blue of the distant peaks fading into the clouds.

Across all of it, there is not a single sign of human presence. It feels profound. "I've lived here my whole life, but I've never seen it like this."

"Did you know this is our last active lookout tower?" Vernie asks as she walks toward the cabin and I follow.

A half dozen steps lead up to where the structure sits perched atop a rocky exposed ridgeline, a lighthouse above a sylvan sea. It's a small thing, no bigger than my bedroom back home, with windows on all sides and a fenced-in walkway that runs all along the perimeter.

"We once had as many as fifty, all throughout the Forest, but they were mostly phased out in the sixties, when they started using planes, and now there's drones and infrared cameras. This one, though"—she pats the handrail of the wooden staircase like an old friend—"this one we still need. The Forest is especially dense through this area, and for some reason, all that wonderful new tech just glitches. Some sort of interference here we can't figure out."

"You know a lot about this place," I observe, studying the cedar shake shingles of the cabin above us and counting the ones with noticeable dry rot.

"I started my career with the Forest Service as a volunteer fire lookout in this very cabin. A good long while ago now," Vernie says with a smile as she slides her hands into her pockets. She must fall in age somewhere between Mama and Gran. "This time of year, you're liable to spot the raptors on their way south for the winter. Hawks, falcons, maybe even an eagle or two."

She holds out the keys, one very small and one a bit longer, on a plain metal ring, and I reach for them.

"The trade-off is no indoor plumbing and no cell signal, but there is the radio in case of emergencies. Daily updates are broadcast by the Forest Service, so you won't get too lonely out here. Speaking of, I don't know if you've got a fella." She doesn't wait for me to respond. "Or whoever. I'm not much inclined to romantic pursuits myself, but I'm not one to judge."

"I don't date." I rush to curtail the conversation.

"I only bring it up because we don't allow overnight guests. There've been some issues in the past. Folks get out here in the middle of nowhere, and it's like all social norms go out the window. Course, it does feel like another world. I've seen some strange things, I'll tell you what. But you'll be fine. I've got a good feeling about you."

"I'm glad someone does." I mean it as a joke, but when I hear the words, I realize it might not be.

"I know this isn't the most glamorous assignment, but we do appreciate your help. This cabin hasn't been touched since the end of the spring fire season. A million acres is a lot of land for less than a hundred employees and volunteers to manage. The rangers out here at the Teays River Station like to welcome new volunteers with a little cookout, so we'll see you tonight after you get settled."

"Oh, you really don't need to do that," I say, shifting the strap on my duffel bag where it's cutting into my shoulder.

Vernie waves a hand, dismissing my objection. She turns to head down the trail to her truck, then pauses and looks back at me. "Do you know why the leaves change color?" she asks, squinting into the sun. "The trees dismantle their chlorophyll, reabsorbing it to store for the long winter. Waste nothing and prepare for anything. That's my motto. Just like the forest." She smiles, then disappears back into the trees.

And then it's just me. I take in the small clearing I'll be calling home for most of the next few weeks, minus the weekends Gran needs me at the diner. Smokebush, with its billowing pink clusters, clings to rocky limestone bluffs. The broad, dark green leaves of the rhododendron burst from the cleft of every hollow.

Yet, after the long, dry summer, much of the foliage is faded and drooping, the canopy of trees overhead patchy with dropped leaves. Some of the conifers have entire sections of brown, with green needles only on the uppermost parts of the trees, and others show signs of bark beetles. Just one errant spark to the invasive grass and overgrown underbrush and this whole mountain could catch.

The cabin is cold and still in that way only places that have never been a home can be. The windows are all shuttered for the off season, and the air is stale, but there's no hiding the thin layer of dust coating everything, motes sparkling thickly in the beam of sunlight that shines in through the door behind me. Cobwebs span the corners of the room, and the desiccated carcasses of several stinkbugs dot the floorboards.

"Gran, what have you gotten me into?" I mutter as I drop my duffel.

The small space consists of a desk shoved under a window with a bed built into the opposite wall, and a small table with a couple of wooden folding chairs by the woodstove. A shelf runs along the top of the windows with some pots, a few books, and binoculars. Across the clearing, there's a small woodshed near the outhouse, opposite the water pump, where Vernie told me I'd find all the supplies I'll need to get the cabin fixed up. The smaller of the keys she gave me must be for the padlock on its door.

I step out of the cabin and around the narrow walkway to where it juts out over the edge of the ravine. The wind is stronger here, and it pulls at me like grasping hands, undoing my hair, tugging at my shirt. I press against the wooden rail and peer down into the ravine. My stomach drops, and it feels like flying. Or falling.

A harsh rattle followed by a screech jerks my attention skyward. I push my hair out of my eyes, disoriented. Something large and dark is hurtling right at me. A bird, I realize, covering my head instinctively. The keys drop from my hand onto the worn wooden planks of the walkway, inches from the edge.

Just before it reaches me, the bird pulls up, soaring toward the trees higher on the ridge. I lift a hand to block the sun for a better look. Roughly the size and shape of a crow, the bird is black, except for a patch of white across its chest, like a vest, and an iridescent blue gleam to its wings.

"Magpie?" I speak the word out loud in surprise.

There are no magpies in West Virginia. But the sound of my voice is enough to startle the bird from its perch. It takes flight again, and I watch until I can barely make out the dark smudge against the bright sky. Maybe it's possible that the bird was blown off course by some distant storm and ended up in these mountains by mistake, but there's something about the sight of it that leaves me uneasy.

CHAPTER FIVE

THE SKIES are already darkening to the color of faded denim when Vernie steps off the long path into the clearing, two other forest rangers in tow. I grab a jacket and head down the cabin's steps to meet them. The temperature falls fast this time of year up in the mountains, and there's already a chill in the air that draws a shiver across my skin.

"Rowan James." Vernie gestures to me. "Meet Rangers Harshbarger and Carson." She swings her arm toward the two men in uniforms that match her own. Both are younger than Vernie, but probably not by much.

"Welcome." Harshbarger, who appears to be the older of the two, steps forward and holds out his hand. He's about my height with deep-set eyes and a slight sunburn across his nose, which I'd guess is perpetual, given his job and how fair-skinned he is. "We were surprised someone your age would be willing to work out here away from all your friends in the land of no internet."

"I prefer trees to most people," I answer as I shake his hand.

"Then you'll fit right in." Carson chuckles. He's a few inches taller than Harshbarger, with a well-trimmed beard, deep brown skin, and a welcoming smile.

Both men get to work building a small fire in the pit. Vernie and I bring down the folding chairs from the cabin and set them up next to the thick logs beside the fire pit for some more comfortable seating. When the fire burns down enough for cooking, Harshbarger drags over the cooler he brought with him while Carson makes a frame above the embers of the fire with some wood and sets a big frying pan on top.

"Caught these beauties in that cold river water up the mountain just today," Harshbarger tells me as he pulls four whole trout from the cooler.

He rubs each of the fish down with butter and salt, then cooks them up in the hot frying pan with some lion's mane mushrooms and sprigs of thyme. Carson sets a cast-iron Dutch oven of cornbread next to the fish, scooping some embers on top of the lid so it will bake evenly, while Vernie and I wrap potatoes with onion and garlic in foil and bury them under the fire.

At this elevation, far from the lights of Caball Hollow, the stars are so bright it feels like a blanket of sky, a comforting weight holding me to the earth. There's something about eating outside in the crisp air, scented by woodsmoke and lit only by the flames of the campfire and the light of the moon, that makes everything taste so much better. The skin of the trout is crispy and salty, and the fish itself is flaky and filled with flavor. The buttery cornbread and baked potato soak up all the juices. Before I know it, I've eaten everything on my plate.

Harshbarger pulls out a pocketknife and uses it to carve a point at the end of a long stick for s'mores. "You have a knife with you?" he asks as he hands me the stick.

I nod, showing him the long, slender mushroom knife I always keep on me for foraging.

"Good. Never know when you might need it out here," he says as he sharpens another stick for Vernie. "I've had this one for about twenty years now, and it's come in handy more times'n I can count."

A bird caws in the distance, and I'm reminded of the strange one from this morning. "Have you ever seen anything unusual out here?" I ask as Vernie passes out marshmallows. I take one and spear it on my stick over the fire even though I'm too full to eat it. "Like a non-native species?"

Vernie pauses and looks meaningfully at the other rangers before meeting my eyes. "What do you mean, exactly?"

"I thought I saw a magpie earlier." I point up toward the ridge. "It flew off that way."

"No magpies 'round here," says Harshbarger. "Not for about a thousand miles."

"And thank goodness for that." Vernie gestures with the stick in her hand for emphasis, waving a partially charred marshmallow in the air. "Don't get me wrong, I love all creatures. But there's something about the way those birds laugh that makes my skin crawl."

"They steal things, too," Carson chimes in from his perch on the other side of the fire pit. "A friend of mine is a ranger out in Montana, and he told me they had one that kept snatching tools anytime someone left the garage door open."

A breeze blows through the trees, rattling the dry leaves like teeth chattering in an empty skull. I pull my jacket tighter.

"When you asked if we'd seen anything unusual, I thought you meant really strange," Harshbarger says as he pulls an old-fashioned pipe out of his pocket and taps out the bowl.

"Maybe we shouldn't frighten the girl on her first night, Hager," Vernie warns. She uses two graham crackers to pull the marshmallow, now completely burnt, off the end of her stick.

"Well, I'll tell you the strangest thing that ever happened to me." Carson stirs the fire, then leans back as far as he can without falling off his log and crosses his arms. "It was during my first year as a ranger. I was out doing trail maintenance. Not far from here, actually." He gestures vaguely westward. "It took longer than expected, and it was already getting dark by the time I got done. But I still needed to hike back to my truck. So I packed up all my gear and set off at a pretty brisk pace, when I heard something, like a faint buzzing sound, off in the distance. The farther

I went, the louder it got, like it's gaining on me. When I was about a hundred yards from my truck, the sound was so loud, I was convinced the damn Moth-Winged Man or something was right behind me. I hightailed it out of there so fast."

Carson slowly shakes his head. He's been staring at the fire while he recounted his memory, but now he looks up, meeting my eyes through the haze of woodsmoke. "It wasn't until I got back to the station that I realized, in my haste, I'd tossed my phone into my tool bag and my end-of-shift alarm was going off, buzzing around into everything."

Harshbarger chuckles, and a slow grin spreads across Carson's face. I shake my head at the ridiculous story, but I can't stop the small smile that tugs at the corner of my mouth. "That's pretty funny, but I've heard scarier ghost stories at sixth-grade camp," I tease.

"You want scary? All right, I can give you scary," Vernie says, the flicker of firelight casting gruesome shadows across her face. "It was maybe twenty years ago. I was out cleaning up trash near the river when I heard strange whispering. It wasn't like any language I'd ever heard before. The harder I tried to listen, the more difficult it was to hear. When I got to that old dead tree that straddles the water, a man stepped from behind it out of nowhere. He didn't have any gear with him, just the strangely old-fashioned clothes on his back. After I got my heart rate back under control, I approached him to see if he needed any help, but by the time I'd reached the tree, he was gone.

I checked the missing person reports for months after, but there was nothing."

"Woo, boy," Carson says. "A real haunted hillside story right there. That one gave me goose bumps." He examines his arms, then leans closer to the fire.

A chill crawls down the back of my neck, too, and I resist the urge to look over my shoulder. There's not a hint of a lie in Vernie's words. And, unless my ability is malfunctioning again, *knowing* that the person telling the ghost story isn't lying about what they saw makes it decidedly more frightening.

"These mountains are older than oceans, older than trees, older than bone," Vernie says. "When the Appalachians rose into existence, nothing walked on this earth. They've borne witness to a half billion years. Something that old is bound to have secrets. But it's humans that are the most dangerous thing in this Forest."

"You can say that again," Harshbarger agrees. "Lots of rough types think they can hide their illegal activities in the vastness of these woods."

"Like ginseng poachers?" I ask, thinking of the town hall meeting just a few days ago.

"Hmm." He nods. "Could be. They get caught, it can be a hefty fine and jail time. They don't, and they can make more in a day than a lot of people do in a month. That's enough to make people risk it." He pauses and chuckles, lightening the mood. "Course, not all of them are criminal masterminds. I once caught some would-be poachers with a five-pound sack of poison ivy. They mistook the leaves for 'sang and were both covered head to toe in a pretty vicious-looking rash."

When I open my mouth to respond, a huge yawn escapes instead.

"Well, gentlemen, I think that's our cue," Vernie says, slapping her hands on her knees and slowly getting to her feet. "Rowan, welcome to the team. We're very grateful to have you. If you run into any trouble, just use that radio, and one of us will be up here in a jiff."

We all work together and have the dishes cleaned up and the fire put out in no time.

"Here ya go." Carson holds out the rest of the cornbread, wrapped in foil, and a glass jar that he jiggles. "Fresh buttermilk. I made it myself. Some crumbled cornbread in this will be good eatin' come morning."

"Thank you," I tell him as he presses them into my hands.

Carson and Vernie head toward the path, but Harshbarger hangs back to help me carry the chairs inside. "We haven't seen any sign of poachers in this part of the Forest," he says. "It's not the best area for 'sang. Case you were worried."

I watch from the doorway as he joins the others. When I can no longer see their flashlights bobbing down the path, the night presses in. There's a fullness to it somehow, now that I'm truly alone, miles deep in the vastness of the National Forest.

And Harshbarger's words would have been a lot more comforting if they hadn't been a lie.

CHAPTER SIX

A QUICK, staccato burst of laughter shatters the quiet like a shot, waking me from a dead sleep. I jerk upright, unsure if I'm still dreaming. My watch tells me it's just after four in the morning. The incongruence of the sound in the middle of nowhere and the darkest part of night sets the hair on the back of my neck on end before I'm even fully awake.

Slowly, I rise to my knees in the center of the thin mattress, summoning the courage to investigate. The windows are all still shuttered, but I don't reach for the battery-powered lantern. Some instinct tells me not to make myself any more conspicuous. I eye the radio, weighing whether I should call for help.

The silence closes back in, like water around a stone thrown into the river. I listen hard for any noise. Any sign there's someone out there. I'm breathing too loud. It's all I can hear now. When the quiet feels so full it might burst, I peer into the darkness, straining to make anything out. But all I can see is the peeling paint of the thick shutters. I lean in, pressing my ear against the glass to listen.

A sharp tap strikes the window.

I leap from the bed. Stumbling over my feet, I go sprawling across the hard floor. Another burst of laughter reverberates through the night. This time, it goes on forever, the sound traveling like a pack of kids running along the walkway outside the cabin. I try to track the movement, but it's coming from everywhere all at once.

Until it stops, cutting off so completely it's like it never happened. Except my heart is still racing. The temperature has dropped dramatically overnight, but I can't tell if my teeth are chattering from cold or from fear.

Then I remember Vernie's comment about magpies and the unsettling way their cries sound like laughter. Maybe the bird I saw yesterday really was a magpie. One that doesn't seem to want me here. But no matter what it was, the likelihood of falling back to sleep now is zero. I've tossed and turned most of the night anyway, thanks to the chill in the air and a mattress that feels like a half-full bag of livestock feed, both lumpy and hard. I sit in the dark, my quilt drawn around me, until the radio crackles to life at seven a.m. as the sun begins to rise.

"Good morning, National Forest Service team members and volunteers! Ranger Eugene Hatfield here with this morning's weather report. A bit of a chilly start today with lows hovering around fifty-six. But we'll see those temperatures climb with a high in the seventies this afternoon. Current fire conditions are moderate. Remember, thunderstorms in West Virginia are often sudden and severe. Be aware of your surroundings, stay alert, and enjoy your day in the most beautiful place on earth." There is a brief burst of static, and then silence.

The lookout tower is elevated on stilts above the ridge and the cold wind cuts beneath it, turning the floor to ice. I climb out of bed, hopping from foot to foot as I try to quickly pull on my clothes without falling on my butt. My first order of business this morning is to figure out the woodstove. A quilt and a double layer of sweatpants don't cut it.

I make quick work of Ranger Carson's cornbread and buttermilk, then lace up my hiking boots. The woodpile sits out behind the shed, partially in a stand of red spruce. But first, I walk around the exterior of the cabin. I'm not sure what I'm looking for, but a single iridescent black feather is all I find. As I walk into the woods, I watch my step in the rocky areas and thick leaf mold. It's copperhead season, that time of year when the new young emerge all over the South. With their bright burnished heads and the distinctive hourglass pattern along their backs that seems to taunt *time's up*, copperheads are West Virginia's most prevalent venomous snake. Like most pit vipers, they lie in wait to ambush their prey, the neonates using the bright green tips of their tails as a lure. Common folk wisdom is that if you smell cucumber, it means they're nearby.

When I reach the stack of firewood, it doesn't take long to realize that all the logs are much too big to fit into the woodstove. Some of them are enormous, like a downed tree has been chopped up to clear a trail. I reach for a smaller one that seems somewhat manageable, but it's heavier than I expect, and I have to bend way down to get a good grip on it. My face is low to the ground when something detaches from the darkness of the woodpile and races toward me.

"Shit!" I drop the log and fall backward, cursing my own foolishness. Everyone and their brother knows woodpiles are ideal hiding places for snakes.

But just as quickly as it moves, the snake stops, coiling its long body just inches from my boot and lifting that distinctive triangle-shaped head that means venomous.

"Impossible," I exhale in barely a whisper. Not a copperhead or even a rattlesnake, it's pale gray with a darker zigzag pattern down its back. This isn't a snake that belongs in these mountains. It's an adder, *Vipera berus*.

I scramble backward, digging in the heels of my hiking boots and kicking up dirt. The snake watches me, its head bobbing up and down, before dropping back to its belly and slithering into the long shadow cast by the squat little supply shed.

Slowly, I get to my feet and lift the fallen log. My instinct to turn tail and run back to the cabin wars with my desire to figure out what the hell is going on. Adders not only don't belong in West Virginia, they don't belong on this continent. So how did this one end up here?

I brush the dirt off my pants with a sigh. When the unexplainable happens around here, there's really only one place that makes sense to start looking for answers. But there's no maintained Forest Service trail where I'm going. I'll have to take my chances trudging through the piles of leaves and across rocky outcroppings. Because the tree Vernie described near where she'd seen the ghostly figure is one I know well.

The Bone Tree is deep in the heart of the Forest. A liminal place, stretching from one bank of the creek to the other. Five thick branches, like fingers, reach for the opposite shore. No matter the season, it's bare of leaves, and the bark is as stark white as sun-bleached bone.

For generations, the women of the James family have gone to the Bone Tree for divination, spirit work, and spells that need a little extra boost. Even the plants we forage for our tonics and tinctures are extra potent from the area surrounding the tree. The location is one we keep closely guarded, a secret passed down from mother to daughter for more than two centuries.

But it wasn't until this summer that my sisters and I discovered its true purpose. It wasn't a naturally occurring place of power, but a forcefully made doorway between this world and the one beyond. One born of desperation by the founders of Caball Hollow, who had feared death in a land far from home. And now there might be something wrong with it. A few weeks ago, we discovered a jagged crack right through the middle of the trunk, so deep it nearly split in two. None of the family books mention anything like this ever happening before. And no one seems to have any idea what it could mean.

The cabin overlooks the valley where the Bone Tree stands, so when I still haven't reached it after nearly an hour, I pause to get my bearings. I'm pretty sure I've passed that same pin oak with the boulder next to it a couple times already. Slowly, I spin around, taking in my surroundings. I've hiked here many times before and know my way well, but somehow, I've been going in circles. There's a strange languidness in my joints and a level of exhaustion that goes beyond a hike and lack of sleep.

There's always been a feeling of wrongness near the Bone Tree, an eerie sense that even the wildlife must pick up on. I've never seen a bird land on its branches, or a squirrel run up its trunk, and the vines that claim the other dying trees have never stretched a tendril toward it. I suspect it's what keeps other people away, too, the feel of its power in the animal parts of their brains. But I've never felt it like this before or from this far away.

I drop my pack to the ground, remembering something I once read in one of the old James family books about breaking enchantments, and pull off my jacket and sweater, turning both inside out before putting them on backward. Almost immediately the fog begins to lift.

I reach for my pack to check the compass attached to its zipper, and my eyes snag on something half-buried at the base of the pin oak. Among the spleenwort and black cohosh, the soil has been turned over and a single stick stands straight up from the dirt. I pull on it, and it slips out easily, the other end sharpened to a point. Someone else has been here. And relatively recently, judging from the color of the earth.

It takes another twenty minutes to finally reach the Bone Tree. The crack that runs through the center is even deeper than I remember. I make a slow loop around the tree, so focused on inspecting the trunk that it takes too long for me to notice the Forest has gone quiet. I'm immediately on edge. There are precious few reasons for nature to stop and hold its breath. None of them especially good. Something else is out here. Something dangerous. A predator large enough for the Forest to take notice. I draw my gaze slowly along the trees lining the edge of the creek, searching for the threat and careful not to make any sudden movements.

A burst of laughter erupts from somewhere above me. My head jerks up, and I freeze. Seven magpies watch me from the branches of the Bone Tree, and my breath catches. When I saw the first one yesterday, I'd assumed it was a black-billed magpie, *Pica hudsonia*, the most likely in North America. But now, seeing the birds more closely, I'm almost positive they are common magpies, *Pica pica*. Another species, like the adder, that doesn't belong on this continent. My gaze drops to the fissure in the sun-bleached white of the trunk. Or maybe it's even more than that. Maybe they don't belong in this world at all.

I back away, the old nursery rhyme echoing in my head: *One for sorrow, two for mirth, three for a funeral, four for a birth, five for heaven, six for hell, seven for the devil, his own self.*

CHAPTER SEVEN

WHEN THE radio crackles to life Friday morning, it startles me from deep in a dream full of rotten leaves and slithering things. I jolt out of bed and land hard on the floor with a thud I feel in my bones.

"Good morning, Forest Service staff and volunteers," the voice from the radio continues. "This is Ranger Carson, and the forecast in the mountains today is cool and cloudy with a low of fifty-four and a high of sixty-eight. We have a low pressure system moving in today and bringing with it a strong chance of thunderstorms in the afternoon and evening hours, so let's batten down the hatches."

Stumbling to my feet, I pull on the pants I left draped over the back of the wooden kitchen chair last night. I've spent my first week at the cabin scraping off peeling paint and chopping firewood until my shoulders ache. Other than the rangers who came by for dinner that first day, I haven't seen another soul. I'd thought that would be one of the main benefits of taking this job, but after growing up in a house of seven people, it's a strange thing to have only myself for company. Am I even the same person when no else is around?

Each morning is colder up here on the ridge. By lunchtime, the western sky is a bilious green-gray haze, with heavy, distended clouds rolling in. It's going to be a bad one. The window shutters are still up so that I can paint them, and I'm all the more glad of it now. Any added protection during a storm is a good thing when you're three thousand feet up in a tiny glass box.

I've taken to hiking through the Forest each day, looking for signs of the unexplainable or anything that doesn't belong. When I step onto the trail today, the birds chirp a warning at my intrusion. The message travels from one to another, moving through the trees ahead of me, the song shifting and evolving as it goes. I haven't made it very far when a shrill beep amidst the crunch of leaves and the buzz of insects stops me in my tracks. It's an electronic pulse that sticks out like a fart in church.

I follow the sound to a stand of sourwood trees surrounded by a cluster of rhododendrons and find discarded wire clippings and plastic ties scattered across the ground. A battery pack is hidden among the glossy green leaves of the rhododendron with a thick cord that leads up to a camera tacked on to one of the tree trunks, sticky pale sap oozing from the wounds. Nearby is a plastic covering that must have blown off only to get stuck in another thicket a few feet away. More wires go up into the foliage, and I have to shade my eyes from the sun to pick out some sort of solar panel and a metal antenna that's been painted green to better blend in.

I spot a little winking sun logo on the bottom of the camera, and a white-hot rage rolls through me. The first rule of the National Forest is to leave no trace. I rip down the wires and cords, then search the ground for a sturdy fallen branch to knock the rest of the equipment out of the trees. The batteries and solar panel are relatively easy to dislodge, but the camera won't budge. I wedge the stick in behind the camera to pry it off. When it finally pops free, I'm puffing like a dragon and bleeding from a slice on my thumb.

A single pink rhododendron blossom floats down and lands at my feet. I bend to retrieve it. Clearly, it's been pressed between the camera and the tree for some time. But at this elevation, the rhododendrons drop their flowers by the end of July, early August at the latest, which was well before the YouTube team got to Caball Hollow. Unless they've been watching the Forest longer than anyone realized. The antenna is too high for me to reach, so I pull myself up into the lowest branches and swing the stick like a club until I knock it from its perch. Then I gather up everything, down to the last centimeter of wire, and stuff it into my pack, determined to return it all back to its owner.

I'm now covered in a thick coat of dirt and sweat, and still too het up to go back to the cabin, so I veer toward the creek instead to splash some cold mountain water on my face. Dropping to my knees on the soft bank, I dip in my hands and scrub my face, then dab it dry with the slightly cleaner inside of my shirt. The water works its magic and already I feel my temper starting to cool.

I haven't been to this part of the Stillhouse before, but the rich soil of the low-lying bottomland is an ideal spot for foraging, and I'm not surprised to spot the telltale patch of big broad leaves. When I get closer, I find pale green pawpaws ready to harvest and, miraculously, not already in the belly of an opossum or a raccoon. Gently, I shake the small tree and only take the ones that fall, nestling the delicate fruit in my pack to bring home so Mama can make some of her spiceberry pawpaw jam. It only takes a few minutes, but in that time the temperature drops sharply as thick clouds roll in, chilling the remaining moisture on my skin.

As I'm zipping up my pack, there's another sound beneath the gurgle of the creek that I can't quite make out. Slowly, I stand and move closer to the trees. The clouds overhead are growing dark and thick. I need to get back to the cabin. But there's the sound again, and this time I know what it is. Not the call of a bird or chitter of chipmunks but voices, coming from somewhere in the trees behind me.

I move a little deeper into the woods, curious. There's not a marked trail back here, but maybe they're hikers who got turned around or are on their way to a secret fishing hole. I can make out at least three distinct masculine voices. As I move closer, one of the voices gets louder, sharper. They're arguing.

I pause, reconsidering whether I should make myself known. They could be lost and need help, but Vernie's list of poacher warning signs comes rushing back, and I remember the sharpened stick I found under the pin oak that couldn't be more than a mile from here as the crow flies.

"You must come with us," the deepest of the voices says loud enough for me to make out the words. "We mean you no harm." Even though I'm too far away to pick up the smell of a lie, there's something in the tone that turns my blood cold.

"I do not concede!" The second voice is younger and strained with fear.

His words are followed by a shout and the scuffling sounds of a struggle. I search frantically for some sign of where they are. But there's not so much as the rustle of a leaf or a flash of color between the trees. Nothing.

"Hurry," the third person shouts, voice shrill. "We haven't much time."

A sickening crack echoes through the trees, like a pumpkin falling on cement, followed by a low groan. My stomach drops. I reach into my pocket and wrap my hand around my mushroom knife. But even if I could take on two grown men, I can't help a person I can't find.

"Is there someone out there?" the first man shouts.

I do the only thing I can do. I run.

Retracing my steps, I race back to the creek, then past the sourwood stand where I found the camera equipment. It's at least three miles to the cabin, mostly uphill, and by the time I reach it, my heart is beating an echo in my fingertips. I dig for the key in my pocket, and nearly fumble it before managing to unlock the door.

Tossing my pack on the floor, I rush for the radio. "Fire Lookout One to National Forest dispatch." I release the button and wait. Several long moments tick by with only the sound of static coming across the channel.

"This is dispatch. Go ahead, Fire Lookout One," a voice crackles through the radio at last.

I let out a long breath in relief. "Three men were fighting out near Stillhouse Creek, due southwest of here. I couldn't see anything through the trees, but it sounded like one of them could be pretty severely injured. And there's a good chance they might be poachers," I tell him, explaining my earlier discovery of the sharpened stick and disturbed earth.

"Ten-four, Fire Lookout One. We're sending a team to investigate." There's a pause and then another transmission. "Rowan, stay in the cabin and keep the door locked until you get the all clear," the voice I now recognize as Ranger Carson instructs, his usual good humor noticeably absent.

The door stands wide open with my pack in front of it, and just beyond is the edge of the approaching storm. A rim of thick clouds as dark as char. In two long strides, I cross the room and bolt the lock.

Thunder rumbles off in the distance, and the wind kicks up, howling ominously between the trees. Low pressure makes the air heavy with anticipation, sending birds flittering to find refuge, insects to fly low on weighted wings, and worms to flee rising groundwater. It's a silence like the inhale before the raging howl.

A big gust blows across the ridge, and something strikes the wall with a thud. I back away from the door.

There's a soft noise from just outside. A light footstep against the walkway. Though that's not exactly right. It was more of a shuffle than a step. I try to convince myself it was the leaves blowing across the wooden boards. But the quiet that follows is heavy with anticipation, more acute even than that of the impending storm. It isn't proof nothing is there. It's the opposite.

Something, or someone, is out there. My breath comes faster as I strain to hear. A muted thud. Then a crash against the door hard enough to make it shudder in its frame. I race to the woodstove and reach for the metal poker.

There's no one to call for help. No one who could get here before a person determined enough could break through the flimsy piece of old wood standing between us. There's only me. Holding the poker over my shoulder like a baseball player at bat, I slide back the lock and yank open the door.

There, lying across the doormat like something the cat dragged in, is a bloodied and unconscious Hadrian Fitch.

CHAPTER EIGHT

I SLAM the door and lean back against it, counting my heartbeats until I don't feel like screaming anymore. Of course he would show up here tonight of all nights after leaving without so much as a goodbye weeks ago. Of course he would somehow find me here when he's in such a state that I can't turn him away. Hadrian Fitch seems to be my special burden to bear, though I'm not sure quite what I've done to deserve him.

I switch on the lantern, hoping that when I look again there somehow won't be a bloodied, unconscious man outside. It wouldn't be the first time he's disappeared, but I won't be so lucky twice.

When I open the door, he's managed to pull himself up against the wall of the cabin. He sits slumped over, his unruly hair especially wild. One of his eyes is mostly open. The other appears to be swollen shut.

"What happened to you?" I ask, kneeling to better assess how to get him inside, all the while replaying the argument I overheard in the Forest earlier. None of the voices sounded like Hadrian's, and yet it's like the violence conjured him. What are the chances he would show up on my doorstep looking like this so soon after something like that?

"I half expected you'd leave me out here," he says through a split lip.

"Thought about it." I pull his arm over my shoulders, and he blinks, or maybe winks, at me. I can't be sure as it's only the one eye that currently has the ability to open. I slide my other arm around his waist, and the muscles of his abdomen, honed through hard labor, tighten beneath my fingertips. He sucks air through his teeth.

"Planning to carry me?" he asks after a couple quick, shallow breaths.

"It's either this or drag you. Makes no difference to me," I tell him. "I'll count to three. Ready? One, two, three." I lift up, and we both grunt. Me because he's heavier than he looks. Him, I assume, because it hurts like hell.

I'm tall, but he's a good deal more so, and we stumble into the cabin together in an awkward tangle of limbs. I drop him into the small wooden chair by the table. He groans and holds his ribs while I grab the first aid kit off the shelf and the half-full kettle from the stove.

And then it hits me, the reason why *he* in particular might be here so soon after that awful fight.

The legend of the Moth-Winged Man, a portent of death with the wings of a moth and the body of a man, told around the Hollow isn't the whole truth. The diablerie, the oldest book of James family knowledge, tells a slightly different tale.

Not a monster, but one of the graveyard watch, the Moth-Winged Man is among the ranks of those who had their lives cut unfairly short and are now responsible for protecting souls who have met a tragic end on the road between death and the hereafter. It was folklore the Scots-Irish immigrants who settled here brought with them, this belief in the good folk. And like the Otherworld, it is all too real.

Not long after Hadrian took off last month, Linden confessed the whole truth. She'd discovered that Hadrian hadn't been searching for his brother but his killer. Almost nineteen years ago, he'd gone missing as a boy and, in the time since, had become something else entirely. Linden suspected he had gone back to the Otherworld for good. Still doesn't explain why he couldn't have given us a heads-up. Maybe even said goodbye first.

"What happened to you, anyhow?" I ask again as I move closer to wipe the dirt and blood from his face. Needing to know and yet afraid to hear the answer. If the fight I'd witnessed was as bad as it sounded, perhaps Hadrian was here because someone had died.

"A man was killed not far from here." He sighs, and my breath catches. My gaze jerks to meet his, searching for answers. "It was a car accident," he clarifies. "After I helped him cross to the other side through the Bone Tree, I was attacked."

"Attacked?" I repeat, surprised. Could this have anything to do with all the other strange things that have happened in the Forest near the Bone Tree lately? "Wait, a car accident? You mean the ginseng poacher that crashed into the tree just outside the Forest? That was almost two weeks ago."

"Time passes differently in the Otherworld." His words are slightly nasal and soft-edged, like maybe his nose might be a little broken.

"Slower?" I attempt to clarify, pressing my hand against his cheek to turn his face to check for more injuries. I can feel his eyes on me, like he's searching for something, but I don't know what.

"Differently." He lifts one shoulder in the barest suggestion of a shrug.

It's strange to talk to him about this. To tacitly acknowledge what he is. He winces when I touch the cloth to his split lip.

I clear my throat and take a step back. "What attacked you?"

"I'm not sure, it was too dark. Too fast. But I don't think it was random. Whatever or whoever it was knew that I'd be coming and was lying in wait."

"How?" I lift his right hand so I can better see to clean out the broken skin across his knuckles.

"I don't know, but the strangest part was that it didn't happen on the Otherworld side. It happened on this side."

I look up into the vibrant green of his eyes. "Why is that strange?"

"Because it means someone in Caball Hollow knows what I am," he answers, his gaze heavy on mine. "And what the Bone Tree is."

I move away, using the act of rinsing out the cloth to give myself a moment to think. All of this makes me uneasy. So many unexplainable occurrences. Disparate pieces with no clear connection, other than the looming sense of foreboding that sits heavy in the air. "What are you going to do?"

He waits until I look at him to answer. "I need your help."

I stare back a moment too long. There's an earnestness in his expression that somehow makes me feel too exposed. I'm comfortable with hating him. Or even with the childish bickering between us before he left. But this. This is too much.

"What does it look like I'm doing?" I ask, pressing a cold compress from the first aid kit against his eye.

He ignores me and puts his hand over mine, removing the compress. "You can tell if someone is lying."

This time I can't keep the surprise from showing on my face, and it doesn't even occur to me to try and deny what he's said. "Why do you know that?" I pull away.

"Because you're terrible at hiding it. What do you think I was doing all year, telling pointless lies around you? You get a little wrinkle right here every time." He taps a finger against the top of my nose, and I jerk backward.

"No, absolutely not." The compress is freezing my hand in sharp contrast to my rapidly heating anger, and I toss it onto the table. "Where do you get off coming here and asking me for a favor? You left without so much as a word. After a year of my gran feeding and housing you, relying on you, while you lied to our faces about who you were. You didn't think you at least owed us a goodbye?"

"I was called back to the Otherworld," he starts, then flinches and wraps an arm around his ribs.

I wait for him to continue, but he doesn't. "That's it? That's all you're going to say? You should have just stayed gone."

He looks at me, clenching his jaw so hard it looks like it hurts, then nods. He stands and turns toward the door. "If you change your mind, burn this." Reaching into his pocket, he pulls out a maple key, the little seedpod with its papery wings still bright green despite the season.

I take it, puzzled, and when I raise my eyes, the door is closing behind him just as the sky opens up and the rain begins with a vengeance.

The call goes out over the radio not long after the storm ends. An injured man, unconscious and nonresponsive, found near the East Fork trail shelter. My heartbeat stutters as my mind goes to the very injured man I sent away just a few hours ago. Has Hadrian been lying out in the pouring rain all this time?

I grab the first aid kit and shove it into my pack. And then I run.

It's less than a mile from here, but it's through dense hardwood forest and slick mud that slides underneath my feet and pulls at my ankles. The rain may have stopped, but it's still dripping from the canopy overhead, and I have to wipe it from my forehead over and over just so I can see.

When I reach the shelter, breathless and panting, a ranger is pressing her fingers to the throat of the person lying on the muddy ground, motionless. The structure is really just a lean-to with three walls, a roof, and a wooden floor for backpackers to get out of the elements. It's remote, not in one of the popular hiking areas, so it's only used sporadically. He's lucky someone happened to find him out here at all, let alone with this storm.

I push the wet hair out of my face and force myself to walk closer. The man has one arm tucked behind him as though he was turning when he fell. The other is thrown across his forehead; a mess of hair the color of shallot skin springs up around it. He doesn't have a coat or shoes, and his clothing is ripped and covered in mud. Sharp-featured and vulpine, his face could be carved from marble and compels attention despite the blood and dirt. But he's not dead. And he's not Hadrian.

CHAPTER NINE

THE WIND whips through the trees, chilling the moisture on my skin at a rapid pace. The lips of the unconscious man—or perhaps boy, it's difficult to tell quite how old he is—are blue around the edges. He groans as one of the forest rangers unfurls a shiny foil blanket from the first aid kit and wraps it around him. She swipes his arm with an alcohol swab and slides a needle under his skin.

He flinches without waking, and I study the lines of his face, trying to determine if maybe it could match up with one of the voices from the woods. Is he the second man—the younger one who was clearly afraid of the other two? It's impossible to know, but the sounds of the sickening crack and the groan after it still echo in my ears.

"Rowan!" someone shouts, breaking me out of my spell.

When I turn, Ranger Harshbarger is walking toward me. He's wearing one of those wide-brim hats the rangers have to keep the rain out of his eyes, but despite that and his waterproof jacket, he looks soaked to the bone.

"Good work today." He claps a hand on my shoulder. "If it weren't for your call, we wouldn't have been near this area, and we might not have gotten to him in time. Was he one of the men you saw fighting?" He watches me closely for my reaction, but there's only one answer I can give.

"I only heard their voices." I shake my head. "I looked, but I never saw anyone."

He nods, satisfied. "Well, we'll figure all that out in due time. Right now we need to get him to safety." Harshbarger crosses to the ATV and pulls out a bright yellow backboard.

"How can I help?" I ask the other ranger.

"Take this and climb into the back of the vehicle," she says, handing me the IV bag that connects by tubing to the needle in the unconscious man's arm. The name badge on her uniform says ELLIS. "It's gonna be a bumpy ride on the way in. I'll need your help keeping him stabilized."

I hold the bag up so gravity can do its thing while the two rangers work together to carefully slide the backboard underneath the victim, then lift it between them. I scramble into the ATV as they load up the injured man. Ranger Ellis climbs in after him, and Harshbarger jumps into the driver's seat.

"Hang on," he calls out, and we take off, rumbling over the rough terrain back to the trail as fast as we dare.

"Is he a poacher?" I shout to be heard over the roar of the engine and the rush of wind.

"I didn't see any ginseng or digging tools on him," Ranger Ellis says. "But the skin of his hands is torn up pretty bad like he's been digging, there's a considerable amount of dirt under his fingernails, and he's missing the very tip of his left fifth digit. It's an old wound, but it healed badly, most likely without proper medical attention."

"What happened to him?" I ask, cataloging the amount of blood and bruising clearly evident.

"Hard to tell. He could have slipped on wet rock somewhere but managed to make it to the shelter before he passed out."

"You don't think it was foul play?" I ask, surprised.

"Sure, it could be. Ginseng hunters can be fiercely territorial. Maybe he was poaching somebody else's patch. Maybe he was double-crossed by his partners. Or he was the double-crosser. But we can't rule out it being an accident."

"He doesn't have a coat. Or shoes," I remind her, as if it were possible to forget.

"I've seen some weird stuff out here. Mental health crisis. Drug use. People do some wild things." She reaches out to tuck the blanket more closely around the man.

"He's lucky you happened to check the shelter," I tell her. It wasn't the most obvious place to search, based on where I'd reported hearing the argument.

"It wasn't luck." She shakes her head, the dark braid down her back like a kite tail. "The Teays River District office got an anonymous voicemail."

My eyes go wide. She may not be ready to rule it foul play, but why else would someone call for help and not give their name?

An ambulance is waiting when we reach the trailhead, flashing lights painting the trees in red. The EMTs quickly transfer the unconscious man from the ATV while Ranger Ellis updates them on his condition and the medical aid she provided in the field. In a matter of minutes, they're speeding off toward the closest hospital, which is still nearly twenty miles away.

"Do you think he'll be all right?" I ask.

"We gave him the best chance we could." Ranger Harshbarger looks over at me, taking in my mud- and rain-streaked appearance. "Come on, kiddo, I'll give you a ride home. It'll be a lot easier to get cleaned up with hot running water."

By the time we reach the farm, the sun has long since set. I stomp up the porch steps, trying to knock some of the muck from my boots, but it's hopeless. They'll need to be hosed down tomorrow. I shuck them off and leave them by the back door.

"Mama?" I call out as I step into the kitchen of the old farmhouse, the hardwood cold against my stocking feet. "Gran?"

Footsteps echo down the front hall and then Gran appears in the doorway on the other side of the kitchen. She has her glasses on and a stack of old books in her arms like I've interrupted some late-night reading.

"Rowan?" Surprise registers at the sight of me, but she must see something in my face that tells her not to push for answers right now. "Well, you look like you've got quite a story. Why don't you go get cleaned up, and I'll fix you some supper, then you can tell me all about it."

I don't think I've ever fully appreciated the luxury of a shower, but a week without running water has changed my perspective. One bathroom shared by four teenage girls means rarely getting the chance to take my time. Now I stand in the claw-foot tub, so old there's barely any enamel left on the bottom, and let the room fill with steam as the water sluices off me and runs down the drain, slowly turning from muddy to clear. All the aches in my muscles that I ignored come screaming back, and I stay under the spray until the hot water heater gives out.

When I go back downstairs, towel drying my hair, Gran already has a plate of cider-braised pork shoulder, green beans with bacon, acorn squash, and a cathead biscuit on the table waiting for me. It may be reheated leftovers, but it's the best-looking thing I've seen in days. Yet she still doesn't pry. Sitting across from me, she picks up what I now recognize as a volume of the James Family Book of Mountain Wisdom and resumes her reading.

I wait to speak until I've finished every bite. Partly because I'm famished, but also because I need time to organize my thoughts. When I finally push my plate aside, Gran sets down her book and listens as I recount the discovery of the unconscious man and the argument that came before it.

It's on the tip of my tongue to tell her about Hadrian's sudden reappearance and his request for my help, but I swallow back the words. There's no guarantee he'll stick around anyhow. Best not to bring it up until I know for sure.

"Sometimes I think we're too much alike, you and I. Both stubborn to a fault." Gran shakes her head, rueful. "Maybe this was one of my more harebrained notions. It certainly wouldn't be the first. I guess I still haven't learned my lesson about trying to force the people I love into doing what I think is best for them.

"I've been looking through all the old books, searching for a way to bring your great-aunt Zephyrine back." Gran gestures to the book on the table in front of her. "It may be time for me to admit there's only one place I'm likely to find a solution." She chuckles softly, but there's no joy in it. "I guess it's a bit poetic that the book we fought over so much would hold the answer to bringing her home. I wished it gone so many times, and now that it is . . ." She trails off with a sigh.

The diablerie isn't only our oldest book, it's also been the source of more than a few family disputes over the years, including the one between Gran and Zephyrine. The magic it holds is unlike the other books, a more potent and forceful sort that comes at a price. Zephyrine thought all James women should have access to the book and decide for themselves if it was worth the cost. But Gran believed the diablerie spells were too powerful and had the potential to exert undue influence on anyone they were used upon.

She kept it locked in a drawer in the summer kitchen. Until Linden made a bargain with the Moth-Winged Man, trading the diablerie to save the life of the person she loves.

"Zephyrine has been gone for more than twenty years now." Gran studies her hands. "Almost as long as she was here. But something changed over the last month. It feels like I'm running out of time." When she looks up to meet my eyes, hers are wet. "A bird got into the house this morning. Your mother found it flapping around in her bedroom, trying to get out the window."

Like a cow that moos at midnight or a whip-poor-will singing at noon, if a bird flies into the house, it is a warning that death is coming.

"What kind of bird was it?" I ask, something uncomfortable pricking under my skin.

"I'm not sure." Gran pauses, surprised by the question. "She said it was big as a crow."

I push away from the table, needing to move so I can focus while I tell her about my own strange wildlife encounters from the last few days with the magpies and the venomous snake.

"Are you sure it was an adder?" she asks once I'm done. "Lots of snakes around here. Could have been a hognose."

I pause to give her a look and lift my shirt to display the tattoo on my hip. "I know what an adder looks like, Gran." It was an impulsive decision, I'll admit. But for months, I'd had this recurring nightmare about a snake wrapped around the branches of a rowan tree, biting its own tail. I thought maybe if I put it on my skin, I could finally get it out of my head. "There's something going on. In the Forest and here, too."

Gran sighs with a shake of her head. "There's been a strangeness in the air since this summer that hasn't gone away. Something has been put into motion. I only hope we realize what it is before it's too late."

I fall asleep like I'm drowning, pulled under by a riptide before I can struggle. And I wake, hours later, gasping for breath. The whole house is quiet, yet I can't shake the feeling of being startled awake, whether on this side of consciousness or the other. The moon shines too brightly through the window, and I stare back at it, my throat dry and achy, before reaching for my phone. If the four of us sisters were one body, Linden would be the heart, Juniper the spirit, and Sorrel the brains. I'm not sure what they'd say I would be. Maybe the muscle. Or the mouth.

"Hey." Sorrel answers on the first ring. She has always been nocturnal, and not even university class schedules can change her ways. "The news about Caball Hollow's very own Sleeping Beauty is all anyone can talk about."

"Is that really what people are calling him?" I ask, disgusted. The poor man was found unconscious and bleeding in the mud. Talk about adding insult to injury.

"Yeah, well, it might not be clever, but there's a photo, and they're not wrong."

I shake my head, then go quiet as I listen to her breath across the distance and work up to the words I called to say.

"Hadrian is back." I close my eyes so I can't see her empty bed, pretending she's here with me like normal, whispering late at night, long after everyone else has gone to sleep.

She doesn't say anything at first, and I count the seconds until she responds. "How do you feel about that?"

"Honestly? I'm angry," I tell her, and my voice shakes just a little in a way I would never let it with anyone else. I swallow against the pressure building in my throat. "And, also, maybe a tiny bit . . . relieved?"

I rush on to explain before she can get the wrong idea. "It's been like waiting for the other shoe to drop, you know? Always wondering if he'd show up again or not."

She hums in acknowledgment, and I keep talking, explaining how he'd appeared out of nowhere at the cabin, bloody and broken, and asking for a favor.

"So, what are you going to do?" she asks.

I think of the hopelessness in Gran's face tonight when she sat across the table, and an idea begins to take shape.

"What if I can convince him to make a trade?" I venture. "My help in exchange for the diablerie."

"Do you think you can trust him?"

"Not even a little bit," I answer immediately.

"There's always one way you could get the truth." There's a rustle of fabric under her words like she's settling in. "And all it would take is a couple drops of blood."

The best way to keep a secret is to say nothing at all. I can't detect a lie that hasn't been told. But there's another side to my ability, one we discovered as children when Linden bit me and promptly told on herself. I've only done it intentionally once, when we needed information to protect my sister. But compelling someone to speak secrets they may not want to share isn't something I take lightly.

"Why should I care about what he's hiding anymore?" I sit up in bed and rub my eyes. "I just want the diablerie. And then to never see him ever again."

It doesn't really matter anyway. Whether I trust him or not, Gran deserves every chance she can get to find her sister. And maybe that book has some answers. I'll do anything I can to protect my family, even if that means playing nice with Hadrian until I figure out what the hell is going on.

"I don't know, Rowan, this could be dangerous. We know he was attacked. If you start asking too many questions, what's to say the same won't happen to you? Maybe I should come home for a bit," she starts, but I cut her off.

"No, you focus on your classes. I'll handle this." I throw off the blankets and get to my feet. "Don't worry, I know what I'm doing," I tease.

"That absolutely does not reassure me," she says, but I can hear the smile in her voice.

After I hang up with Sorrel, I dig through the hamper in my closet until I find the pants I was wearing earlier. The cuffs are stiff with mud, and the pocket where I thought I shoved that damn maple key is empty.

I pull out the rest of the dirty laundry until, finally, I find it stuck to an old sweater near the bottom. I fish it out, terrified that the delicate wings of the seedpod will rip and all this will be for nothing. There's a box of matches next to the candle on Sorrel's dresser, and I pocket them on my way to the bathroom. Now that I've made up my mind, I don't want to waste any time.

After I lock the door, I tear a match from the book and strike it against the friction strip on the back. The maple key has dried out enough that it catches immediately, burning down so fast I have to drop it into the sink so it doesn't singe my fingers.

A stream of black smoke spirals from the top of the flame. There's a strange solidity to it as it slowly makes its way to a gap around the seal of the bathroom window, pushing through to the outside. Then, just as quickly, the fire goes out. Nothing is left of the seedpod in the sink, and all the smoke has seeped through the crack without leaving so much as a scent behind. It's as if it never existed at all.

CHAPTER TEN

SUN SHINES through the wide front window of the Harvest Moon, casting the shadow of the leaping stag logo across the wide-plank floors.

It's only been a handful of days since I was here last, but it doesn't quite fit the same. Like when I accidentally wore Sorrel's muck boots instead of mine and, even though they were the same size, the wear pattern of her gait was different, too low or too high in all the wrong places, and I felt it with every step.

Caball Hollow, though, seems in quite a fine fettle. The dining room is packed full, which is a good indicator that there's gossip afoot. Hillard Been sits at his usual table, and I watch from the front counter as Linden approaches to take his order.

"Will Buck be joining you today?" she asks, pulling a notepad from her pocket.

"He can't get away for lunches too often these days," Hillard tells her, folding his newspaper. "You know how it is at the post office. Ramping up for holiday crunch time."

"Oh, sure, sure," she agrees, even though it's only September.

At the other end of the counter, a group from the Caball Hollow Historical Society chatter loudly about the upcoming mayoral election.

"Any council member who wants my vote better get to the bottom of this," a woman in a bright blue sweater declares. "If the rash of petty thefts lately wasn't bad enough, now we've got folks losing memories, too."

"Mighty troubling," the man with the impressively bushy mustache agrees.

"If you ask me, they oughtta get somebody out there to check that old mine for gas leaks. Wouldn't be the first time a town was being unknowingly poisoned."

And over in the corner by the big window, the better to be seen and admired, is the YouTube crew, laptops and books spread across the two tables they've shoved together. I grab my pack from under the counter, slinging it over one shoulder as I approach.

Sonny Vane turns his face toward me, his too-wide smile already spreading to show off his expensive teeth. "Couldn't stay away, could you?" he says. "I'll have you know you were wrong. We've already filmed . . . Was it three eyewitness accounts about the Wampus Cat?" He turns to the others for confirmation just as I upend my pack and dump all the equipment I pulled off the sourwood trees onto the table in front of him, sending wires splashing into lukewarm coffee and battery packs bouncing off laptop keyboards.

"What the hell?" Sonny squeals, jumping to his feet to prevent the splatter from landing on his artfully ripped jeans.

"You left this in the Forest." I jab a finger toward the mess on the table and the annoying little winking sun logo stuck on the camera. "Next time I have to clean up your mess, I'll make sure you're fined out of every last dime you're making with this nonsense and have you banned from ever filming in a National Forest again!" I have no earthly idea how, exactly, I'm going to do that, but I'll damn sure figure it out.

Sonny is turning a shade of puce even the thick stage makeup he's wearing can't hide, but before he can say a word, his assistant pops up between us. "I'm so sorry," she tells me, her golden-brown eyes going wide as she tucks a long strand of hair that has escaped the pencil holding her bun in place behind her ear. "You're completely right. I'm Ona. Production is my responsibility, so this must have been an oversight on my part. I'll make sure it doesn't happen again."

She starts to gather up everything on the table, prompting the rest of the film crew to help. All except Sonny, who is too busy sulking. "We need to get that shot set up, or we're going to lose the light," she tells him.

"Yeah, and maybe we should look into a new workspace," he grumbles, slowly returning to his normal shade of artificial tan. "This one doesn't seem to appreciate our business." He tosses some cash onto the table and a scathing look in my direction.

"We should be so lucky," I mutter under my breath as they all troop out of the diner. But the feeling of satisfaction I'm expecting doesn't come. Not even knocking Sonny Vane down a peg can distract me from everything else.

"What was that all about?" Linden asks, tucking her order pad back into her apron as she crosses the dining room toward me.

"Oh, you know, *celebrities*," I say, rolling my eyes. "So temperamental."

The knock on the kitchen door comes that evening, when I'm helping Mama clean up the supper dishes, and the sound draws my spine up tight even though I've been waiting for it all day.

"It's open," Mama calls from where she's wiping down the countertop around the sink, and I brace myself.

But it isn't Hadrian who pushes open the door. It's my father. He's in uniform, his shiny sheriff badge pinned to his chest, and he pulls off his hat as he steps inside.

"Hi, Daddy." I set the plate I've been drying onto the shelf.

"Lyon," Mama greets him. "We didn't hear you pull up. What brings you out this late?"

"I went to the hospital this afternoon to check on the accident victim from the Forest," Daddy says. "The rangers that brought him in asked for help in tracking down identification. His fingerprints haven't shown up in any database, and none of the usual searches have turned up anything yet, so he's a John Doe for now. They mentioned that you were there, too, Rowan, when they found him."

"I heard the call over the radio and went to see if I could help."

"Have you eaten?" Mama asks, waving him toward the table.

"I grabbed a bite on the way back into town, but I wouldn't say no to a slice of that pie." He nods toward the chocolate chess pie on the counter and shrugs off his jacket before taking a seat.

"Sure thing." Mama turns to the cupboard to grab the plate I just put away.

"Did you notice anything strange?" Daddy asks me as I slide into the chair across from him.

"Yeah, he was barefoot. And he didn't have any rain gear, or even a jacket, despite the forecast predicting it would storm. So if he was a hiker, he was a bad one." I shrug, thinking back. "I overheard an argument a couple miles from where they found him that might have been poachers. But even a ginseng poacher would have enough sense to be outfitted for the weather."

Mama startles as she sets the slice of pie in front of Daddy, and I realize I haven't shared that part with her yet.

"Did the rangers tell you about the anonymous message?" I ask. "Any progress tracing the call?"

Daddy shakes his head as he takes his first bite. "Dead end. It came from the pay phone out at the hospital."

"So, someone who knew he was injured went to the hospital *without him*?" I ask. "Don't you find that suspicious?"

"Could have both been injured and gotten separated. No sign of an abandoned vehicle yet, either." He shrugs. "We don't know until we know. But we're looking into it."

Which means, he's not telling me anything else. I slump in my chair. "Maybe he came into the Forest with the person who made the anonymous call, they got up to something not exactly legal, John Doe got hurt, and the caller ran instead of trying to get help."

"Could be," he allows as he lifts another forkful of pie. "Course there's no signal out there, so the caller would have had to leave to get help regardless of whether or not there was anything nefarious going on."

"But why not come forward? Why not leave a name? Why leave the Forest at all instead of going to the ranger station?"

Daddy shrugs again, focused on finishing his dessert. I know all these questions must have already occurred to him and, no matter how much I badger him, he's not going to give me any information on an ongoing investigation, but I have to make the point anyway. Whatever happened in that Forest was no accident.

"Do the doctors have any idea when he might wake up?" I change my line of questioning.

"When I spoke to the staff at the hospital today, they said they're not sure why he hasn't yet. His head injury wasn't especially severe, but they can be unpredictable."

"Substances?"

"None of the ones they routinely test for," he answers. "They're having some more extensive testing done, but it'll take some time. Listen, I don't know what happened out there, but it's all suspicious. Maybe it's not the best time for you to be volunteering at a remote cabin alone."

"I agree," Mama chimes in from over by the stove, where she's making a cup of tea. "I'll call Vernie in the morning and let her know you won't be back until all this is settled."

She wasn't too keen on the idea of my volunteering out in the middle of the Forest, miles from anywhere, in the first place. And now that her fears prove to have merit, I brace myself for a full argument over what I'm about to say.

"No, I'm not quitting."

"Really?" Mama asks, surprised. She brings her mug over to the table and sits next to me. "I thought this whole thing was another battle of wills between you and your grandmother. It means that much to you?"

"Don't tell Gran I said this"—I lean back in my chair, pensive—"but I don't think she was wrong. As hard as the work has been, I was able to help when that man was injured. And the rangers are counting on me to get the cabin ready for fire season."

"You're eighteen, which means legally you can make your own choices," Daddy says. "But you're still my little girl, which means you better keep this pepper spray with you at all times." He clips a canister off his belt and slides it across the table to me. "If something seems off, trust your gut, don't take any chances, and get out of there immediately."

I look at Mama, sure she'll protest. But she reaches across the table and puts her hand over Daddy's, looking up at him with soft eyes, shiny with gratitude, before pulling away. It's so fast, I could almost think I've imagined it if not for the surprise on his face.

Since their split last year, Mama and Daddy have always been civil but distant. I'm not sure what to make of this decidedly warmer exchange.

"Well, I've got to get back to the station." Daddy stands and drops a kiss on the top of my head. "Stay safe, baby girl." He reaches for his empty plate, but Mama stops him.

"Oh, leave it, Lyon, I'll take care of it."

He nods, and the tops of his ears pink. "Thank you for the pie. It was delicious, as always."

Mama walks him to the door, then watches as he drives off. He holds a hand up through the open car window before he turns out onto the road, and she mirrors the gesture.

"What was that all about?" I demand when she turns around with a tiny smile, just at the corners of her mouth. "Were you *flirting*? With *Daddy*?"

"Don't be ridiculous." She reaches into her pocket, and I watch for the shine of metal from the locket, but it doesn't come. A confused look crosses her face, and she pats along the sides of her jeans.

"Lose something?" I ask.

"No," she hesitates. "No, I don't think so."

There's no hint of smoke in the air, no charcoal-scented untruth. I recall the conversations around the diner this morning about missing items and lost memories and a weighty suspicion sinks in my stomach.

"Mama?" I ask, then hesitate.

"Yes?" Her hands pause as she scrubs the pie plate in the sink.

"Do you remember what you told me about falling in love with Daddy? About creating a whole world just between the two of you?"

"Oh, Rowan," she sighs. "I have no earthly idea what you're talking about. It's been a long day, I'm going to turn in. Don't stay up too late."

I watch her head up the back stairs, my thoughts whirling. Buck Garland and the missing pocket watch. The man who forgot his car outside the Pub and Grub after his keys went missing. And now Mama without her necklace and no memory of a story she told me only a week ago. People aren't just misplacing objects, they're losing the memories connected to them. That's why I couldn't detect any lies. Buck and Mama believed they were telling the truth. A chill slithers up my spine and digs its fangs into the back of my neck.

But are these things being lost? Or are they being stolen? I think of the magpies, which don't belong in West Virginia, not avoiding the Bone Tree like other animals but roosting in its branches instead. Could they have come from the Otherworld? If normal magpies are known to swipe interesting objects, maybe these birds can take even more. Yesterday, there was a bird in Mama's bedroom. I let out a slow, shaky breath. Getting the diablerie back from Hadrian just became more important than ever because it's the only book I know of that might have answers.

I race up to my room. Closing the door behind me, I lean against it as I squeeze my eyes shut.

"Rough day?" a deep voice asks.

My eyes fly open, and with my next breath, I've sent Sorrel's heavy ceramic candle from the dresser sailing across the room.

Hadrian catches it easily from where he's sitting on my bed, legs stretched out in front of him and crossed at the ankles.

"You asshole." I slide down the door until I'm sitting on the floor and try to get my heartbeat back under control. "You are so lucky I left the pepper spray in the kitchen."

"What changed your mind?" he asks with no preamble.

I study him. He already looks better than he did yesterday. Both eyes are now open, and the swelling has gone down significantly.

"I haven't," I tell him, then hold my breath to avoid the stench of my own lie. No need to let him know just how desperate I am to make a deal now. "At least not yet."

He gestures for me to keep talking, then pulls the lid off the candle to smell it. I'd forgotten how much space he takes up. How all the air in the room seems pulled toward him like gravity has shifted.

"The diablerie." I push myself off the ground and step toward him. "I want it back."

He sets the candle down on my nightstand and slowly rises from the bed. "I *earned* that book."

I shrug, aiming for nonchalance. "It's a family heirloom. It belongs here."

"It's part of a bargain." His sharp eyes narrow as he moves closer. "I can't just give it back."

"Linden offered you your life back, no more summons from James witches whenever they wanted to make a deal with the devil." I press a finger against his chest to make my point. "So keep the pages about the Moth-Winged Man. The deal stays intact. No future James will ever know about you, but we get the rest of the book back. And in return, I'll be your human lie detector."

Hadrian tilts his head, studying me as he considers the offer. We're standing way too close now. I look up, and I can see the flecks of amber deep in his eyes and feel the whisper of his exhale against my cheek. "Clever," he murmurs. "Fine, you have a deal."

He steps back and extends his hand, the one with *hell* tattooed across his fingers. I hesitate. I don't trust him, but there's no other choice. I slide my hand into his.

CHAPTER ELEVEN

LATE SUNDAY afternoon, after we close the Harvest Moon, Sissy drives me back up the mountain in the old Bronco. A cold front blew in overnight, settling deep into the valleys and hollows and bringing with it a haze that blurs the yellows, reds, and oranges of the trees into a wash of flame.

When she pulls into the dirt turnoff, where the small trail to the cabin branches off, she reaches into the back seat for a small pouch. "Put a protective ward around that cabin if you haven't. No need to tempt fate." Sissy hands me the bag.

"I will," I promise, grabbing my backpack and reaching for the door. "Be careful going home." These mountain roads can be dangerous, especially in the fog. After all, that deadly car accident had happened not far from here, when the poacher swerved off the road and straight into a tree.

I'm well on my way up the path before I hear the rumble of the Bronco pulling away. Sissy must have watched until I disappeared into the trees. When I reach the clearing, I find I'm not alone. Two of the rangers, Carson and Harshbarger, descend the cabin stairs, one of the heavy wooden shutters balanced between them.

"Well, there she is!" Carson calls out.

They walk past me to set their burden down on top of the other shutters they've piled up beside the shed. Harshbarger brushes his hands against his uniform pants. "We saw you'd gotten them all painted and knew they'd be near on impossible for one person to take down."

"I've never seen the cabin without them." I stare up at the lookout. Only one of the shutters remains, the glass of the windows so wide and clear, I can see straight through the cabin to the sky on the other side. It's beautiful, even more like a tree house than before. I imagine the future fire lookout will be able to spot even the faintest hint of smoke anywhere in the valley with this view. But there's also an uneasiness in the pit of my stomach at the idea of being so exposed.

"Glad to see you back." Carson nudges me. "We weren't sure you would be after all the excitement last week." He takes off his hat to wipe sweat from his brow, and I notice his hair is just beginning to gray at the temples.

“I’ve still got a job to do,” I tell him, and his smile widens.

“Let’s get this last one off,” Harshbarger calls, walking back toward the cabin. “We’re losing daylight.”

I follow behind them, pausing to drop my stuff by the cabin door. The last shutter is the one on the far side, where the walkway hangs over the ridge. When I catch up, Carson already has his side unlatched and is holding all its weight while Harshbarger struggles to get his disconnected.

“It’s caught on something,” he grunts.

“Looks like the paint leaked a little around the edge on this side.” I point out the problem area. “It’s sealed to the frame.”

“Anyone got a utility knife?” Harshbarger asks.

“Not to rush you, but I am holding fifty pounds while dangling over the side of a ravine,” Carson complains. An icy wind whistles across the ridgeline as if to emphasize his point. “Just use your pocketknife.”

“I don’t have one,” Harshbarger grumbles. “That’s why I asked.”

My eyes go wide. On my first night here at the cabin, he was so proud to show me the pocketknife he’d carried for more than twenty years. Now it’s gone. Is this another stolen item on an ever-growing list?

“I’ve got it.” I flip out the blade of my mushroom knife and slice through the paint seal, freeing the shutter.

Once we get it stacked with the others, the rangers say goodbye, eager to get back to the station for the end of their shift.

"Oh, by the way." Carson stops at the top of the trail. "We searched all over down by the creek where you heard yelling. No sign of poachers. Maybe just some disgruntled fishermen?" He shrugs, then waves.

It should be reassuring, and yet it isn't. I don't know if what I heard was poachers, but I do know it wasn't nothing. I pull my jacket tighter against the chill in the air and head back up the stairs to the cabin, digging the keys out of my pocket.

By the time I unlock the door and carry in my gear, the sky outside the windows has deepened to a sooty blue. Tossing my pack onto the bed, I toe off my boots, then open the pouch Sissy gave me. I spread the contents out on the desk: a small mirror, a candle, and local Appalachian salt, sourced from the ancient ocean that sleeps beneath these mountains.

First, I take the salt outside and lift the rough, worn doormat to pour a protective line in front of the threshold. When that's done, I stand the candle in the center of the table and light a match. As I move the flame toward the wick, I begin to speak.

"This fire shall burn away all ill will." When the candle catches light, I pick up the mirror and pass it through the smoke. "I infuse this mirror with the energy of the fire that it may cast any negativity back to its source." I repeat it three more times, then blow out the candle and set the mirror onto the windowsill beside the front door, facing outward.

When I turn back toward the table, a light in the distance catches my eye. It's too dark to make out quite how far away it is, but from this angle, it looks about the size of a golf ball floating in the air. My first thought is a flashlight, but it's moving too erratically to be in the hands of someone walking. Unless they're doing it intentionally.

The strange light disappears while I'm looking directly at it. I blink a few times, then switch off my lantern so I can better see outside. An uneasy feeling heats the back of my neck like I'm being watched. Slowly, I turn in a circle in the middle of the cabin, straining to see whatever I can make out in the darkness through the walls of glass.

A flash in the distance has me spinning toward the back of the cabin. Another light, just like the first. I press my face against the window to try and get a better look at whatever's down there. And that's when I realize where the lights are coming from. If my estimation is correct, it's just beyond Stillhouse Creek and through the trees. Exactly where I heard the voices. The small glowing light disappears, then reappears farther away for just a brief moment before it's gone for good.

I don't sleep for hours, instead searching the horizon for any pinprick of light until I can no longer keep my eyes open.

It's the coldest morning yet. There's a chill in the air here on the mountain that reaches down into my bones. I pull on a pair of thick socks and move the kettle onto the top of the woodstove, then open the heavy cast-iron door to stir the ashes and add some more wood, all the while stealing glances toward the windows that look out over the top of the Forest.

I've tried to come up with answers for what might have caused the strange lights, from the natural to the uncanny: Foxfire, the bioluminescent fungi that grows on some decaying trees, or some especially large lightning bugs, though it's too cold for both. It could have been glowworms, *Orfelia fultoni*, except they glow blue and are found mostly in caves. And then there's will-o'-the-wisps, the ghostly lights that lead travelers from their paths. But, of course, they don't really exist. Unless they do.

The rangers have already searched for signs of poachers and ruled it out. But knowing what it *isn't* only makes me all the more determined to figure out what it *is*.

When the kettle finally whistles, I pour the water into the coffee press and let it sit, my gaze pulled once again out toward the valley beyond. As I turn away, something crashes into the window behind me.

I drop to the floor on instinct alone. After several long minutes, I slowly get to my feet, expecting the window to be cracked in half. Instead, there's the perfect outline of a bird, wings outstretched, each individual feather remarkably clear, left behind on the glass like a fingerprint.

I've read about this. It's a phenomenon caused by a fine dust called powder down that only certain kinds of birds produce to protect their feathers. A ghostly imprint of what is likely its final moment.

Leaning over the desk, I peer down to the walkway outside, but I can't see anything. I move to another window and try to look back toward where the bird must have fallen after it hit the glass, but there's not so much as a loose feather.

"It couldn't have hit that hard and flown away," I murmur to myself as I hunt for my boots.

The first one is under the kitchen chair next to the stove, the other so far under the bed that I have to lie on my stomach to retrieve it. I shimmy back out from beneath the wooden bed frame and tug the boots on, not bothering to lace them as I reach for the doorknob and find it already unlocked. Had I gotten distracted by the lights and forgotten to lock it last night? I pull open the front door and stop fast, reeling back just in time.

There, on the worn-out old welcome mat, like some morbid gift, is a dead magpie, the keys to the cabin trapped beneath its wing. *One for sorrow.*

CHAPTER TWELVE

I STOP to listen whenever I hear a rustle in the underbrush or the crack of a twig, pausing to search the deeper parts of the Forest, between the trees, for any sign of the uncanny, any evidence of what caused those lights and who I'd heard arguing near the creek. And, even still, I nearly miss the footprint pressed into the dry, chalky clay just off the path.

One large center pad and four toes that taper at the ends. It's clearly feline, yet way too large to be a house cat. I search the ground, calling up Daddy's tracking lessons from when my sisters and I were kids, and spot another. And then another. The outlines of the prints have softened, the edges no longer crisp, meaning they aren't fresh. With the temperatures lately, I'd guess they're from very early this morning.

West Virginia officially only has one big cat. Bobcats aren't rare, but they are elusive. Solitary predators, mostly nocturnal and almost preternaturally silent, they can weigh up to forty pounds and stand two feet at the shoulder. Not especially large, but still able to take down a deer with one strong bite to the back of the neck.

There are rumors, though, of other sorts of cats. Once there were cougars in these woods. The eastern cougar is extinct, but that hasn't seemed to stop the sightings. It isn't called the ghost cat for nothing. An ambush hunter that liked to pounce on its prey, it could weigh more than a man, with retractile claws and a powerful jaw.

Curious, I follow the tracks away from the path and deeper into the Forest, winding my way downhill. This cat was heavy enough for its paws to press prints into even the drier earth. It had pushed through the undergrowth of the sourwood and heath shrub beneath the towering oaks, skirting a thicket of dense laurel and cutting a path too wide to be a sleek bobcat. Whatever this cat is, it's big. I lose the trail not long after, the last trace a tuft of black hair caught on the branch of a rhododendron, standing out starkly against the newly turned crimson of the leaves like a calling card.

Was I wrong? Had I somehow mistaken a bear print for a cat? No, my tracking skills may be rusty, but I still know how to count toes. A black bear would have five, a cat only four. And yet West Virginia has never been home to a large black cat.

Unless, of course, you believe the legends. A fearsome feline with fur that ripples with shadows like the darkest depths of the river. But the Wampus Cat is only a legend. There are many versions of the story, some older even than the European settlers that laid claim to this land. The most well-known begins with a woman who was cursed to live as a cat and bring ill fortune to all she encountered.

It's impossible. But I've got Sonny Vane's annoying voice in the back of my head telling me he interviewed three eyewitnesses. Too bad I just picked a fight with him, or I might have been able to convince him to give me the real stories behind the claim, not the sensationalist version I'll likely be able to look up on YouTube in the near future. Because, with the evidence in front of me, either the Wampus Cat is real or someone wants to make people believe that it is.

I consider the placement of the camera I pulled out of the woods and the location of these tracks. Would Sonny Vane stoop so low as to fake a Wampus Cat for his channel? Of course he would. But did he?

I've wandered farther off course than I realized and pull out my compass to get my bearings. There's no marked trail out here, and I have trekked through thick underbrush and dense forest, focused only on the next track in front of me. Carefully, I pick my way through rough terrain and loose rock, drawing up short when I hear a bark of laughter from the trees above me. I look up to find a magpie sitting on a branch above my head, watching me. It cackles once more, then takes flight. I trace its path across the sky until I lose sight of it.

But there, in a patch of sunlight, surrounded by trees, is something clearly man-made. A tower of stacked stone, a lone chimney sitting quite literally in the middle of nowhere.

Caball Hollow was founded in the late eighteenth century, but this is a good distance from the center of town, especially for people who relied on a different sort of horsepower. The latest the chimney could possibly have been built is sometime around 1910, when this land became National Forest.

And yet. There is a presence to this place. A sort of ancient weight that only very old structures have, like every person who ever walked inside its walls left a tiny piece of themselves behind. Like how used books feel heavier than new ones.

Old folk wisdom said that the hearth held the soul of a home, and it could be vulnerable to evil spirits. People would put personal belongings, like old shoes and worn clothing and bits of iron within the walls or under the floorboards near chimneys and thresholds for protection. They believed that these sorts of items could hold some of the essence of their owner. The spirits would then mistake them for their intended victim and become trapped.

If that's true, I don't think it worked here. This place seems haunted, soaked in an oppressive feeling that reminds me of the Bone Tree, an eerie sense of wrongness that would push all but the most determined away.

"You must come with us." A man's voice rings out, and I jump. "We mean you no harm."

My blood turns to ice, recognizing the words from the night the man was discovered unconscious in the Forest. It sounds close enough that the speaker could be standing right next to me. But there's no one else here. And there's no stench of a lie despite the obvious threat beneath the words.

"I do not concede!" the younger voice objects, afraid.

"Hurry, we haven't much time," the third voice shouts.

I press my hands against my ears and squeeze my eyes shut to block out the sickening thud I know comes next. After several long seconds, I slowly lower my hands.

"Is there someone out there?" the first man shouts. "Hurry! The instructions were clear. We must get him to the water now."

Out of the corner of my eye, I catch a glimpse of a shadowy figure rushing toward me, like a man hunched low to the ground to avoid being seen. I whirl around to face him, grappling for the pepper spray in my pocket. But there's no one there.

It's over just as quickly as it began. I freeze, every muscle tense, eyes scanning the landscape for any sign of a new threat. And then I take off. Running as quickly as I can away from this place. Something bad happened here, of that I have no doubt. Hearing the same voices again, closer now, I realize they seem older somehow, the words rounder through the vowels and fuller in the mouth. An echo of another time. And it left a mark, like an afterimage, imprinted on the land itself.

When I reach the trail that leads up to the lookout cabin, bone-tired and stinking of fear, the sun is already sliding down the sky. I went looking for answers and came back with more questions. All I want to do now is collapse onto that lumpy, uncomfortable bed and forget about it all until tomorrow. Instead, when I break through the trees at the trailhead, I find Hadrian Fitch on the cabin's walkway, leaning against the railing.

Despite the chill in the air, he's only wearing worn jeans and a T-shirt, the tattoos that march down his arms and across his fingers on full display. It's a variation of what he wore every day on the farm, and it feels familiar in a way I don't like.

"Hey, there." He watches me as he cuts a slice from the apple in his hand and pops it into his mouth.

I eye his pocketknife and think of Harshbarger's missing one. It's not strange for Hadrian to have a knife. He'd certainly needed one on the farm and likely would in the Forest as well. But the timing of his return to town is suspicious enough already, and I have no doubt he knows more than he's letting on. Sorrel's suggestion to use my blood to force him to tell the truth whispers again in my ear.

"Did you bring the diablerie?" I stalk up the stairs toward the cabin and reach behind him to open the door.

The walkway is only about two feet wide, and he's taking up most of it. He folds the knife with a practiced hand, and it disappears into a pocket as he turns and leans closer, reaching to slide his fingers into my hair. I freeze with the key in the lock. There's a small tug, and he pulls away a twig.

"Rough day?" he asks flatly, flicking it over the railing.

I shove the door open and toss my pack on the floor. "Did you bring the diablerie?" I repeat. Dropping into a chair, I bend to pull off my hiking boots. Something thuds onto the desk above my head, and I jerk upright.

Slowly, I reach for the fabric-wrapped bundle, but Hadrian sets a hand down on top of it.

"First, we talk," he says, when I look up to meet his eyes.

I've only seen the diablerie once before, when I helped Linden with a protection spell that called for dirt from the grave of a recently departed mother. "What's there to talk about? You give me the diablerie, and I become your own personal lie detector." I lean back in my chair and cross my arms.

"Let's think about this logically." Hadrian straightens, and in the tiny cabin he towers over me. "Whoever attacked me must have some knowledge of the Otherworld."

"Like my family?" I offer unhelpfully, needling him. Though he had suspected the James women once before, which led him to Bittersweet Farm in the first place and served as a handy excuse for all his lies.

"This would go a lot quicker if you took it seriously." He gives me the irritated look I know so well, and I bite the inside of my cheek, hiding a satisfied smile.

But while my family may be one of the few to still rely on the old ways, that doesn't mean we're the only ones who remember.

"People often know only a bit of the truth and think it's the whole thing." I stand up, tired of craning my neck to look at him. "Bryson Ivers came into the diner a couple months ago accusing Linden of cursing him because of something his grandmother believed about our ancestors. There's more old knowledge still alive around here than this town would like to admit."

"About old folk magic, sure, but the purpose and location of the Bone Tree?"

"Any one of the descendants of the original founders may know something about the Bone Tree and the Moth-Winged Man. It was their ancestors who created them, after all."

A shared history with long-lasting repercussions. The town founders, who feared death in a strange land, sought the comfort of their old traditions, no matter the cost. Nature may give the Bone Tree a wide berth, but we foolish mortals are sometimes drawn toward that which we should fear the most.

"But, if they did know the truth of what I am, what motive would they have to want to attack me?" Hadrian crosses his arms, the sleeves of his shirt pulling tight against muscles built in the sun. "Most who know the truth seek me out to make a bargain."

His eyes fall to the fabric-wrapped bundle on the desk between us. A not-so-subtle reminder of the summoning spell it contains. Because the Moth-Winged Man doesn't just faithfully guide the souls of those who die too soon from this world to the next. He can grant people their deepest desires, but only at a very steep cost. A deal with the devil.

"Any disgruntled customers lately?" I ask.

"The only bargains I've made have been with the women of your family."

"Why is it so important for you to know who was responsible?" I ask, impatience flaring. All I want to do is search the diablerie for answers. For a way to get Zephyrine back and to stop any more memories from being stolen. "Is it ego? Revenge? Isn't it enough to just be more careful?"

It's such a ridiculous and mean-spirited thing to say, and I know it even as it escapes my mouth. Of course he'd want to know who jumped him. Of course he'd want to determine if it might be part of some larger threat. I swallow back the acrid taste my words leave behind.

There's a flash of something in his eyes, but he snuffs it out before I can identify it. I drop my gaze, and he lets out a slow exhale, clearly battling frustration of his own. Running a hand through his hair, he perches on the edge of the desk in front of me. "I'm not concerned for me, Rowan."

The sound of my name draws me up short, pulling my eyes back to his.

"Dying is a fearsome thing." The words are soft for all their weight. "No one should do it alone."

I nod slowly. Hearing all the things he isn't saying about a little boy who never made it home. The silence stretches as we both sit with our own thoughts, until something occurs to me.

"Maybe we're looking at this the wrong way," I suggest. "What if there's another, more straightforward possibility?"

"Like what?"

"Plenty of folks went out into the Forest this summer, hunting for the Moth-Winged Man. Maybe one of them finally got lucky."

"You think that's who attacked me?" Hadrian asks, clearly skeptical. "One of those fools with their rifles and their six-packs?"

"No, if that were the case, you'd probably have been full of buckshot, not covered in bruises." But there is one person who would want to try to take him alive. If someone was trying to prove the existence of the Moth-Winged Man, the only thing better than capturing him on camera would be actually capturing him.

I raise my eyebrows at Hadrian. "The person who attacked you might not have known what the Bone Tree is at all, he might have just been watching the Forest for weeks, trying to catch his ticket to fame and fortune."

"You're talking about the guy with all the cameras who's been wandering around here like his cornbread ain't done?"

"That's the one."

"You think *that guy* kicked my ass?" He leans toward me, clearly insulted.

I shrug and mimic him, leaning into his space in return. "Only one way to find out. Looks like we just identified our first suspect."

His eyebrows draw down in annoyance.

"To be fair, he would have had four or five other people with him at the time," I cut in before the storm brewing in his eyes breaks. "So, should we get on with it?" I wave a hand toward where the diablerie sits on the table.

He sighs and pushes the bundle toward me. It's wrapped in some sort of floral silk fabric. When I remove it, the book looks no more powerful than an old leather journal. But the diablerie is our oldest history. The very first notes were written inside by our family matriarch, Caorunn James.

Gran hid the book away for years, blaming it for driving the wedge between her and her younger sister, Zephyrine. She didn't believe it was the type of work we should practice, but then she dabbled in it herself and lost her sister to the Bone Tree. Maybe that's why she always told us that the diablerie, unlike the rest of the family books we consult, is filled with a different sort of James magic, a dangerous sort.

I flip through the pages, searching for the entry on the Moth-Winged Man. Then I see it. An illustration with the body of a man, strong and powerful, with eyes glaring red and two enormous sets of gossamer moth wings unfurled behind him. My hands still. Linden told me about this, about what Hadrian looks like when he's the Moth-Winged Man. But seeing it here, in these ancient pages, is something altogether different.

I look up to find him watching me. "You scared?" I taunt.

"Of you?" He chuckles low. "Never."

The smell of a matchstick fills the space between us. "Liar."

I carefully tear the handful of pages, one by one, from the book. The thick, old paper resists at first before it pulls free. I roll them up and hand them to Hadrian. "Pleasure doing business with you."

He takes the pages and drops two maple keys into my open palm. I look down at them, then back up at him. "Can't you just get a cell phone?"

"No signal up here on the mountain." With a wink over his shoulder, he pulls open the door and then he's gone.

But when I look back at the book on the desk, I see the smudgy shape of a large black feline sketched on the page. The words *Beware the Cat-Sìth* are written in bold letters across the top. And the text underneath explains that a cat-sìth is a dangerous witch who can transform into a cat nine times and steal souls before they cross to the other side.

A woman transformed into a cat. I think of the strange feline tracks I found in the woods earlier, and the clump of black fur. Could the legend of the Wampus Cat be rooted in this lore? Could it be yet another tale grown from a kernel of truth?

And then I realize there might be another motive entirely for the attack on Hadrian: to steal the soul he was guiding to the Otherworld.

CHAPTER THIRTEEN

MY FINGERS are stiff with cold as I gather windfallen red oak and sugar maple branches for kindling along the ridge near the lookout. Footsteps crunch on the gravel trail just before Vernie crests the hill.

"Hello, there," she calls when she spots me, waving a hand over her head. Her cheeks are burnished red by the cold.

I grab an armload of sticks from my pile on the ground and signal that I'll meet her up at the cabin.

"It's lookin' real nice out here," she tells me. "You've been busy these last couple weeks."

"Muscles I didn't even know I had ache," I admit.

She chuckles and follows me inside. I stoke the fire in the woodstove, then warm my hands over it until the feeling starts to return.

"Well, we do appreciate all your hard work, but I'm gonna level with you, kiddo," Vernie says, taking a seat in the wooden chair beside the desk. "This morning, a backpack was found not far from here, near the exit road, stuffed with about three hundred ginseng roots. And since we still don't have answers about the man who was injured, the other rangers aren't too keen on having a teenager out here alone. We're going to have to cut your assignment short."

I drop down onto the edge of the bed, a rock sinking in my chest. After being forced to volunteer, then swallowing my pride to stay on, it's all going to be for nothing. "Is there anything I can do to convince them to let me finish the job?"

"I admire your tenacity. You're a tough cookie, and more importantly, a smart one. I wasn't much older than you are when I started out here." Vernie leans forward, resting her forearms against her knees. "But there's something different about the poachers this year."

"Different how, exactly?"

"Hunting ginseng has been a tradition in these mountains for hundreds of years, I don't need to tell you that. It's gotten a lot of families through the winter. The methods, the secret hunting spots, the tools are all handed down from one generation to the next. And I respect that." She sighs, shaking her head. "But this is something else entirely. Poachers usually work alone, maybe with a partner at most. This has to be a much bigger group, and they're organized, almost systematic, in a way I've never seen. They're clearing out whole acres. And they're always a step ahead of us."

"But I thought ginseng could only be sold to registered dealers. How are they moving so much volume without raising suspicion?"

"The local dealers claim they haven't seen anything unusual, but they pay a few hundred dollars a pound, then they turn around and sell to the wholesalers in China and Korea for a few thousand, air shipping fresh roots wrapped in moss and packed in cardboard barrels. A single ninety-three-year-old root was found in Vermont last year and sold at auction for more than a hundred thousand dollars. That's a hell of a lot of money, especially in this county. I suspect they either found a dealer willing to break the law or they found their own wholesaler."

I whistle low through my teeth, looking out across the valley as though I might be able to somehow spot any poachers down below. "That's a lot of reasons to risk it."

"Ginseng grows wild, but it's finicky. That's what makes it hard to cultivate and why the wild goes for about ten times more than farmed. Each seed can take two years to germinate and then another decade to be worth harvesting. Some of these roots they're stealing are forty, fifty years old." Vernie shakes her head. "It's slow growth, not something we can replace quickly."

"So what can we do to stop them?" The heavy weight in my chest turns to fire at the selfishness of a few stealing resources that belong to the many. It's a story we know well enough in West Virginia, where the tops of million-year-old mountains are blown off to get the coal out faster and cheaper, waste dumped into nearby valleys and watersheds, and old-growth forests clear-cut. Moonscapes of pockmarked rubble are all that remain where proud peaks once stood. And politicians who were meant to hold the companies to account choose to line their own pockets instead, taking the money and leaving residents to deal with the mess.

"I wish I knew. But we do have a prescribed burn planned for this area, and our window is coming up in November." Vernie pulls open a couple of the desk drawers until she finds a map of the Forest. She spreads it out between us and points to an area I know well. "There's a large amount of dead vegetation in this area. Right by the creek, which we're planning to use as a natural firebreak." She drags a finger along the map. "My hope is that it'll stop the poachers for a while, or at least slow them down enough that we can get a hold on it."

I stare at the map, watching as Vernie points directly at the Bone Tree. They're going to burn it. I don't know if that's even possible. It's stood for hundreds of years, neither alive nor dead. And what would the loss of it mean for Caball Hollow? No more birds stealing memories or strange snakes or possible Wampus Cats? No more Moth-Winged Man?

Hadrian once told Linden that he can't stay on this side of the Bone Tree for too long. He's not meant for the land of the living. Would he have to stay in the Otherworld? What then of all those souls unable to find their way to the other side? And what of Zephyrine? No gate means no way home.

Vernie folds up the map and gives me a sad smile. "Anyhow, I hope this doesn't stop you from coming back as a volunteer in the future. Or even considering a career in the Forest Service. I see a lot of potential in you, Rowan." She pats me on the shoulder and rises to her feet. "I'll drop by at the end of my shift this evening to give you a ride home."

I watch Vernie hike down the trail until I can't see her anymore. And then I start to pack.

When Vernie drops me off at the farm, I grab my bags out of the back of her truck and wave as she pulls away. We've come full circle from my first day as a volunteer, the tires kicking up a fog of dust as she pulls back out onto the road.

The kitchen is empty when I push through the screen door. I race up the back steps, dropping my duffel on the floor of my bedroom and taking the fabric-wrapped bundle out of my pack. Crossing the hall, I rap my knuckles against the door to Linden and Juniper's room before pushing it open.

"What's wrong?" Linden is lounging on her bed when I come in, a textbook open in front of her and papers spread out across the quilt, but bolts upright when she sees me. "You didn't find another body in the woods, did you?"

"They canceled my assignment early." I close the door behind me and hold up the diablerie. "Can you keep this where you hid it before?"

"You really got it back?" she asks as she takes the bundle from my hands and slowly unties the fabric wrapping in awe. "When you told me your plan, I didn't think there was any way it would actually work."

I drop onto the bed beside her, scattering loose pages and knocking a pen onto the floor. "It took some convincing," I admit. "But eventually we agreed that your bargain for Cole's life really only applied to the pages concerning summoning the Moth-Winged Man, so Hadrian returned the rest."

"I thought we all learned our lesson about bargaining with the Moth-Winged Man," Juniper observes from where she sits at the desk on the other side of the room, tapping the eraser of her pencil against a notebook.

"It's not a bargain." I roll over to meet her eyes. "It's a business arrangement."

Linden flips over a corner of the rug and slides out the loose floorboard, placing the diablerie in the empty space beneath it. Maybe it's not the most creative of hiding spaces, but I want to keep the book close at hand.

"When are you going to tell Gran you got it back?" she asks.

I pause, weighing the options. "Let's wait until we know if there's something in there that could help. The diablerie is her last chance to get Zephyrine back. As long as she thinks it's still out there, there's hope. I don't want to destroy that unless we have to. Which we may if we don't find something soon. The Forest Service is planning a burn next month that would include the Bone Tree."

Linden freezes after replacing the floorboard, eyes wide. "Would it even burn?" she asks. "The Bone Tree is a physical manifestation of the bargain, but it was the creation of the first Moth-Winged Man buried at its roots and the arrival of Caorunn James that created the actual bridge all those years ago."

"I don't know, but I think the Bone Tree might have something to do with the strangeness out in the Forest. I heard voices in the woods again, the same ones as before, but it was different this time. Like a haunting, but not quite. More like the ghost of a memory. Is that possible?" I ask Juniper.

She leans back in her chair, her unusual eyes, blue but for a vertical line of brown through the left iris, go unfocused as she gathers her thoughts. "I've only encountered something like that once, but Granny Sudie wrote about it in her notes, too. I think traumatic events can leave behind indelible marks on places just like they can on us. We can be haunted by our own memories, there's no reason the same couldn't be true of the places those things happened."

"But I must've hiked past that area dozens of times and never heard voices before," I tell her. "Why now?"

Juniper shrugs. "I don't know, but I've noticed it, too. The spirits have been restless lately, like when the veil between worlds is thinner. I thought it might mean the upcoming equinox would be an especially powerful one, but with all the other weird things you've seen, I wonder if somehow it's the Bone Tree itself."

"What do you mean?" Linden asks.

"Maybe it's weakening," Juniper suggests. "And things that don't belong here are getting through."

"I think you're right," I agree.

"But how do we stop it?"

"Maybe the answer is in the diablerie," Linden suggests. "It's the only book I know with any sort of information at all about the Bone Tree. I can look for a way to keep anything with ill intent from crossing over."

"Good idea. And while you do that, I'm going to try and figure out what the hell is going on."

The Pub and Grub is on the outskirts of Caball Hollow, just off the switchback that leads into town. Judging by the softball team photos that line the wall to the bathroom and the selections on tap, the place hasn't been updated in at least fifty years. The menu is mainly an afterthought of greasy burgers and tuna melts, except for the Brunswick stew. With its smoked meats, tomatoes, potatoes, butter beans, onions, and rich, hearty, and tangy broth, it's the best in the county, but they only make it in the fall. Gran has been trying to get the recipe for years. It's also the only other restaurant in town, which means when Sonny Vane decamped from the Harvest Moon, there was only one place for him to go.

When I pull into the parking lot, two men in stained white aprons stand in the glow of the security light over the back door, smoking.

"Hey," I call as I walk past. "You got a light?"

The taller one reaches into his pocket and tosses me a matchbook with the Pub and Grub logo stamped across the front. Nodding my thanks, I tear off a stick, then drag it across the brick wall as I go until it catches. I take one of the maple keys Hadrian gave me from my pocket and hold it to the flame. Blowing out the match, I flick the burning seedpod into the dark and watch as it flares bright, then disappears into a plume of dark smoke.

At the front of the building, I push open the glass door. Inside, there's a small entryway with worn carpet that was once a vibrant red but over the years has dulled to the color of dried blood. A bench sits along one wall under a row of hooks where several jackets hang.

I spot Sonny Vane and his crew at a table near the back of the main dining room as soon as I walk in. They've clearly been there a while, judging by the laptops, empty glasses, and soup bowls. But before I can step inside, Ona, the production assistant, barrels around the corner and nearly plows into me.

"Rowan." She stops me with a hand on my arm. "I'm glad I ran into you. I was going to stop by the Harvest Moon in the morning, but this saves me a trip." She glances over her shoulder at Sonny's table, then tugs me toward a bench near the door where we'll be hidden from view.

"I thought you should know Sonny is planning on filming in the Forest again on Friday. It's the anniversary of the Elam McCoy disappearance, so Sonny is promoting it as a special episode exploring the history of Moth-Winged Man sightings in Caball Hollow and the tragedies they predicted." She pauses as Pastor Boggs passes by on his way to the exit, nodding to us as he goes. "We're camping at the site overnight because he thinks we might even get lucky and catch a glimpse of the Moth-Winged Man at the place where the little boy disappeared all those years ago."

The expression on my face must be alarming, because she rushes to reassure me.

"Don't worry, I'll make sure nothing is left behind this time."

But my mind is filled with the person who is about to walk through the door any minute now. Hadrian Fitch, who was born Elam McCoy. The boy who went missing on a family fishing trip when he was four years old and never came home.

"He's using the disappearance of a child for views?" I ask, my voice gone sharp. "Isn't that low, even for Sonny Vane?"

She shrugs, then shakes her head. "Yeah, I know. It's absolutely terrible, but he's been hyping up this episode on the channel for weeks. There's no way to talk him out of it. I just didn't want you to find out from someone else." Ona grabs her jacket from one of the hooks, then gives a little wave before she leaves.

I let out a slow breath. Now is not the time to start a fight with Sonny Vane. I need to stay on his good side long enough to get the answers I need from him. Then all bets are off.

When I step out of the entryway, I spot Buck Garland sitting alone at the end of the bar. There's an empty stool next to him, and I slide onto it.

His head jerks up from his bowl. "Rowan James? Didn't expect to see you here."

"Yeah, don't tell my gran." I lean forward, pulling a paper menu out from between the salt and pepper shakers on the bar. "But the stew here is even better than hers."

He grins, and I find myself studying his profile, the way his jaw changes when it clenches, the texture of his hair, the shape of his ear, searching for any sign of the brother he lost.

Buck Garland, born Wyatt McCoy, was only a few years older than Elam and the last person to see him alive. There's no way he could know who Hadrian truly is, but does Hadrian know who Buck is? Maybe meeting here was a mistake. Linden is always telling me I jump in without thinking things through. Clearly, she was right this time.

"Hey." A deep voice near my ear startles me enough that I jump, bumping against the chest of the person standing right behind me. I glance over my shoulder to see Hadrian, but he's looking at Buck. His expression is confused, then it goes carefully blank.

"We can sit somewhere else," I tell him, my voice annoyingly unsure.

He looks down at me curiously, then his brow softens in a way I haven't seen before. It's times like these I wish I had Linden's ability to know what others are feeling.

"It's fine, Rowan." He sits on the stool beside mine and steals my menu.

I swallow, turning back to Buck. "You haven't been in the Harvest Moon in a while," I tell him. "You and Hillard still feuding?"

Buck immediately starts shaking his head. "I already told that old fool I don't have his damn watch about a million times."

"Do you know what kind of a watch it was?" I ask, trying to suss out how much of his memory is gone.

He nods. "Yeah, of course. Hillard carried it everywhere with him. It's been passed down in his family from father to son for generations. Always thought that was real neat. To have a family that was close like that." He clears his throat. "And I'm sorry he lost it, truly, but I don't know what the hell happened to the blasted thing."

"Seems like a lot of people have lost things around here lately," I say as I pluck a peanut from the bowl on the bar and crack the shell between my fingers.

"You can say that again," Buck agrees. "On my route alone, I know of five families who've had things stolen."

"So you think it's theft?"

"Would be a pretty big coincidence otherwise, now, wouldn't it? Speaking of." Buck points with his chin. "Don't look now, but I think Whitney's flirting with your date."

Of course I do what everyone does when told this and immediately turn to find Whitney Arkell, who graduated a couple years before Sorrel and has worked at the Pub and Grub ever since, leaning over the bar to give Hadrian what appears to be a very thorough explanation of the menu.

"Oh, no, this is Hadrian Fitch." I put my hand on his arm and ignore the irritated glare Whitney throws me. "He used to work for us out at the farm. Hadrian, this is Buck Garland, one of our favorite regulars at the Harvest Moon."

"Nice to meet you." Hadrian leans across me to shake Buck's hand. "Hey, didn't I see you in the National Forest a few weeks ago, out near Stillhouse Creek?" He phrases this as a question, and I can't help but wonder if it's an investigation tactic or he avoided telling a lie for my benefit.

Buck tenses, then stands, tossing some money onto the bar next to his empty bowl. "The last time I was in the Forest was exactly eighteen years, eleven months, and twenty-eight days ago." He nods to me. "Better hit the hay. I've got an early morning."

"That could have gone better," Hadrian observes wryly, after Buck leaves.

I study his face, trying to gauge his reaction. If he didn't know Buck was his brother before, he surely does now.

"It's fine, Rowan." He looks at me in that way he has that feels like he can see underneath my skin. "I don't really remember much from . . . before."

I clear my throat. "Right. Well, should we see what we can find out from our top suspect?"

The moment Sonny Vane notices me heading his way, he leans back in his chair and laces his fingers behind his head. "Well, well, well," he drawls. "Who do we have here? Come to apologize and win back my business?"

"Yes, missing out on the ten bucks a week you spent on coffee is really breaking us." I can't hold my tongue. One of the older men on his crew guffaws, then tries to cover it with a cough.

"What do you want, then?" Sonny demands, fixing the crew with a scowl.

"I want to talk about that camera you left mounted out in the Forest."

"Not this again." Sonny crosses his arms petulantly. "Is there some sort of fine or something?"

"It's been out there since late August, hasn't it?" I take a shot, thinking of the petal trapped between the camera and the tree trunk.

Sonny's eyes narrow, then dart from me to Hadrian and back. "Is this guy from the Forest Service or something?"

I glance over at Hadrian, doing that sullen, broody thing in his standard T-shirt and jeans, with tattoos saturating every stretch of skin, and shrug. "He's definitely from the Forest."

"Out of the million acres of the National Forest, why did you put the camera in that specific area?" Hadrian asks.

Sonny swallows. "Uh, a lot of the reported Moth-Winged Man sightings were centralized near Stillhouse Creek and the Teays River."

Hadrian glances at me, and I nod. Sonny isn't lying, but I get the sense that he isn't telling the whole truth, either.

"How much do you know about the history of the Moth-Winged Man?" Hadrian asks. And I'm not sure why.

I thought his questions would be focused on what happened the day he was attacked.

"I've read every article I can get my hands on," Sonny asserts, obviously insulted that his expertise is being questioned. "Every folktale ever printed. I've interviewed dozens of people who believe they've seen him. There's no one who knows more than me."

A smell like burning rubber fills the air. A lie. But of all the things to lie about, why his expertise? I signal Hadrian with a tiny shake of my head.

"Why does the Moth-Winged Man fascinate you so much? You're not even from around here. You didn't grow up hearing the legends." Hadrian crosses his arms, and it looks like a threat.

"Be-cause"—Sonny stresses each syllable in frustration—"he's going to make me rich and famous, one way or another. Do you know about the legend? If you capture the Moth-Winged Man, he'll grant your deepest desire."

"No," Hadrian disagrees. "He won't. Not if you don't have something worth trading."

"Okay, well, this has been real fun," Sonny says. "But if you're not going to fine me or . . . I don't know. Can forest rangers arrest people? Then I've got a lot of work to do." He starts tapping away on his cell phone, clearly dismissing us.

I grab Hadrian's arm and pull him toward the alcove near the bathrooms. "What the hell was that about?"

"What do you mean?"

"Why were you asking him such random questions? It's like you're not even trying to figure out who attacked you."

He shrugs. "He's hiding something."

I throw up my hands. "Obviously, but so are you. And that bothers me a hell of a lot more." I didn't mean to say that last part out loud, and I spin on my heel, heading for the bathroom, before he can respond.

The ladies' room at the Pub and Grub is not a place I would normally enter voluntarily, but I need a minute to splash some water on my face and pull myself together. I take a deep breath, plant my palms on the cool porcelain sink, and stare into the mirror.

"Why do you keep letting him get to you? He's never going to tell you the whole truth," I whisper. "So what are you going to do about it?"

After I wash my hands and try to avoid touching anything else in the tiny space, I step out into the back hall. Hadrian is talking to a couple of men near the bar. I'm pretty sure one of them works at the feed store. But just before I take a step in that direction, Sonny Vane's voice stops me in my tracks.

"That's why we don't work at the Harvest Moon anymore," Sonny complains to someone I can't see. I take a quiet step closer. The group is right on the other side of the wall.

"Yeah, that whole family is off like week-old milk in the hot July sun," another voice chimes in. "Rowan, though. She might be nice to look at and all, but there's just something not right about that girl."

"She put a knife to my throat the other day." A third voice joins in. This one I know: Bryson Ivers. His lie singes my nose, but I chuckle under my breath. "I handled it, though. Sometimes you have to put people in their place, just like this summer."

"What happened?" Sonny asks.

"Let's just say, we know who they can thank for the diner's new look." The second man chuckles, and I have to hold myself back from rushing over and grabbing him by the collar. Confronting him won't get me what I really want: the names of the people responsible for trashing the diner.

"I see," Sonny says. "Well, I'm working on a little something of my own. You should check out the episode I'm shooting on Friday."

"What are you planning?" Bryson asks.

"Actually, I could use some more muscle if you're interested," Sonny offers. "We can't drive all the way into the filming location, so we've got to haul a bunch of equipment by hand. The pay is nothing, but if you're lucky, you might make it onto my channel, and I'll definitely tag you on my socials."

The other two men quickly agree, both talking at the same time so I can't make out what they're saying.

"I've got to go shake the dew off the lily," one of them says clearly. I finally identify Kye Hensley's voice just as he's about to catch me eavesdropping. I glance the other way toward where Hadrian is still deep in conversation at the bar.

In a flash of perfect clarity, I realize I can kill two birds with one stone.

I slide around the corner and sidle up next to Hadrian. He's focused on something the feed store guy is saying and doesn't even look at me, but I cast a glance over my shoulder and hook a finger in his belt loop to get his attention. He goes completely still in a way that reminds me he isn't fully human anymore, like a coiled snake before it strikes. Footsteps are approaching behind me, and it's too late to come up with a better plan.

"Kiss me," I whisper so quietly I'm not even sure he can hear me. "Quick."

When he doesn't move, I meet his eyes and he searches mine for a long moment. Then he closes the distance between us, mouth on mine, hands in my hair. I stumble, and he presses my back against the wall, bracing an arm beside my head. My mind goes liquid for a moment, and I forget why we're doing this. I forget every lie he ever told me. I forget how to breathe, and I lean into him like I'm drowning. His teeth scrape across my bottom lip, coaxing my mouth open.

And then I bite my tongue, hard, until I taste the copper of my own personal truth serum.

He pulls back, just enough to meet my gaze. "If your goal was not to draw attention, I think we failed," he murmurs, rubbing a thumb gently against my bottom lip. He pulls his hand away to examine the rust-colored stain. "Did I hurt you?"

I cast a glance around the room at the people blatantly watching us, but Kye is nowhere in sight, and I let out a sigh of relief. "Come with me." I grab Hadrian's hand and pull him toward the ladies' room.

The tiny space isn't anywhere near big enough for two people. I shut the door behind us and push him up against it. His eyes go molten, and I can't stop the shiver that races across my skin.

"What is it you're not telling me?" I ask, and watch the way the words hit.

He moves like a cat. Muscles contracting before he bursts into action. His hands find my waist, and he lifts me onto the edge of the sink, so his hips are bracketed by my knees.

"What have you done to me?" he whispers, resting his forehead against mine. His teeth grit together as he fights against the effects. "It was your blood, wasn't it?" His eyebrows rise at the realization. "Clever."

"There's something else going on here," I press. "And I need to know what it is."

He draws his bottom lip between his teeth and pushes away from me, putting as much distance between us as possible in the small room. "Buck Garland. Have you noticed him acting a little strangely? Not like himself?"

I think back; besides the lost memory, I remember a comment Hillard made at the town hall meeting about Buck not normally being so confrontational. "Sure. Why?"

"He's missing part of his soul. I can see it when I look at him."

"What does that mean?" I ask. "What even is a soul, and how does someone lose a piece of one?"

"Soul is just a word. You can call it whatever you like." He waves a hand like it doesn't matter. "It's the essence of who we are as people: every memory, every hope, every dream, everything. It's the part of us that remains beyond our physical form. And the pieces aren't being lost, they're being stolen."

"Buck's pocket watch." I realize with dawning clarity. I had already suspected that the people who were losing things were also missing the memories attached to them, but it's even worse than that. They're losing pieces of themselves.

"Buck and his watch, that waitress and her earring, Joe from the feed store and his favorite fishing lure."

Mama and her necklace.

"I read about the *cat-sith* in the diablerie. What if the attacker wasn't after you at all? What if they were trying to steal the soul you were transporting, and when they couldn't take a whole one, they decided to try taking pieces."

"That's certainly a theory," he concedes.

"But why? And what does it mean if someone is missing part of their soul?" I ask.

He tilts his head and studies me. "Nothing," he finally answers with a shrug. "They won't remember the missing piece, and one tiny sliver won't change much for most. To others, they'll seem *less* than they were. A person who was known for their kindness will be colder, an angry person slower to lose their temper, like a photograph that's faded over time.

"But once they die, it's different. A soul can't cross over unless it's whole. They'll be stuck here."

There's not even a hint of a lie in his words. My mouth goes dry at the thought of my mother spending eternity as a restless spirit left behind in this world, and I struggle to tamp down the panic that tightens my throat.

As soon as the words leave Hadrian's mouth, someone pounds on the door, and I jump. "Other people need to use the facilities," a voice calls from the other side.

I yank open the door to Whitney's startled face. Her eyes go wide, traveling from me up to Hadrian behind me. I push past her, scanning the people in the bar. When I spot Sonny, I corner him.

"You want me on camera? Fine, this Friday night in the Forest. I'm coming with you," I tell him.

He tilts his head, studying me. "I know you're probably up to something, but I don't even care because viewers love drama. Is your boyfriend coming with you?"

"I . . ." I stumble, knocked off-kilter.

"Yeah, he is," Hadrian says from directly behind me.

Sonny smiles unconvincingly. "Great, I hope you're both ready for an adventure."

CHAPTER FOURTEEN

IT TAKES another full day for Linden to find a spell in the diablerie that might could bind the Bone Tree and stop the things from coming through that shouldn't, like magpies and whatever else might steal bits of souls. We wait until Gran and Mama go to bed, and then Juniper, Linden, and I sneak out to the summer kitchen.

The small stone building behind the main house was used in the dry season by the first James women, more than a century ago, to protect the main living space from excessive heat and risk of fire. Now it's where Gran and Mama make all the infusions, tinctures, and balms we sell, and where we store ingredients, like the lavender, sage, and other simples that dry tacked to the wall and scent the air. It's dim inside and the cramped space is filled to the brim with shelves of jars organized alphabetically and a large, old wooden worktable. We aren't breaking any rules by being here, and yet it feels like we are with the way we whisper and gather close.

"It's this one here." Linden opens the diablerie to a page near the middle that she's marked with an old recipe card. "It's similar to the witch bottle tradition, more of a charm than a spell. It's supposed to contain only that which means to do harm."

"How does it work?" I ask, twisting my dark hair into a knot to keep it out of the way while we work.

"First, we need a few things."

Linden instructs us on what to gather, and Juniper and I fill the workbench with all manner of things: the seeds of black snakeroot that I collected from a ravine in the Forest, useful in preventing those with bad intentions from crossing thresholds; bittergrass root, dug from a roadside meadow, to fend off ill will and unmake any curse; and an iron nail for protection against the uncanny. We add each ingredient to a small ceramic jar made of mud pulled from the creek bed and dried in the summer sun.

Juniper has on an enormous white nightgown trimmed in ribbons and lace that glows in the moonlight shining through the tiny windows. "What are you wearing?" I ask, bumping my shoulder into hers.

"It was Granny Sudie's." She shrugs. "I like it."

"Now, then." Linden consults the book again. "You need to add something from the Bone Tree, like a piece of bark or some dirt scraped from the roots. Once that's done, fill the opening with a bit of fresh clay and bury it upside down at the base of the tree."

"Do I need to offer blood or something?" I ask. The few spells we've done from the diablerie have all required a painful sacrifice of some sort, like blood for the simpler ones, or the exchange of what you hold most dear for making a bargain with the Moth-Winged Man.

"No!" Linden and Juniper both shout, then cast worried looks toward the farmhouse. We all hold our breath for a moment, waiting to see if a light will switch on in Mama's or Gran's windows. When we're sure we're safe, Linden explains.

"If you put a piece of yourself in there, you'll be bound up right along with it." She hands me the bottle. "But after you bury it, salt the earth."

"Our best chance of success will be on the fall equinox this weekend," Juniper adds. "Because it's the most potent time for magic and manifesting, but it's also the most dangerous because it's when the veil between the spiritual and physical worlds begins to thin. And I don't know what that will mean, with the unpredictable nature of the Bone Tree lately."

"What time is the equinox, exactly?" I ask.

"I think it's around two Saturday morning," Juniper clarifies. "But anytime Friday night or early Saturday morning between light and dark, dusk and dawn, should still be more powerful."

"I'll sneak out of Sonny Vane's vulturine production and hike over to the Bone Tree," I tell them, taking out my phone to set a reminder.

"That whole thing is weird," Juniper says.

"What do you mean?" I ask.

"Most of the YouTube channels I watch are self-produced, with maybe a freelance video editor. Sonny has an entire crew like some kinda reality show," Juniper says. "What sort of sponsor does he have to afford all that? His channel isn't exactly small, but it's not that big, either."

"And I don't like the idea of you traipsing through the Forest in the dark of night," Linden says, eyes bright with worry. "Especially when we don't even know what could be out there with you."

"Yeah, maybe you should cancel the Sonny Vane thing," Juniper agrees.

"I can't," I tell them. "This is all the more reason to go. Everybody is lying, and I need to figure out why."

Early the next afternoon, I meet the YouTube crew in the parking lot of the Ick, Caball Hollow's only gas station. The official name is the QuickStop, but no one calls it that. Not since all but three of the letters on the sign burned out long ago, leaving only the unfortunate set in the middle. The Ick is the last stop for supplies before the entrance to the National Forest, and with its location all the way across town from the Piggly Wiggly, the selection is more varied than most convenience stores.

"You can toss your bag in the back," one of the older guys on the crew tells me, jerking a thumb in the direction of the open rear doors of their big white van. "We're still waiting on Sonny, so it could be a while." He rolls his eyes.

The cargo space is full of audio and video equipment as well as several large duffel bags. I drop my pack on top of the pile, then wander toward the Ick to wait. The electronic chime sounds as I push open the door, and Dreama Kinnaird, an old classmate of Gran's who has worked here for as long as I can remember, calls a hello from the back, where I can just make out her blue smock.

A fresh tray of pepperoni rolls sits on the counter by the coffeepots and the rotating hot dog grill. The soft bread is still warm and stuffed with thick sticks of pepperoni, the delicious, spicy oil infusing the dough. There's nothing better for a day at the river than this West Virginia staple, first made popular by the Italian immigrants who packed them for their lunch in the coal mines. I shove two into a take-out bag and carry it to the register.

Dreama Kinnaird meets me at the counter. "Will this be all, honey?"

"And this." Hadrian steps up behind me, then slides a can of sweet tea across the counter and pulls out his wallet.

I freeze, not sure exactly how things have changed between us after the last time, when I used my blood as truth serum against him and had my tongue in his mouth. The tops of my cheeks heat embarrassingly, and it makes me furious.

"You've got to stop sneaking up on people," I mutter under my breath. But his attention isn't on me. It's on a yellowed piece of paper tacked to the bulletin board behind the register.

The edges are curling in around the pushpin, and the page has gone soft with age, but the photocopied image of a young boy with dark hair is still visible under the bold letters in red ink across the top: MISSING. It's a flyer about Elam McCoy that Dreama adamantly refuses to take down until he comes home. She was working here the day he disappeared, and she helped his father make the call to the sheriff's department when his hands shook too much to dial the number. And now the man who was once Elam McCoy is standing right in front of her but can't say a thing.

Hadrian pays and nods his thanks, then heads for the door without a backward glance. I catch up to him in the parking lot, but before I can figure out what to say, I realize the giant white van is gone. Only Sonny's little rental car remains.

"Hey," Sonny greets us from where he leans against the hood. He lifts his sunglasses. "The others headed over to get set up. Looks like you two are riding with me."

The drive to the Forest isn't far—luckily, because Hadrian doesn't say a word and Sonny won't shut up.

"I'm glad you finally came to your senses and agreed to be on camera," Sonny says as he flips on his blinker. "I have big plans for this shoot." He yammers on, about his shot list and his plans to use me to entice new viewers for the special episode, until it all sounds like static.

I glance at Hadrian in the rearview mirror; he's squashed in the small back seat, staring out the window and gilded by the sun. He is beautiful in a way that looks effortless. Beauty may be a little bit of power, but it's the kind every man wants to own and wield for himself. Mine I've had to sharpen. And it cuts both ways.

When we reach the river, the crew has already unloaded the van, so we grab the rest of the gear from Sonny's car and haul it up the trail to the spot on the Teays River where Elam McCoy went missing on this day nineteen years ago.

Sonny unexpectedly snaps into professional mode as soon as we reach the site, and starts ordering Bryson Ivers and Kye Hensley around in a way I quite enjoy, but it's left Hadrian and me all alone, waiting on the sidelines, as I'm determined not to do anything to help that isn't a required part of my agreement with Sonny.

"Will you stop looking at me like that?" Hadrian finally breaks the silence as he leans back against the tailgate next to me.

"Like what?"

"Like you're waiting for me to crack wide open." He crosses his arms, looking out across the valley where Sonny's crew is setting up their equipment and mounting tiny cameras everywhere.

"Is it strange for you to be back here?" I ask the question that's been gnawing at me since the Ick. Or, really, since that moment at the Pub and Grub when Buck Garland declared he's never gone back in the Forest.

"I gotta admit, watching them debate the best way to get the Moth-Winged Man to show up tonight is pretty amusing." A wry smile tugs at the corner of his mouth. "Have you been here since what happened with your sister?"

This is also the place where Linden went missing last year, after her own ill-fated attempt to summon the Moth-Winged Man, part of a foolhardy tradition among graduating seniors and their friends. We didn't know what had really happened, or how bad it could have been, until this summer. But I have vivid memories I'll never forget of standing in this field, begging Daddy to let me join the search, which he adamantly refused. Then watching as he kept going back into the woods, over and over, all through the night, long after he'd officially called off his deputies until morning.

"That was one of the worst days of my life, but it's not the same," I say finally, pulling off my sunglasses to study him more closely. "You almost died here."

"Hey, you!" Sonny calls. "Tall, broody guy. Can you mount this camera up there?" He points to a notch above his head in an old oak tree.

Hadrian gets to his feet, then turns back to face me as he walks backward. "I *did* die here," he says so only I can hear before he strides off to help.

There's a folding camp table set up by the tents where a couple of the crewmembers are taking a break, and I join them to wait for my cue.

"Where's Ona?" I ask the same crewmember I spoke to this morning.

"Cable snapped, so Sonny sent her to get a replacement," he tells me. "I'm Noel, by the way." He holds out a hand, and I shake it.

"Rowan," I tell him. "This all seems pretty intense. Is it always like this?"

"I've only known Sonny for about a month, but he seems pretty serious about his channel."

"Really? I thought y'all were a team."

"Nah, we're all contract. Sonny hired us just for this Moth-Winged Man investigation series. I think he's hoping it will be the thing that makes him famous. I don't know about all that, but he pays on time." He stands and tosses the rest of the coffee from his cup into the grass before putting it back onto his thermos. "I gotta get back to work."

"All right, people," Sonny calls, and claps his hands together. "We've only got a few hours to get ready for the night hunt, which is the most important part of our shoot. But before that, we need to get some B-roll footage of the area for the voice-over, and I'll interview Rowan, Bryson, and Kye."

Bryson and Kye look entirely too pleased at this announcement. But we're losing daylight rapidly, and I still haven't learned anything new. "I'll go first." I raise my hand to volunteer.

Sonny lifts his eyebrows in surprise, but then waves me over to a place away from the noise of the rushing river where they've set up the interview shot.

"After all those weeks of playing hard to get, your enthusiasm is a nice change," Sonny murmurs, and I try not to vomit in my mouth as Noel clips a tiny microphone to my shirt.

"Maybe I could sit in on your interviews with Bryson and Kye, too," I suggest, in as friendly a tone as I can muster. My plan is to lull them into a false sense of security, then hit them with the hard questions when they least expect it.

Sonny shrugs, then Noel cues us that the camera is rolling. "Rowan James," he begins, his voice deeper and pronunciation more carefully precise than normal, like he's impersonating someone from the evening news. "You've lived in Caball Hollow all your life. Have you ever seen the Moth-Winged Man?"

"No, only sketches, like in the newspaper or with the folktales," I answer, truthfully though not completely. I've never seen Hadrian in his Moth-Winged Man form, but I've heard about it from Linden. "What about you? Have you ever seen him?" I ask before he can move on to his next question.

"Ah." He stumbles for a moment. "I've seen things here in the Forest that I truly cannot explain. But whether it was direct evidence of the Moth-Winged Man, I can't say for certain. At least not yet."

I take a deep breath, but there's no telltale stench. I push for a more solid answer. "What would you need to be certain?"

"I thought I was doing the interview here." He chuckles, slightly off-kilter.

"A photo? Video?" I press. "Actually capturing the Moth-Winged Man?"

"There would always be the naysayers who claim a photo or video can be faked." Sonny's expression changes, an intensity that I've never seen in him before creeping in. "No one could deny the validity of what I do if I were to bring in an actual specimen."

I study him, trying to read between the lines to the whole truth. But now it's his turn to jump in before I can regroup.

"And what about your family?" he asks, glancing at someone off camera. "I've been told you have a closer relationship to the Moth-Winged Man than most."

I follow his gaze to see Bryson and Kye watching us. "What do you mean by that?"

"The most recent sightings of the Moth-Winged Man were connected to the murder of a friend of your sister's. In fact, your sister helped solve the case and was nearly killed herself. Right here, I believe." Sonny holds out a hand, taking in the landscape behind us. "But all of that happened after she attempted to summon the Moth-Winged Man by calling his name three times on the anniversary of Elam McCoy's death. Did she succeed?"

I stare at him for a moment, then throw my head back and laugh. "That old urban legend? If it was really that simple, don't you think *you* would have found him by now?"

It's clear this was meant to be some sort of gotcha moment, likely worked out in advance with Bryson and Kye, so I switch tactics, putting them on the defensive instead.

"What about your family, Bryson? Wasn't your cousin there when Dahlia Calhoun's body was found?"

Bryson's mouth drops open as the camera swings around to point at him. "It wasn't like that," he argues. "He was just working late in the area."

"Right. And, Kye, didn't you join the hunting parties that went out into the Forest looking for the Moth-Winged Man? Done anything like that lately?"

"What? No," he scoffs. "Why would I? No one's seen the Moth-Winged Man in months." He realizes what he's said and gives Sonny a sheepish look.

"You know who vandalized the Harvest Moon, don't you?" I ask, while he's still off-kilter.

"Of course not!" Kye shouts. The lie is so potent I reflexively cover my nose before I can stop myself.

Sonny quickly wrapped up our interview, unamused by my attempts to steer the conversation. Later that evening, after a simple dinner of sandwiches and chips from a folding table set up near the van, Noel points me to my tent. Sonny warned me that he'll likely want me on camera again later and I'll need to behave myself, but right now they're getting ready to film the portion of the video where he hunts for the Moth-Winged Man using night vision cameras, which I can only imagine is all for the drama.

The tent they've assigned to me is a small green one at the back of the campsite, and when I push through the flap, my pack is already waiting for me inside, along with a bedroll and Hadrian Fitch.

"What are you doing in my tent?" I ask with a sinking feeling. I thought Sonny was kidding when he called Hadrian my boyfriend, but I'd never corrected him.

Hadrian glances up from the book he's reading, one arm underneath his head. "I think you mean *our* tent, my love."

"Do not call me that," I object as I drop down onto the second sleeping bag. I don't plan on sleeping for more than a handful of hours anyway, but there is something I need to address before I can do even that much. "Are we going to talk about what happened at the Pub and Grub?"

He closes the paperback, marking his place with a finger and resting it against his stomach. "You certainly are full of surprises."

I can feel his eyes on me, but I don't meet his gaze. "Is it going to make it difficult for us to work together?"

"Did it ever occur to you to just ask me without the truth serum and subterfuge?" His voice is even, but there's something simmering underneath.

"Would you have answered?"

"I guess we'll never know." He shrugs. "Don't worry, it doesn't really matter either way, does it? We live in different worlds. Help me figure out who attacked me and then there'll be no reason to ever have to see each other again."

I swallow hard, gathering my thoughts, then push aside everything else to refocus on why we're here. "Did you hear what Sonny said about his hunt for the Moth-Winged Man?"

Hadrian nods. "You still think he's the likeliest suspect?"

"He's definitely hiding something," I tell him. "But I can't ignore the fact that right around the time you were targeted, something started stealing pieces of souls from the people of Caball Hollow."

And I still want to get answers out of Bryson and Kye. Either they know who vandalized the Harvest Moon or they did it themselves.

"I've been talking to the crew," Hadrian says. "I don't think they'd jump someone with Sonny or cover for him this long. They aren't especially loyal to him or his mission. They're just here doing a job."

He's right. I heard as much myself from Noel. "They might if he paid enough. The source of Sonny's funding is another mystery I'd like to look into." I roll onto my side, facing Hadrian, and prop my head up with an elbow. "It really doesn't bother you, how they've turned your death into this urban legend and the Moth-Winged Man into something to be hunted for curiosity's sake?"

He's quiet for so long I start to think he won't answer. "Their false beliefs about me don't change anything. I don't remember much from that day. But what I do remember is being afraid and very cold and wanting nothing more than to go home to my mother, which was the one thing I could never do again. I know how important the job I do now is, because I would have been lost without those who were there for me then."

He rolls over and switches off the light with a mumbled good night, but I stay awake, staring at the sky through the mesh window and thinking about his words for a good long while.

CHAPTER FIFTEEN

MY PHONE buzzes at one a.m., and I ineffectually slap at it until I wake up enough to remember where I am. The small tent is cozy with trapped body heat. I jerk upright as last night comes rushing back and lunge to silence the reminder I'd set before I knew I'd be sharing a tent with Hadrian. I glance toward his sleeping bag to see if I've disturbed him, blinking my tired eyes until they focus in the darkness. But I'm alone.

I look around like there's somewhere Hadrian could be hiding in a space that can't be more than four feet across. Logically, I suspect he's gone to find a nice bush to water. But if Sonny is still out there trying to spot the Moth-Winged Man by the river, part of me hopes Hadrian went to mess with him.

As silently as I can, I pull on my jacket and grab my pack. Bracing for the bite of the wind, I step out of the tent and into the crisp mountain air. It's dark, but the sky is clear and the moon is waxing. If I'm careful, I should be able to make it to the Bone Tree in under an hour.

The rest of the small camp is quiet, a handful of tents scattered across the valley. I take careful steps, waiting until I'm several feet into the trees before flipping on my flashlight. The Forest is a different place at night. The flutter of bat wings and the call of owls in the canopy overhead, the chirp of crickets in the long grass and the song of mountain chorus frogs in the shallows of the creek. But it doesn't just sound different, it looks different, too. The colors are all muted, shadows stretch and obscure landmarks that would usually be easy to identify, and distance is harder to gauge with a limited field of vision. And then there's the wildlife, bolder when the Forest belongs to them.

When I finally reach the clearing, the Bone Tree glows bright in the moonlight like a warning, and the urge to stay away from it builds beneath my skin. This is the epicenter of the strangeness happening in Caball Hollow, just like it's always been. I know it in my bones.

The shape of it usually brings to mind a hand, coming up from the ground and reaching over the creek, but now it almost looks like a person standing, with two long legs widespread on the ground, two arms reaching as if to break a fall, and a head hanging down in defeat, frozen in time.

The spell bottle is wrapped in muslin at the bottom of my pack. I pull it out and step closer to the tree, running my hand along the trunk until I find a loose piece of bark. I pry it off with my mushroom knife until I have a large enough slice to add to the bottle. When it's done, I plug the opening with a bit of fresh clay, then use my spade to dig a hole in the soft dirt at the base of the Bone Tree, near where the largest of the roots protrudes from the ground, and bury the bottle upside down.

Next, I take out the bag of local salt. As much as it can protect, it can also destroy. Salting the earth will prevent the threat from growing. It'll prevent just about anything from growing. I turn my back on the buried bottle, take three long steps, then pour out a circle of salt to seal in the spell and prevent future ill fortune from taking root.

As I'm packing up the spade and the rest of the salt, the hair on the back of my neck stands up like lightning is about to strike, and I freeze. It takes me awhile to spot it. A smudge of darker black against the sky.

Movement draws my gaze, and as I search the night, I can barely make out the edges of a large, distinctly feline shape just beyond the range of my flashlight.

It's at least the size of a bobcat, maybe even a mountain lion, yet it looks formed of shadow. Its ears twitch, and I freeze until I'm barely even breathing. Slowly, its large head turns until it's looking right at me. But I still try to convince myself it's my mind playing tricks, crafting monsters that aren't really there, until the moment I see the metallic flash of its eyes. Two bright orbs staring back at me across the distance.

Then, between one breath and the next, the cat loses substance, blurring around the edges and bleeding away into the darkness of the trees. Once I lose sight of it, I question if it was ever really here at all. But my throat has gone so dry, I struggle to swallow. I need to get out of here, away from the Bone Tree.

Before I can even stand, the cat bursts out of the underbrush, racing toward me with a speed I have no prayer of matching. I lose my footing, falling backward as it leaps across the twisted center of the Bone Tree. My flashlight crashes to the ground and shuts off.

Reality flows like water off its fur. Even staring directly at it, I struggle to map its form. But there are claws. And teeth, glowing in the light of the moon. It lets out an angry yowl that sounds like a scream. My heart gives a painful lurch, blood gone thick in my veins. All I can do now is squeeze my eyes shut, waiting for the inevitable explosion of pain.

But it doesn't come.

When I blink open my eyes, the cat is gone. I search the shadows for any sign of the creature. It must be playing some game, wanting me to run so it can chase me. My pulse echoes in my ears, drowning out other sounds as I push off from the trunk of the Bone Tree to get to my feet.

I wait until my muscles ache from resisting the urge to flee. And when I can't hold back any longer, I force myself to walk away slowly, following the creek toward the river.

It's faster to cut through the woods, but the dense Forest offers too many places for a predator to hide.

Yet, as I make my way south, I start to question if I'm going the right way. The landscape looks strange, with massive trees unlike any I've ever seen before and enormous moss-covered rocks. I stop to get my bearings, sure I must somehow be lost. But this doesn't just look unfamiliar; it looks *wrong*. Like a different sort of forest altogether has grown into mine.

A sound, like the trees are breathing, the faint creaking of wood expanding and contracting. It's soft but unmistakable, coming from several directions at once. The deeper I look into the forest, the longer the shadows seem to stretch, murky and indistinct. No matter how many times I look over my shoulder, I can't shake the feeling of eyes watching me.

I pick up the pace. Following the creek will eventually take me to the river, and from there I should be able to find the camp.

Then I hear something familiar. Hadrian. He's close. And he's angry.

I follow the sound into the woods and find a small clearing. There's a circle at the center with evidence of past fires in the dirt marked by ash and charred wood fragments. Beside the fire pit, Hadrian stands with his back to me, facing a man I've never seen before. He's older, probably somewhere around my father's age, with a thick beard shot through with gray. His shirtsleeves are rolled up, and he has dark tattoos in shapes I can't quite make out inked across his forearms. Some instinct tells me to hang back, and I watch from behind the trunk of an oak.

"The Bone Tree grows weaker every day, son." The man speaks with a commanding voice and the hint of an accent I don't recognize. "What have you learned?"

"Not enough," Hadrian answers, his frustration obvious. "There isn't much to go on."

"What of the James women?" the man asks, and I have to hold back the gasp that threatens to escape and give me away. "Could they be involved?"

I wonder for a moment how this stranger knows about my family, and when Hadrian speaks, I realize I'm looking at the answer.

"No," he says. "They are concerned about the theft of souls but don't yet seem to be aware of the consequences of a failing Bone Tree."

A sinking feeling, like tripping on uneven ground, drops my stomach, and I have to press my hand against the ivy-covered tree trunk beside me for balance. I knew Hadrian couldn't be trusted, but even I didn't suspect him of spying on us. How long has he been reporting back to this strange man? And what else has he told him?

"They don't know who is responsible for the thefts?" the man demands.

"No, but I'm sure it's just a matter of time," Hadrian admits.

"That's the one thing we don't have, boy," the man growls. "And I'm running out of patience, too. Stop it your way, or I'll do mine. Because if we don't act soon, there'll be nothing left." He reaches out, grabbing Hadrian's arm, just below the sleeve of his T-shirt. "Remember where your loyalty lies, son. You disobeyed me once—there won't be a second time." As he speaks the words, a light beneath his hand begins to glow, and below it the tattoos on Hadrian's skin start to move.

Hadrian grits his teeth, his jaw going tight. When the man finally lets go, he gives Hadrian an insincere smile and a pat on the shoulder before walking away. Once he disappears deeper into the woods, Hadrian drops to his knees.

I step forward without thinking, and a harsh chatter breaks out above me. The branches overhead are filled with more than a dozen magpies, each picking up the warning call.

"Rowan?" Hadrian stares at me, face slack with shock.

I turn and run, racing back through the trees.

"Wait!"

I don't stop until my lungs ache. Then, when I'm gasping for breath, I risk a look back.

A hand claps over my mouth.

"Don't scream," a woman's voice whispers into my ear. "I mean you no harm. I just want to talk."

The hand peels away, and I spin to face her, breathing deeply to test her claim. She's shorter than I am, but not by much, with long dark hair the color of coffee beans and eyes as bright blue as cornflowers. Just like my mother's. I step back. She looks like she could be an older version of Linden.

"Aunt Zephyrine," I whisper, the realization knocking the air out of my lungs. "We've been looking for you."

Her eyes widen, as if she's surprised I recognize her. I can't believe, after years of Gran searching for her sister, this is how I'm meeting her for the first time. There are so many questions I want to ask her. I'm not sure where to even begin.

"I know." She grabs my hand and pulls. "But you must forget what you saw here. It isn't safe. Not for you."

"Why? Who was that man?" I ask.

"I mean it. Forget you ever saw him," she warns.

"But he knew about our family," I insist. "Is he dangerous?"

"Shh!" She whirls to face me, leaning in close. "Don't draw any more attention. Even the trees here have eyes." She points up to the magpies in the branches above us.

The crack of a twig echoes like a shot.

"We need to go. Now," Zephyrine insists. And then she's pulling me behind her through the trees at a reckless pace.

Her feet are more sure than mine in this strange place, and I stumble, breaking her hold on my hand. But before my knees can connect with the rocky ground, an arm hooks around my waist and hauls me to my feet.

"Rowan, wait," Hadrian murmurs. His chest heaves against my back, heart racing. "Let me explain."

"Let her go, Hadrian," Aunt Zephyrine commands. "The Otherworld is no place for her, as you well know. Besides, it sounds like you have other matters to attend to. Investigation not going well?"

"Interesting you should ask." Hadrian drops his arm, stepping in front of me and leveling a steady gaze on her. "The culprit would have to be someone with something to gain from throwing into question the power of the current leadership. Perhaps someone with a debt to pay or . . ." He pauses, and the corner of his mouth tips up in the faintest hint of a smirk. "The need of a distraction. So tell me, have you been playing a dangerous game?"

Zephyrine's eyes flare with anger and what I think might be a touch of fear. "Certainly if someone were to gamble, they'd have to be willing to lose what they have. Hear me when I say I am not that person."

Hadrian's eyes go to mine automatically after her statement, checking for a lie. I scoff through my teeth. He told me he wanted a lie detector. I was the fool who thought it could ever be anything else.

"What was it you said? All I had to do was ask, and you'd tell me the truth, huh?" I knew I couldn't trust him, and yet seeing the proof of it still stings. "And have you been spying on my family the entire time we've known you or just since your latest return?"

"This place isn't like your world, Rowan," he says. "The magic here is everywhere. It's in everything. It's the very basis of who the good folk are. There's a careful balance of power that must be maintained."

"You knew where Aunt Zephyrine was this whole time, you saw how much Gran missed her, and yet you never said a word."

"It would have done no good," he insists. "She's made her choices, and now she must live with them."

"You can't lie if you don't say anything, right?" My voice is low, barely hanging on to control.

"There are things I can't tell you, Rowan. Deals I had to make to survive in a world where no one cared if I did." He leans down to meet my eyes. "You don't have to trust me—hell, you probably shouldn't—but I am trying to keep you safe, that I promise."

"And telling that man about me and my family, that's keeping me safe?" I demand. "You honestly believe that?"

A pained look crosses his face and he grasps his arm, just over where the bright light had been.

"It's a yes or no question, Hadrian."

"Yes," he grounds out, his jaw clenched.

The most dangerous lies are the ones you want to believe. As Hadrian looks at me with eyes begging for understanding, the air fills with the smell of woodsmoke and ashes.

"Come on." Zephyrine holds out her hand again, and I take it.

Hadrian watches me leave, but he doesn't try to stop me.

"No one here is who they seem," she says once we're farther away. "I don't know what you think your relationship with Hadrian is, but his loyalty is to one person and one person only. He'll never be honest with you as long as he bears the mark of another. You must look out for yourself first and foremost, because no one else will."

When we reach the Bone Tree, Zephyrine pulls a knife from her boot and grabs my hand, slicing clean across my palm before I even realize what she's doing. I hiss and try to pull away, but she holds tight, pressing the cut against the white bark of the tree. She whispers something in a language I don't understand, then waits. But nothing happens.

"What's wrong?" I ask. "Why won't it open?"

"Something is blocking you from crossing." She lets go of my wrist, grabbing my shoulders instead. "Is there anyone who would want to trap you here?"

"There's no way anyone could have known I'd be here." I shake my head, bewildered. "*I* didn't even know I'd be here."

Could someone have followed me when I snuck out of my tent in the wee hours of the morning? Linden and Juniper warned me about the danger of being bound with the spell. Had someone tampered with it to trap me here? But how would anyone know what it was? We hadn't even known of the spell until a few days ago.

The sound of something large moving through the trees echoes behind us.

Zephyrine turns to look, then grabs my wrist again, pressing my hand against the tree and whispering the words a second time, faster now, like a prayer. A light blinks to life underneath my palm.

"Go." She pushes me toward the opening threshold. "Quickly."

"Come with me," I plead, grabbing her arm with my other hand. "Gran has been waiting so long for you to come home."

Her eyes fill, and she looks away. The rising sun cuts through the trees, shining on her face. I know she's quite a bit younger than Gran, but she looks like she could be the same age as Mama.

"I made my own binding agreement when I was desperate and didn't fully understand the consequences," she says, still not looking at me. "Now I'm cursed to only be able to leave this place in a form no one would recognize." She casts another glance at the trees, then leans forward and lifts her sleeve just enough to expose a tattoo on her forearm of a cat with smudged shadow edges.

"You?" I gape at her in disbelief. "But you can't be the one stealing souls." I may not know Zephyrine, but I know she's a James and she wouldn't do that to Mama.

"No," she agrees. "I've had to keep my claws covered, but I've done what I can to protect you from spying eyes and thieving beaks. Now you must do the rest."

The image of the dead magpie on my front porch flashes in my mind, then morphs into Hadrian bleeding in the same spot. But before I can ask Zephyrine anything else, the tree falls away beneath my hand. I stumble and go sprawling across the ground. In the canopy above me, I make out willow and pin oak, sourwood and spruce. The stark white branches of the Bone Tree reach across the sky. I'm back in my Forest.

I sit up and blink hard at the sight of my sisters. Linden and Juniper stand in the midst of the broken shards that used to be the spell jar, concern pulling their faces tight.

"Oh, thank goodness. It worked." Linden breathes a sigh of relief, bending to help me to my feet.

"What are you doing here?" I blink up in confusion as I reach for her hand.

Juniper picks up the iron nail from the pile of debris on the ground. There's a dark hair wound around it that perfectly matches the color of my own. "Someone tampered with the spell."

"When you didn't come home, we started to worry something had gone wrong," Linden says, holding me out at arm's length to check me over from head to toe.

"Didn't come home? I can't have been gone for more than a couple hours," I object, looking from Linden to Juniper, alarm prickling under my skin.

"Rowan," Juniper says. "It's nearly sunset. You've been missing all day."

CHAPTER SIXTEEN

"WE NEED to get a move on if we want to make it home before dark," Juniper says, slipping the iron nail into her pocket.

We hike back toward the trail that leads out of the Forest as the sun goes down, and I tell them how I didn't realize I'd been pulled into the Otherworld until I tried to hike back to where Sonny Vane's film crew was camping and everything looked different.

"We covered for you when you weren't back this morning in time for your shift at the Harvest Moon," Linden said.

"But then Sonny Vane's crew came in. His assistant asked if you'd made it home all right from the shoot because she hadn't seen you. And then Sonny made a scene, complaining loudly that you and your boyfriend had left early and he hadn't been able to finish filming," Junie chimes in, picking up the story. "Which really confused Mama, so we had to tell her that Hadrian was back in town and then she seemed to understand why you two might need some time to talk."

"And why would she think that made any kind of sense?" I demand.

"When you weren't back by closing, we started to get really worried," Linden says, ignoring my question. "We thought something might have gone wrong with the spell, so we dug up the jar, only to find you'd been bound to it."

"That's the part I don't get," Juniper says. "How would anyone know to do that?"

I reach out, pulling them both to a stop and wait until they look at me. "That's not the only strange part." I recount the conversation I overheard between Hadrian and the man in the clearing. And then I tell them about meeting Aunt Zephyrine.

"So there's nothing we can do?" Linden asks.

"We should keep searching for a solution, but Zephyrine studied the diablerie more than anyone before she disappeared. If there were a way, I'm not sure why she wouldn't know it."

We agree not to tell Gran until I figure out how best to broach the subject. How do you explain to someone that the person they love is alive but can never come home again? There's no way it won't break her heart.

Just as we reach the main road that leads out of the Forest, headlights cut through the trees. Two Eldritch County Sheriff's Department trucks are pulled off on the shoulder about a half mile ahead. We exchange a look and pick up our pace.

Daddy and Ethan Miranda, his youngest deputy, are standing in front of the vehicles near a massive outcropping of limestone, earnestly discussing something in low voices.

"What are you girls doing out here?" Daddy calls when he spots us.

"Just heading home," I tell him. It's the truth, but not all of it, and I hate the way it reminds me of Hadrian's lie of omission. But I don't have the wherewithal to deal with the can of beans I'd open if I told him everything right now. "What's going on?"

Daddy crosses his arms and sighs. "Come on, I'll give you a ride." He nods to his truck, then murmurs something to Deputy Miranda before he heads for the big Suburban.

We all climb in, but he doesn't answer my question until after we pull away. "I'm reopening the investigation into the crash that killed the alleged poacher."

"Is there new evidence?" I ask.

"No one has come forward to claim the body." He flips on the blinker, then heads down the road that leads to the farm. "And you know me, I hate a coincidence. Two strange cases in the same month have me wondering if they might be connected."

"That's where the accident happened?" I turn around in my seat to try to get a better look when Daddy hums in acknowledgment. "Or do you think it wasn't an accident?"

He gives me that look that means he's not answering.

"Is there any news about the John Doe from the Forest?" Juniper asks from the back seat. "Has he woken up yet?"

"No, no change." He purses his mouth, clearly frustrated by the situation. "And the doctors can't figure out why."

If the two cases are connected, that would likely mean both men were ginseng poachers. Unless the accident wasn't an accident. I'm not sure what, exactly, that would mean. But thinking about the crash makes me realize something else. There was another witness to Hadrian's attack. The spirit he was guiding to the Otherworld.

Daddy pulls into the driveway and throws the truck into park. I clamber out, then open the rear door for Juniper. Daddy does the same for Linden on the other side.

"Thanks for the ride." I start to follow the others back to the house, but he stops me.

"Rowan," he asks. "What happened to your hand?"

"Oh." I look down at the gash across my palm. "It got sliced by something out in the woods," I answer vaguely and hate myself a little.

He watches me with his investigator face, not giving anything away and waiting for me to say something to incriminate myself. He does this when he suspects we're up to something. I've learned to wait him out.

"Make sure you clean it real good," he says after several long minutes.

"I will."

"Lyon?" Mama calls as she steps out of the barn. She pulls the rolling door shut behind her and makes her way toward us. "Did you eat? Come on inside. I'll fix you a plate."

A smile spreads across his face at the sight of her, and I use the distraction to escape toward the house.

"Rowan Persephone, you and I need to have a little chat later," she calls just as I reach the screen door.

I shower until the water goes cold, trying to fit all the different bits of information into one cohesive story. But I'm not even sure if I'm solving one mystery or several. When I finally climb out of the claw-foot tub, skin pink and puffy, I clean the wound on my hand and apply some of Gran's famous yarrow balm for healing.

"Rowan?" Mama knocks softly.

I open the door, and she leans against the jamb as I comb the tangles from the ends of my hair. "I know you're eighteen," she starts, and my muscles clench, realizing where this conversation is heading. "But you will always be my child, and if you ever plan on ditching work again, you better tell me yourself. Because if I have to hear it from your sisters, I'll ground you till you're thirty." She reaches out and grabs my face, pulling it toward her to drop a kiss on my forehead before she leaves.

It's an uncharacteristically mild lecture, and I can only imagine the one I would have gotten had she known where I really was. But her just forgiving Hadrian and easily accepting that he's back after everything he's done, especially with what I know now, makes me want to scream.

I grab my pack and haul it to the laundry room. Turning it upside down and dumping the contents into the hamper, I almost miss it when a tiny leather-bound book falls to the floor. I bend to pick it up, confused. It's only a handful of pages, and the paper is thin as onionskin, the text so tiny it's hard to read:

There once was a child born
Of oak, ash, and thorn.
In a time of great dismay.

To preserve for him his crown,
A human decoy was found
And he was sent to live far away.

But the child of flesh and bone,
Wanted the throne for his own.
A cunning and violent usurper.

With a hungry cat black as night,
He convinced others to fight.
Igniting in them a great fervor.

The rightful lord was soundly felled,
Buried in a bed of dirt and weald,
His kingdom left to plunder.

And there he will lie,
Till the bone's day to die.
Two worlds torn forever asunder.

I flip through the pages again, but there's nothing else. Someone had to have snuck this strange little fairy tale into my pack for a reason. Could it have been Aunt Zephyrine before she sent me back through the Bone Tree? Or could it have been left by whoever tampered with the spell jar in the first place? But regardless of who sent it, if this is a message, I don't know what it means.

Shame on me for thinking Mama would let me off easy for missing work. Instead, I've spent the past week pulling double shifts and taking on all the farm chores that are long overdue now that we don't have help. Plucking the thick, green hornworms from the tomato vines. Mucking out the sheep pens and spreading fresh straw. Composting all the spent stalks from the summer harvest. By Friday night, I'm more exhausted than I was during my time at the fire lookout.

The door to Linden and Juniper's room is open, and I pop my head in. Juniper is sprawled out across her bed and scrolling on her phone.

"What are you up to?" I ask, leaning against the doorframe.

She flinches like she's been caught doing something she shouldn't. "I was just checking the latest news about the boy in the coma." She locks her phone and tosses it onto the bed in front of her.

I tilt my head and study her for a moment, confused about why she'd be embarrassed. And then I remember Sorrel's comment about what everyone has been calling him. Sleeping Beauty. My baby sister has a crush.

"I've been thinking about what Daddy said." She pauses, nibbling the corner of her lip. "If the two cases are connected, the first victim may know something about what happened to the boy. The reason or maybe even who might have hurt him."

"Yeah, maybe," I agree. I'd had a similar theory about what happened to Hadrian, though the one bright spot in being so busy was not having the time to ruminate on what I'd overheard in the Otherworld. But coming from Juniper, this line of thought is giving me a bad feeling.

"So what if we ask him?"

And that's exactly what I was worried about.

"No, Juniper." I cross my arms. "Absolutely not."

A few months ago, she was able to make contact with the spirit of Linden's murdered friend, but the information we were able to get wasn't worth the toll on Juniper. It took so much out of her, we'd had to carry her to bed after.

"I've been searching through Great-Granny Sudie's notes, but the spell we used this summer won't work. We'll have to try something else."

"We're not doing it."

"Doing what?" Linden asks from behind me. I turn and she walks into the room, arms full of notebooks and her school-assigned laptop.

She's determined to go to Georgetown with Cole next fall, and she's working her ass off to make that happen. I'm happy that Sorrel got to go to college; Linden and Juniper deserve that chance, too. But I know there's no way my parents and Gran can afford to send all of us.

"Don't worry, we're not doing it," I tell Linden.

"I found something that might work in the diablerie," Juniper presses on.

"Just how long have you been thinking about this?" I demand.

She shrugs. "Pretty much since Daddy drove us home last weekend."

Linden drops her stuff on the desk she shares with Juniper, then perches on its edge. "You're not leaving me out of this."

"I'm not completely sure we can even do it," Juniper admits. "The car accident was weeks ago now. Although violent deaths are more likely to leave a connection. But our best chance of success is during the dark moon, on Friday the thirteenth."

"No." I throw my hands up in frustration. "It's too risky, Juniper."

Her nostrils flare. "The thing is, I don't need your permission, Rowan. I'm doing this. With or without you."

Linden meets my eyes, and the look she gives me says Juniper is acting just like me. I let out a breath and sink down onto the corner of Linden's bed across from Juniper.

"But I would like your help," she admits quietly. "I don't suppose we could get our hands on anything belonging to the victim?"

"I don't see how," I tell her honestly. "We don't even know his name."

"What happened to the truck he was driving?" Linden asks. "Don't totaled vehicles normally get towed to the junkyard? If it hasn't been scrapped yet, maybe there's an item of his we could use there. I can do a little digging—"

"You need to focus on school," I interrupt. "I'll do the digging."

"Please hurry," Juniper warns. "I'm pretty sure the next dark moon will be our only chance before he moves beyond our reach."

I fall backward onto the bed behind me, soundly steam-rolled into the one thing I didn't want. I have no problem throwing myself into danger to get answers, but I'll do whatever I can to keep them out of it. Even when they seem bound and determined to race in headlong.

October

Hunter's Moon

As we transition from light to darkness, it is a time to turn inward and examine our beliefs and understanding. This life requires both sturdiness and grounding. Look closely at what you attempt to hide away. Under the Hunter's Moon, we honor the dead, but it is also a time to cut out and bury that which we wish to leave behind. Now is the time to remember our ancestors, commune with the spirits of the dead, protect against evil, and dream our wildest dreams.

In Season

Garden: apples, beets, broccoli, Brussels sprouts, cabbage, carrots, cauliflower, celery root, eggplant, fennel, garlic, greens, leeks, onions, parsnips, pears, potatoes, pumpkins, radishes, shelling beans, spinach, squash, tomatoes, turnips, zucchini

Forage: passionflower, wild comfrey, wild fox grapes, chanterelles, cauliflower and pheasant back mushrooms, chestnuts, spicebush berries, black walnuts, teaberry, arrowhead tubers, rosehips

Charm for Undisturbed Slumber

When uninterrupted sleep is a necessity, gather mugwort and agrimony under the dark moon and place them in a square of fabric cut from a child's nightgown. Add a sprinkle of local salt, then sew the edges together with black thread. Place under the pillow of the one who needs to rest. Remove to awaken, after a maximum of thirteen hours. If limit is exceeded, waking may become difficult.

—Sudie James, 1954

CHAPTER SEVENTEEN

THE CABALL Hollow Public Library makes up one half of the old brick municipal building in the middle of town that also houses the Eldritch County Sheriff's Department and a handful of township offices. At the center is a clock tower that loses time, sometimes skipping whole hours or ticking randomly into the past.

The library is closed on Sundays, so on Monday I speed through my morning chores, then head over, parking the Bronco on the street out front. Leaves skitter across the sidewalk in a swirl of faded colors.

I push through the wide glass doors and make my way to the reference desk.

"Hello." Opal Parrish, the library director, greets me, her white hair cut precisely at her chin. "Can I help you?"

Our local newspaper is mostly high school sports updates, car dealership ads, and garage sale notices. Predictably, there's no online version I can easily search through. Because nothing in this town is ever easy. But the library does keep an archive.

"I'm looking for a copy of the *Caball Hollow Observer* from a few weeks ago."

"Ah, the most recent months haven't been converted to microfiche yet, but you can find the hard copies over in periodicals."

She leads me over to an area of metal shelves filled with the latest editions of various newspapers and magazines displayed on a ledge at the front, which folds up to show stacks of past issues. I thank her and get to work, digging through pages of newsprint until my fingers are shiny with ink. It isn't until the issue from the first week of September that I finally find what I'm looking for:

> CABALL HOLLOW—*Last night at approximately 11:52 p.m., the Eldritch County Sheriff's Department responded to a fatal single-vehicle crash. An older-model white Ford Ranger, driven by a 25-year-old male from out of state, was exiting the National Forest when it left the roadway and struck a large boulder. The male driver was found deceased at the scene. He was the sole occupant of the vehicle and was not wearing a seat belt. The sheriff's department is withholding the name of the victim until next of kin has been notified. The incident remains under investigation.*

I make a copy of the article, and then return all the papers to their proper places. Now I at least have a make and model to look for, but no name for the victim and no idea which salvage yard might have his vehicle. I can't exactly ask Daddy without tipping him off that I'm investigating on my own, something he explicitly forbade. But salvage yards are only required to keep a vehicle for around forty-five days without it being claimed before they're allowed to scrap it. That may not apply here, since Daddy reopened the case, but that's not something I'm willing to rely on this close to the cutoff date. We're running out of time.

I find an open computer between two elderly ladies checking their email on 200 percent zoom, and search for local salvage yards. There's a ridiculous amount. Twenty in Eldritch County alone. I switch to map view and note the closest one to the scene of the accident. But it's also possible, maybe even probable, that the sheriff's department has a contract with a particular company. I open another tab and search again, then scroll through the results. Most of them are about towing, but there's one that explains what to do if you think your car has been impounded, and it lists the name of the company the sheriff's department uses. I write that one down as well.

Just as I'm about to close the tab, I notice a logo at the bottom of the website. It's the security company they use, and I recognize it. It's the same logo that's on the uniform Kye Hensley and his friends wear when they come into the diner for lunch.

When I get back out to the Bronco, I call both places and leave voicemails asking if they have a rear panel for an older-model white Ford Ranger.

I don't hear back from the first place until Wednesday, and it's just to tell me they don't have what I'm looking for. I call the second place several more times, but they never answer the phone, and I don't want to leave multiple voicemails and become too memorable.

I'm considering the merits of driving over to the salvage yard and asking in person when I get a call from a blocked number at seven in the morning on Friday. Luck must finally be on my side, because when I answer, it's a man from the second salvage yard who says he might have a rear panel from 1999.

"The front end is crushed, but the back panel looks to be in pretty good shape," he tells me. "Want me to give ya a shout when we're released to scrap it? It'll probably be about another week or so."

I thank him and tell him I'll be in touch if I still need one by then, a plan already forming in my mind.

When I arrive for my shift at the Harvest Moon that day, after breakfast and before the lunch rush, the dining room is nearly empty except for Ona and Sonny Vane. He started coming in again after the video shoot as though he hadn't left in a snit for the Pub and Grub, vowing never to return. I found out later that Brett Hawley, the manager over at the Pub and Grub, had told him if he kept camping out at their tables they were going to start charging him rent. Knowing Brett, he really would.

I grab the coffeepot from the wait station behind the counter and make my way over to warm up their mugs.

"I've gotta head over to the library to use the Wi-Fi," Ona tells Sonny as she packs up her bag. "Otherwise it'll take all day to upload these clips."

"I don't know how you two could stand growing up here," Sonny interrupts as he taps away at his phone. I've never met anyone who loves the sound of his own voice as much as Sonny Vane. "There's barely any cell signal, and where there is, it's slower than molasses on a cold day."

"Ona's not from Caball Hollow," I say reflexively. It really shouldn't surprise me that he's so self-obsessed he doesn't even know where his own assistant is from.

"I thought you were?" Sonny looks slightly confused but mostly uninterested as he searches the bowl in the middle of the table for the coconut sugar he knows we don't have. "Doesn't matter, all these small mountain towns are the same." He digs in further, completely oblivious to the stricken look on her face.

"Where are you from, Ona?" I ask, because somebody should care and it sure as hell won't be Sonny.

"Oh." She looks startled, and I wonder how long it's been since someone showed an interest in her life. "Here and there, you know how it is. Anyway, I better get going."

Ona looks at me apologetically when she leaves, just as lunch rush begins in earnest and all the tables start to fill up.

"Morning," Deputy Ethan Miranda greets me when he comes in around half past eleven. Even in his uniform, he looks too adorable to be law enforcement, with his dimples, long eyelashes, and thick, dark curls.

"Staying out of trouble, Deputy?" I ask. Or some such thing. There are moments when I'm waiting tables that even I don't listen to the words that come out of my mouth. "What can I get you?"

"I'll take the buttermilk fried chicken and honey," he says, handing me his menu.

I nod, then make another round of the other side of the room. I've been liberally refilling Kye Hensley's coffee in an effort to drive him to the bathroom so I can corner him. It looks like it's finally starting to work when he excuses himself from the table where he's eating an early lunch of a pimento cheese biscuit and a side of ham with two of his co-workers. I leave the coffeepot on the hot plate in the wait station and cut him off from the other side.

"What the hell?" Kye blurts out, more in confusion than anything, as I shove him into the bathroom and lock the door behind us.

"Shut up." I lift a finger to silence him, and he steps back in surprise. "There's a deputy right outside this door, and if you don't want me to tell him everything I know about your involvement in vandalizing the diner, you're going to tell me everything *you* know about the security at the salvage yard."

His mouth drops open in surprise. "I didn't trash the diner!"

"But you know who did, and unless you want to spend hours in an interrogation room until you give them up, start talking."

When his face goes bright red, I fear I've miscalculated.

"They'll do worse to me," he mutters. Then he pulls at his collar and starts talking.

Five minutes later, I walk out of the bathroom with a smile on my face because I know exactly how I'm getting to that truck, and stop dead in my tracks. Hadrian Fitch is standing at the front counter. We lock eyes, and then his gaze goes up and to the left as Kye pushes past me, adjusting his shirt.

"Hadrian, I heard you were back in town," Mama greets him, coming around the counter to pull him into a hug. "Welcome home."

"It's good to see you," he tells her. I approach slowly, my earlier excitement fading fast. "Rowan, can I talk to you outside?"

I nod, and he heads toward the door. Before I follow, I turn back to where Mama is refilling the silverware drawer under the counter. "Why aren't you angry at him for everything he took from you?" I whisper fiercely.

"I thought you two talked about all this." She takes a deep breath and shakes her head. "He didn't *take* anything from me, Rowan. It was my choice. And in return, he gave me back your sister's life."

Hadrian is waiting for me around the corner, leaning up against the side of the building, arms crossed. My gaze falls to the tattoo just below his sleeve, where the man in the Forest pressed his hand. It's a flower, but I can't quite make out which one.

"What are you doing here?" I demand.

"I still need your help."

"Too damn bad." I lean in, pressing my finger against his chest. "Because I quit being your little lie detector the moment I discovered you were spying on us. Who was that man you were with? And what did he mean about the Bone Tree?"

He sighs, and his gaze goes distant for a moment before it lands back on mine. "The man is Ciaran Nimh. He is the leader of the Otherworld and the only one who cared if I lived or died when I ended up there alone at the age of four. He asked me to look into why the Bone Tree is failing and what, or who, is causing it."

"So I was right? That's why things that don't belong here are getting through, like the magpies and the adders?" I ask.

He shrugs. "If the condition worsens, more things that don't belong could seep through. But if it fails, the connection between Caball Hollow and the Otherworld will be lost forever. I won't be able to guide souls to what comes next, they'll be left here to fend for themselves."

"How will you stop it?"

He leans back against the wall again. "Any interest in helping me?"

I hesitate to tell him that my father is reopening the investigation into the crash that killed the poacher, but I realize it could be connected to his own attack and decide not to be petty. The whole time I'm speaking, his brow furrows more and more until it looks like his eyebrows are trying to work together to become a mustache.

"I'm doing a little research into the victim of the accident to see if he and John Doe are connected."

"That's a terrible idea," he says with no preamble.

"Why, because I came up with it?"

"No, because if someone caused the car accident to kill the poacher and then tried to kill John Doe, what do you think they might do if you go putting your nose where it doesn't belong? You're right, you should be done with this case."

"I said I'm done with you, not the case," I say. "I'm not stopping until I figure out what the hell is going on in this town and get back the missing piece of my mother's soul."

Hadrian sighs as he rubs his forehead, probably because all that brow furrowing must hurt. "Fine," he says at last. "I'll help you."

"When did I ask for that?" I hold up my hands to stop him. "I've got plenty of help. We're all good here. No more volunteers needed."

Behind Hadrian, movement through the window of the Harvest Moon catches my eye. I watch as Daddy walks in, dropping his uniform jacket and hat off at the table where Ethan Miranda sits, then crossing the dining room to the counter. Mama sees him coming and smiles softly. She says something, and he leans in, giving her his full attention.

"When Mama lost her memory, she forgot about falling in love with him. All those moments, just erased." I'm not sure if I'm talking to Hadrian or myself. "But now she's doing it all over again. What will happen to the bargain she made if they get back together?" I whisper the fear I've been afraid to admit.

"If they're starting all over again, then it's new," he says after a long pause. "A new love doesn't change the bargain. She can fall in love again as much as she wants, even if it's with the same person."

My eyes drift back to meet Hadrian's deep green ones. If Mama had kept her memory, she never would have allowed herself to fall in love with Daddy again because of the guilt she felt for causing him so much pain and heartache. She didn't think she deserved it, and she didn't want to risk the deal she'd made for Linden's life. But the Moth-Winged Man's bargains are always more serpentine than we realize. And he always seems to be one step ahead.

CHAPTER EIGHTEEN

I WAIT until just after two Monday morning to attempt my very first break-in. Every single crime series I've ever watched has convinced me that junkyards are more dangerous to burgle than banks, so at least I'm an overachieving criminal. Despite being the daughter of the sheriff, almost all my knowledge about breaking the law comes from television, which is probably why I've chosen to dress head to toe in formfitting black.

The last time I snuck out, my sisters were with me, so we could push the truck up the hill before we started it. But this time I'm on my own. I'm not risking Linden or Juniper getting bitten by a guard dog or arrested after a silent alarm. Although the latter shouldn't be a problem if Kye knows what's good for him. I'm already trusting him to be right about there being a smaller staff on Mondays, after the rush of their busiest days over the weekend.

"Hey." A disembodied voice emerges from the darkness, and it's almost enough to make speaking to the dead a whole lot easier. I grab my chest where my heartbeat just stopped then increased threefold.

As my eyes adjust to the low light, I can make out the shape of annoyingly broad shoulders and wild black hair. "Hadrian," I whisper fiercely. "What the hell are you doing here?"

"I had a feeling you might be up to something." He shoves his hands into his pockets. "And would try to do it all alone."

I make a face. "Don't act like you know me so well."

"Come on." He tilts his head toward the farm truck in the driveway. "You steer, I'll push.

When we get to the salvage yard, there aren't any snarling guard dogs, just a tall fence, a locked gate, and a few security cameras that, according to Kye, have a very limited field of view. The sign out front says BAYLOR'S SALVAGE YARD AND LICENSED GINSENG DEALER. Ginseng is a seasonal business, which is why it's usually part of something like this, salvage or scrap metal, and often the buying and selling of other roots like black cohosh, bloodroot, and mayapple. I drive past and then loop back to park down the street.

"What are we doing here?" Hadrian asks.

"I don't know what *you're* doing here." I climb out of

the truck and dig around behind the seat for the old barn jacket that's always back there.

I start down along the side of the chain-link fence, far enough to find the cameras' blind spot Kye told me about. It's the narrow space around a fence pole with junk stacked up on either side. The night is especially dark. The moon, a crescent, and waning. But I can't risk a flashlight, so I pick my path carefully. When I find what I think must be the spot, I climb the chain-link fence, tossing the jacket over the barbed wire at the top.

I'm still brushing myself off when Hadrian lands effortlessly beside me. I blow a strand of hair out of my face and ignore him, turning to make my way toward the racks of cars. There must be some sort of organization system here, but after nearly an hour of looking, I haven't figured it out.

"We've been here a while now," I start. "Maybe we should call it . . ." I trail off as I finally spot the crushed front end of a white Ford Ranger peeking out from behind a huge van. The driver-side door is locked, but the window has been completely smashed out. I reach in and open it. It's darker inside the cab, so I make sure my flashlight is below the level of the dash, then risk switching it on. There's surprisingly little in here, not even empty paper coffee cups or soda cans rolling around the floorboards. Our unfortunate poacher must have traveled light.

I reach over to try the glove box, but it's jammed. Hadrian opens the passenger door and pounds a fist against the top of the dash. When the glove box pops open, I find a strange assortment of items inside: a sharpened iron railroad spike, a small bottle of water, bear spray, a tiny bone on a leather tie, a small sack of meadow rue, and a tiger's-eye stone.

Underneath it all, I find the vehicle registration. It's from Florida, and the name listed is Lucien Ballard. I've never heard of him, but the items he keeps in his truck don't say poacher to me. I can understand why law enforcement would think that, but there are better tools for digging ginseng than an iron spike. And if the water in that bottle has been blessed by a priest, then everything here is used in various folk practices as protection against the paranormal. That spells out one thing to me. This guy was looking for the Moth-Winged Man, just like our resident YouTubers. I'd put money on it.

"Did he say anything to you?" I ask, and Hadrian looks up at me blankly. "I mean, I don't know how it all works, but when you were guiding him to the afterlife, did he say anything?"

He considers, or maybe he's trying to remember. "He said a lot of things. Most people do at the end. But if you're asking if he told me he'd been murdered or named his killer?" He shakes his head. "That isn't most people's concern at the end."

"Then what is?" I ask, surprised.

"The ones they're leaving behind, mostly. Some plead for their lives, some say nothing at all, but most just want to know their loved ones will be all right." Hadrian looks away.

Somewhere in the distance, a coyote yips as a crisp breeze rustles through the leaves, a sound like whispers murmuring all around us. And then a light flips on in the salvage yard office. I stifle a gasp and crouch down, hiding in the shadow of the truck as I feel my way around. When I reach the end, I make a run for it, staying as low as I can, then pressing myself against the building.

I can make out two distinct voices, but not what they're saying. Though they don't seem to be here because of a silent alarm. The voices are too calm for that. I risk a glance into the window and spot a Forest Service jacket draped across the chair. I press back even farther. There must have been some sort of poaching bust to get someone out here this late at night. But if I'm spotted by someone who can immediately identify me, there's no way I'm getting out of this. I take a deep breath and slide along the wall to the corner of the building, then race toward the fence.

Hadrian is right behind me. I hook my feet into the chain link and scramble over. We race back to the truck and jump in. Pulling the door closed as quietly as I can, I shove the keys into the ignition, then drop my head against the steering wheel so I can catch my breath.

Beside me, Hadrian scrubs a hand over his face. "There are things I can't tell you." He looks over at me in the dim light from the dash. "About the work I do and about the Otherworld. But that doesn't mean I don't want to."

"All right." I draw out the words, not sure where this is going.

"I've been thinking about that night at the Pub and Grub."

I feel the tops of my ears go warm, and I want to look away, but I don't.

"Your blood is a truth serum, so there might be something we can try," he continues. "Do you trust me?" He studies my face, his gaze intent.

I let out a slow breath, considering the question. Considering all our history and what Zephyrine said in the Otherworld. "No," I admit in a whisper.

"What if there was a way you could?" he offers.

I glance away, but there's something inside me that has to know more. "How?"

"There is a tradition in the Otherworld. Tattoos aren't like they are here," Hadrian explains. "They are spells, for protection, for power, for fealty, and they are earned." He pulls out a long knife that looks wickedly sharp.

"What's that for?" I ask, the waver in my voice betraying my nerves.

"It'll be all right, but I need to concentrate," he murmurs. His eyes drift closed, and his lips start moving, forming words I don't recognize the shape of, but I know magic when I see it.

Hadrian slices the blade across the palm of his other hand. "Lift your shirt."

"Why?" My voice wavers as I lean away from the knife as far as I can in the small space.

"I need to touch your tattoo," he rasps, squeezing his injured hand enough that blood wells up, glistening darkly.

I watch him for a long moment, considering, then take off my jacket and lift the bottom of my shirt to expose the snake tattoo that curls along my right hip. Hadrian leans closer and presses his bloody palm against the ink. Slowly, a light begins to glow between his skin and mine.

"What the hell is that?" I whisper, awed.

He doesn't respond, all his attention focused on the task. The light turns hot, heat flaming beneath his touch, and I squirm. Then I realize it's not just me. There's something moving beneath my skin, and it's growing. My stomach roils at the wrongness of it.

Hadrian pulls away, and I watch as, under the smear of red, the inked snake swells and slithers like it's awakening. Nausea rises in the back of my throat.

"I'm going to let it out now, all right?" He looks up to meet my eyes, and I hesitate for just a moment before I nod.

Hadrian picks up the knife and slides it across my skin, making a small cut above the snake's head. The blade is so sharp that I barely feel it until the line turns red and the sting sets in. I grit my teeth as he puts his hand over it, blood to blood. The snake moves, sliding from my hip and into Hadrian's palm, slithering up around his forearm before it stops, then begins to flatten until it looks like an ordinary tattoo again. Only now it marks his skin instead of mine. "I pledge my loyalty to you," he says. "And even if you don't believe that, you know your blood in my veins means I will always tell you the truth." He lifts his hand, and the cuts on both our flesh have disappeared like they were never there. I examine my hip, and where the snake had once been there's now only a shed skin. He runs his thumb gently across it, and my eyes lift to meet his in the low light of the truck's cab.

But who is Hadrian Fitch if not a liar?

I bring everything I found in the truck's glove box home, even though I'm not sure any of it will be useful for Juniper's purposes. They don't feel very personal to me, but I suppose if these were tools for Lucien Ballard's passion, then maybe they were to him.

In the morning, I call her into my room, closing the door softly behind her, to present the items. She was in the middle of getting ready for school, her hairbrush still in her hand.

"Will these work?"

"I guess there's really only one way to find out." She shrugs. "The dark moon is in three days. I've read through the instructions and gathered up the rest of the supplies we'll need, so we're as ready as we can be." She clenches her jaw, resolute.

"It's not too late to back out," I tell her.

Reaching across the veil to connect to those on the other side is physically taxing for her in the best of circumstances. But this, making contact with someone who may have been murdered and is likely in a state of unrest, this will take its toll on her both physically and mentally. She may be the one sister who faces her gift head-on, but that doesn't make it any easier to handle.

"If you don't want to do this, we'll find another way to get the information," I insist, ducking my head to catch her eye and convey how much I mean the words. How much I want her to take me up on them.

She shakes her head. "There is no other way." Reaching out, she puts a hand on my shoulder. "It'll be all right. I can do this."

And then I feel even more like shit, because she's the one reassuring me.

CHAPTER NINETEEN

THE SPELL Juniper found in the diablerie is very specific in that it must be performed between eleven and midnight at either the gravesite or the location of death. As Daddy already told us, Lucien Ballard's body is still in the funeral home freezer, and I've done enough breaking and entering for the week, which leaves us with one option.

We have a general idea of where to find the crash site from the information in the newspaper article and where we saw the cruisers parked the night Daddy reopened the case. But as we drive out toward the National Forest in the pitch black of a dark moon night, we watch for signs that will lead us to the exact point of his final moments.

"I think there's something over there," Juniper says from the back seat, pointing out the window at an outcropping of massive limestone.

"If he hit that, it's no wonder he didn't survive." I pull over and use the headlights to illuminate the spot.

The ground in front of the rock face is still furrowed and turned up from the tires, even after all these weeks. We climb out of the truck and make our way toward the sheer wall of rock. The silence is heavy and full, but none of us break it. This would be about the time Sorrel would tell us what absolute fools we're being, but she's back at school, and so we carry on.

Linden takes the salt from my pack and carefully pours a sacred circle around us. I light the beeswax candles she and I will hold at the left and right of the circle. Juniper stands in the center with a small round mirror.

"Don't look into the mirror once I start the spell," Juniper tells us. "The diablerie was adamant about that." She blows out a long, nervous breath. "All right, here we go."

Juniper pricks her finger with a sewing needle and uses the bloody tip to trace along the perimeter of the glass. Then she holds her other hand out, palm up. I place the smaller items I found in Lucien Ballard's car in her palm: the iron spike, the tiger's-eye stone, and the tiny fragment of animal bone. She closes her hand over them and shuts her eyes. Almost immediately, they start moving back and forth beneath her lids like she's falling into a deep sleep. Or searching for something.

"We call upon the spirit attached to these items," Juniper's voice rings out, clear and confident, then she repeats the words twice more.

When she utters the final syllable, the glass of the mirror begins to ripple. A gust of wind blows down the ridge, flinging Juniper's dark hair out behind her. With the glow of the candles reflecting up toward her face, she looks like some sort of ancient priestess or goddess.

Juniper keeps her eyes resolutely closed. And then the mirror goes solid black, no longer reflecting any light. I avert my gaze from the dark surface, but out of the corner of my eye, I catch a glimpse of something moving inside the glass.

"Lucien Ballard, we've summoned you here to ask you about the day you died." Everything around us goes impossibly quiet. "Was your death an accident, or was it murder?" Juniper asks the spirit.

There's a long gap of silence, and I'm sure it hasn't worked, like maybe our connection is bad. But then there's something else. What answers isn't a voice at all. It's like the static between radio stations or the rustle of the breeze through dry leaves. It's a whisper that barely touches the edges of the words, and I strain to hear each jagged fragment.

"No accident."

A chill cuts through me, both from the absolute wrongness of the sound and from the confirmation of murder. I look across at Linden, and her gaze meets mine, eyes wide.

"Who killed you?" Juniper continues.

"Betrayed . . ."

"Who betrayed you?" she pushes.

"She of the dark . . ."

A giant boom like thunder echoes against the mountain behind us, and I feel it reverberate through the ground. Juniper's eyes fly open as the mirror in her hand shatters into a thousand tiny fragments, spraying shards of glass into the air. Both candles gutter out and we're left in complete darkness.

"Is everyone all right?" I ask. It takes a few moments for my eyes to adjust, and when they do, I see Juniper on her knees in the dirt. Crouching down next to her, I cup her cheeks and turn her face so I can look into her eyes. "Are you all right?"

"Cold," she murmurs.

Linden and I exchange concerned glances. This gift of Juniper's seems to take more from her than it ever gives. We help her to her feet and half carry her between us back to the Bronco. Linden climbs into the back seat, and I help Juniper lie across her lap. Then I go back to the circle to collect our things and scatter the salt.

On the way home, I watch Juniper in the rearview mirror, and I can't help but think about another night like this one over the summer when we were driving an exhausted Juniper home. Only then we'd been so sure the spell hadn't worked, and this time I'm afraid it might have worked too well. Maybe Juniper's ability isn't something that should be amplified.

After work on Sunday, I borrow the old Bronco and drive to the hospital two towns over with a pawpaw cheesecake Linden made for me buckled into the passenger seat.

It's somehow already been an entire month since we found John Doe unconscious in the Forest. And yet he remains in a coma the doctors can't explain, still unidentified. When I reach the nurses' station on the intensive care floor, I find a man in scrubs sitting in front of a computer, and a woman searching for something in the cabinets behind him.

"Hello." I announce myself as I approach the first nurse. He looks to be in his mid to late thirties, with his hair leaning more salt than pepper and thinning, probably from his habit of shoving his fingers into it in frustration, which I've already witnessed twice. "I'm Rowan James." I set the cheesecake onto the counter between us. "I was with the team that found John Doe out in the Forest, and I just wanted to thank you for taking care of him all this time."

"Well, would you look at that!" He completely abandons whatever he was doing on the computer to lift the lid on the covered dish.

"How's he doing?" I ask, hungry for whatever information I can get, any of which is more than Daddy is liable to give me.

The woman opens a file cabinet drawer and pulls out small paper plates and an assortment of plastic cutlery from what looks to be every take-out restaurant in the county. She's younger than the man and wiry in that way that means she never stands still. "You want to see him?"

"Can I?" I ask, like this wasn't what I'd wanted all along.

"Visitors are good for patients. And who knows, maybe knowing someone out here cares about him will be just the motivation he needs to finally open his eyes."

"He's just down the hall," the man—whose name is Kurt, according to his plastic photo badge—tells me. "Room 306."

I thank them again and head down the hall in the direction he points. When I reach the room and pull the door closed behind me, the only noise is the regular beep of the heart monitor hooked up to the chest of the man asleep in the hospital bed. A blanket is tucked tightly around him, and his arms are pressed to his sides.

He looks impossibly young. And it's no surprise Sorrel's friends are calling him Sleeping Beauty. He looks like some fairy-tale prince. Even the light shines through the window like it's trying to caress his face. I move closer to the bed, unsure now that I'm here why exactly I've come. It's not like he can tell me who he is or answer any of the questions I want to ask him.

I've been going over and over what we learned from communicating with Lucien Ballard's spirit, but I still can't figure out what any of it means. Other than each case having its own set of strange circumstances, and no one stepping forward to claim them, there doesn't seem to be any connection between the two. There's no evidence that John Doe and Lucien Ballard even knew each other.

I lean forward, close enough now to see his chest gently rise and fall beneath the blanket. "Who are you?" I whisper, and—I might have missed it if I wasn't so carefully examining his face—his eyebrows draw together. Just barely, like the ghost of frustration. But I notice something else, too. A scent I know well.

Not like a lie, but the opposite. An aroma that belongs tacked on the wall in the summer kitchen, concentrating as it dries, the smell of spicy apricot and bitter green growing stronger as everything that diluted it fades away.

I sniff the air around him until I identify the pillow itself as the source of the smell. Gently, I lift his head and pull the pillow out from beneath him. I shuck off the plain white case and examine it: a cheap, standard-issue bulk hospital pillow, but there's a line of thread along one part of a seam that's a slightly different color and definitely not a machine stitch. I pick it apart with my fingers and find a tiny sachet inside among the polyester fluff.

I sniff again to make sure it is what I already know: agrimony and mugwort, known to aid sleep. There's a passage in one of the family books that notes agrimony placed under the head of a sleeper will keep them from waking until it's removed. I slip the sachet in my pocket and place the pillow back in its case, then beneath his head where it belongs.

Perhaps this wasn't a wasted trip after all. Only there's something bothering me. If John Doe was attacked by whoever's been stealing souls, they wouldn't use this kind of charm to keep him asleep.

This is James family magic.

When I get home, Linden is waiting for me at the kitchen table, homework spread out all around her.

"How did it go at the hospital?"

"Your cheesecake worked like a charm," I tell her as I toe off my boots. "They let me right in to see him. But I found something strange."

"About John Doe?" The scratching of pencil against paper stops and she meets my eyes.

"Sort of," I allow. "This was sewn into his pillow." I toss her the sachet of agrimony and mugwort.

Linden examines the stitching on the small cloth bundle. "The last time I remember Gran making something like this was back when Parlee Wilkerson was on hospice."

"Do you think someone might have bought a sleep aid from Gran in the past and was desperate enough to try and use it to keep John Doe from waking up?" I slide in the chair across from hers.

"Maybe, but it wouldn't work." She passes the sachet back to me. "Gran would never make one that strong. It would be too dangerous."

I stay in the kitchen alone, long after Linden has left for her study group, puzzling over the words I could make out from our conversation with the spirit of Lucien Ballard. There's one part that I almost missed because of everything that happened after. When Juniper asked him to identify his killer, it sounded like he said *she*. Only, none of my suspects are women.

Unless I include the names of my family members.

CHAPTER TWENTY

GRAN IS slow-roasting a pork shoulder with onions, apple cider vinegar, and sorghum syrup, and the aroma must reach clear across town, judging from the crowd at the Harvest Moon this morning. Yet the table in the corner where the YouTube crew sits is conspicuously empty.

I've been replaying every single detail I can remember about the night John Doe was discovered unconscious in the Forest over and over again, searching for anything that could be a clue to what happened. So many times that it wasn't until last night that it finally occurred to me to go back further. Back to the beginning. Because the first thing I did that morning was discover a camera in the middle of the woods.

I'm watching for Ona so intently through the wide front window that I almost miss Vernie. She removes her hat when she steps inside and uses it to give me a little wave.

"Just the person I came to see." Vernie smiles, crinkling the lines that bracket her eyes as she sidles up to the front counter.

"Hey, Vernie." I can practically smell the sunshine wafting off her uniform, and a twinge of something that feels a little like envy hits me. "Can I get you some coffee?"

"I left Ranger Harshbarger to run the station alone, so I can't stay, but I wanted to drop this off for you." She sets an envelope down and slides it across to me.

"What is it?" I ask, turning it over to open the flap.

"It's a letter of recommendation."

My hands freeze with the envelope half opened, and my eyes fly up to meet hers.

"Now, I don't want to interfere with your family business here." Vernie holds up a hand. "But I think you should consider applying to the Forest Service. There are all sorts of career paths, lots of which don't require a degree if college isn't your thing."

I'm so touched, it takes me a moment to respond. "Thank you. I'm not sure what to say."

"Say you'll think about it." Vernie pats the countertop, then steps back toward the door.

"I will," I promise, sliding the letter into my apron pocket.

"Good. You light up in those woods. And if there's anything I've learned in my fifty-odd years on this earth, it's that life is meant for enjoying."

Not long after, Ona finally shows up. She smiles when our eyes meet, then slides into her normal spot, dropping her bag onto the floor beside her. Ona is usually the first of the YouTube crew to arrive. The rest of them will likely filter in over the next hour or so. She always orders the same breakfast, too: coffee and two eggs over easy with a cathead biscuit. Out of the whole team, she is the most reliable. I grab the coffeepot from the hot plate and cross the room.

"Mornin'." I fill the mug in front of her while she takes her laptop out of her bag.

"Thanks," she says without looking up from the screen, until I pull out the chair next to her and sit down.

"Do you remember when I returned that equipment I found out in the Forest?" I ask.

"Yeah, of course." She nods, but her brow is furrowed in confusion. "You dumped everything out on the table. It's the first time I've ever seen Sonny Vane speechless."

"Could I see the footage from that camera?" I ask. "From the day the injured hiker was found?" I intentionally don't say the word *poacher*, even though it seems more likely, so as not to scare her off with the mention of a crime. Lots of people don't want to get involved, even if they'd be helping.

Her eyebrows, dark slashes against her pale skin, lift in surprise. "But I thought the paper said the man was found near the East Fork shelter? Wasn't the camera over by Stillhouse Creek somewhere?"

"It was," I admit. Would footage from a camera mounted more than a mile away and pointed in the wrong direction have captured anything that could be useful to the case? Probably not, but it seems like something we should at least check.

She studies my face, clearly torn. "Sonny has really strict rules about who is allowed to look at raw footage. And he gave me a chance when no one else would," she says apologetically. "Maybe I can take a look at it for you?" she offers, grabbing her laptop and logging on. "What is it you're hoping to find, exactly?"

"I'm not really sure, to be honest." I rub at a water spot on the table with my thumb, thinking. "Anything unusual from the morning John Doe was found or even in the days leading up to the incident. And any people who might have been in the area. Someone may have seen something and not even realized it could be a clue."

Ona pulls up the file directory and scrolls for a long time, searching. "Sonny never follows the proper file naming conventions," she mutters.

"Did Sonny share any of the footage with the police or the Forest Service?" I ask while she searches.

"No, I doubt it occurred to him that it might be useful," she says. "I don't think anyone has even looked at the footage yet." Ona leans closer to her screen. "Huh, weird. The file format is different from what we normally shoot. I thought that camera was strange."

"What do you mean?"

"It looks like it was uploading stills whenever it connected to a mobile signal." She turns the laptop so we can both see. "Which was often, thanks to the booster antenna it was connected to. More like a cheap security camera or those trail cameras hunters use to track game. It was just shooting low-res images whenever it detected movement." She opens a folder and clicks randomly. A grainy close-up of a squirrel pops open.

"You said you were responsible for the camera being left in the Forest. But you didn't know it was out there, did you?" I study her face, trying to get a read on her. I don't trust Sonny, but Ona? I'm not sure. There's something about her golden-honey eyes and bright smile that feels familiar.

"It is my responsibility to manage the equipment, but no, I didn't know that stuff was there."

"So why would Sonny put a camera in the woods that only shoots grainy stills instead of something like the digital cameras he mounted for his special episode last month?"

"My guess? He was probably watching the area for signs of the Moth-Winged Man or that Wampus Cat. I've heard cameras like that can be set up to notify your cell phone when motion is detected, and they don't need a very strong cell signal to work, which would definitely be useful out in that part of the Forest."

I grab the coffeepot, then pause. "Can I ask you one more thing?"

"Sure." Ona shrugs and closes the laptop.

"You said Sonny gave you a chance when no one else would. Does that mean this is your first job as a production assistant?"

"Is it that obvious?" She chuckles. "Yeah, I'm kind of figuring it all out as I go along. Sonny is the sort of boss who would teach you to swim by throwing you in the deep end. But he had to hire an entire crew fast, so a lot of us are pretty green."

I thank Ona for her help, then head back to the kitchen. Her explanation for using what amounts to a glorified trail cam doesn't fit with what I know about Sonny. He wants proof the Moth-Winged Man exists. Why would he risk his chance at getting evidence with a grainy image when he could have just as easily used a different, better quality camera? Then he would have usable video footage for his channel if he managed to miraculously catch something on film.

Stranger still is where he put the camera. If he was trying to get proof of the Moth-Winged Man, why not at least put it near the creek? Instead, it was sitting in one of the most remote areas of the Forest. The only thing that camera could have seen, I realize, was the trail I was on when I found it. It's the same trail I'd take from my cabin to the Bone Tree. Lucky coincidence? Or does Sonny know more about the truth of the Moth-Winged Man than he lets on?

"Rowan, must you antagonize our customers?" Gran asks from the prep station, where she's busy chopping vegetables for stew.

"I wasn't," I object, then consider. "This time." I pluck a chunk of raw potato from the pile in front of her and pop it into my mouth.

"Quit buzzing around like a vulture at the slaughterhouse." Gran gives me a look without her knife slowing down in the slightest. "We've got a dining room full of people to feed."

"Speaking of customers, you been entertaining any of those video folks out at the summer kitchen?" I ask, raising an eyebrow. "Whip up any simples, tonics, or tinctures for Sonny Vane? Maybe something to help him sleep?"

She scoffs. "You think that fool would have any use for our kind of cures? Not unless we're paying for advertising, I tell you what."

Gran isn't wrong. But someone wants to keep John Doe asleep, and that means there's at least one person in town who knows who he is.

"You gonna tell me what's wrong with your sister?" Gran slides her knife under the chopped vegetables and scoops them into the pot.

"You're going to have to be more specific." I hand her the jar of bay leaves from the pantry.

"Odette just got a call from the school." She pauses stirring the stew long enough to point her wooden spoon at me. "Juniper got written up for falling asleep in class today. Twice."

"Did Mama go pick her up?" I can't hide my concern, and Gran eyes me from across the counter. Juniper hasn't been able to shake off the exhaustion after contacting the spirit of Lucien Ballard. She spent most of the weekend napping in the sun like a cat.

"Mm-hmm, she's taking her over to the urgent care." Gran leans over the stove, the steam from the pot curling the hair around her face. "Funny thing, though, she had to take the farm truck because the Bronco was out of gas even though it had a half tank Friday morning and, far as I know, it was parked in the driveway all weekend."

She raises her eyebrows at me. "Now, what's this I hear about you saying the Pub and Grub makes better Brunswick stew?"

When I get home from my shift at the Harvest Moon, I check in on Juniper. She's wrapped in a blanket on the sofa with a mug of ginger lemon tea, reading webtoons.

"How are you feeling?"

She shrugs. "The doctor couldn't find anything wrong with me, so he said it might be my period. But I got to skip pre-calc and I took a really nice nap, so I'm feeling pretty good."

"You weren't this exhausted last time. Or for this long."

"True, but that spell wasn't this powerful, either. I think it might just take longer to wear off."

After making Juniper promise to tell me if she gets any worse, I head to my room. Sprawling across my bed, I open YouTube and type in Sonny Vane's name for the first time.

I scroll back through the lists of videos. All the most recent ones were clearly filmed here and focus on his hunt for the Moth-Winged Man, with a handful investigating the legend of the Wampus Cat. He has a lot of followers, but Juniper is right, it's not a number that I would imagine supports the kind of money his production must cost. So where is the money for the fancy equipment and crew coming from? There is no mention of a sponsor in any of Sonny's videos that I can find.

But when I scroll further back, to videos from other locations about other folklore monsters, they don't have as much audience interaction and the filming style is different, much less polished. Interesting. Sonny Vane acted like a big shot as soon as he rolled into town, but it looks like Caball Hollow did a lot more for him than the other way around.

After a bit more digging, I find a possible reason for the format change that turned his fortune. Just before he started his series on the Moth-Winged Man, he posted a video titled "Face Reveal" and appeared in front of the camera for the first time. He had been anonymous until then, known only by the name of his account: Monster Encounters. And the obnoxious tagline he still uses: "Sunlight on the truth."

I watch a few of the oldest ones from several years ago. The footage is almost charmingly earnest. Most of it is voice-over. But in the rare moments he actually appears on-screen, wearing a face mask and a hat pulled low over his eyes, he moves like he's uncomfortable in front of a camera. Younger and scrawnier. Not at all like the Sonny of today. I guess time can change people.

But more than that, I'm curious about what's underneath the one mask he still wears. I start watching a couple of the videos every day, studying them in between work and chores, dissecting them to try and get to the truth of the most elusive creature of them all. Sonny Vane, who showed up in Caball Hollow to make his fortune, definitely has secrets he wants to keep buried.

CHAPTER TWENTY-ONE

ON THE night of the full moon, I couldn't have been asleep for more than a couple of hours when I awake to someone shaking me. Opening my eyes in the hazy darkness of the middle of the night, all I can see is Linden's face peering down at me, her long curtain of hair tucked behind one ear. At the concern etched into her face, I sit up before she's even said a word.

"It's Juniper," she half whispers. "Something's wrong."

I stumble out of bed and follow the candle of her bright white nightgown across the hall, padding barefoot on the icy floor. The house feels like a stranger. Cold air seeps in around the window frames, curling along the baseboards, and trailing bony fingers around my ankles and down the back of my neck, stealing away the last dregs of sleep.

The lamp on the table between their beds is on, casting a gentle glow over Juniper, her skin pale and pulled taut against her cheekbones, writhing like she's in pain. She must have been at it for a while because her blankets have been kicked off and the sheets are twisted around her legs and damp with sweat.

"Have you tried to wake her?" I ask, fear sharpening my voice. Linden ignores the ridiculous question.

I press my hand to Juniper's forehead. She feels clammy to the touch and unnaturally cool. "Run a washcloth under some cold water and bring it to me."

Linden dashes from the room, likely glad for something to do in a situation that feels so out of our control.

"Dà shealladh." Juniper speaks the words, but it doesn't sound like her. They seem to force their way out of her throat, churning and scraping along the way.

I've never heard that phrase before, but the cadence sounds familiar, like when Zephyrine spoke the words to open the Bone Tree. Linden rushes back into the room with the cool cloth, and I gently wipe Juniper's face, then fold it into a compress and lay it across the back of her neck.

"Should we wake Mama?" Linden whispers from the other side of Juniper's bed.

"Not yet," I say, though I'm not sure why I want to wait. Maybe because, once we sound the alarm, it becomes all too real. "We need fennel. Seeds for the keyhole and flowers for the window. And rabbit tobacco—I think I saw some drying in the summer kitchen."

The old ways say fennel can keep away ghosts, while the smoke of rabbit tobacco, also called white balsam or sweet everlasting, can ease restless spirits.

"And amethyst," Linden suggests with a snap. "I think Junie has one somewhere in here." She digs through the contents of their bedside table.

I rush downstairs, pulling the gardening snips from their peg on the wall by the door without stopping. The outdoor air of the wee morning hours is hungrier than the cold inside, biting at my toes and pulling at my hair. I cut several of the dried-out flower heads from the fennel, then run to the summer kitchen for a bundle of rabbit tobacco, and hightail it back to the house. Dropping the snips on the counter, I pull open drawers and cupboards, collecting a matchbook, a paper bag, and the twine Gran uses to truss up her roast chicken.

When I get back to Juniper's room, I tie the flowers together, put them in the paper bag, and shake them until they release their seeds. Linden has already set an amethyst on Juniper's forehead. I close the bedroom door, then carefully pour fennel seeds into the keyhole and hang what's left of the flowers in the window. Striking a match, I light the rabbit tobacco, blowing out the flame once it catches and passing the smoke over Juniper's restless form before setting the bundle in a dish on the table.

"Now what do we do?" Linden asks. When she smooths back the damp hair from Juniper's forehead, her hand shakes.

"Now we wait," I tell her with more confidence than I feel.

We sit side by side on her bed, watching Juniper sleep until slowly, so slowly I don't realize it at first, her body seems to unclench and the pain in her face eases. Long after Linden curls up on the bed behind me and gives in to sleep, I stay and keep watch.

In the morning, Juniper wakes with a low-grade fever and dark circles like bruises under her eyes. But at least she wakes. She stumbles into the kitchen, so drawn and pale that her skin nearly matches the color of her nightgown.

"How are you feeling?" I ask, pouring us each a much-needed cup of coffee.

"I had some really strange dreams last night," she answers after a long pause, like she barely has the strength to push out the words.

"This doesn't sound like your usual exhaustion after a spell." I grab the spoon from her hand before she can stir salt into her coffee instead of sugar.

"I don't think it's the spell." She slowly shakes her head, sliding her thoughts into order. "It's almost like the connection was too powerful. It feels like . . . I don't know, like it's still there in the back of my head."

"You mean you're still connected to the spirit?" I ask, trying not to panic.

She considers, and it's like I can see her feeling around in her mind the way someone with a toothache would prod around their mouth with their tongue.

"Not exactly like we're connected," she clarifies. "It's more like just before someone answers the phone, but you know they're about to because the sound of the silence changes. I guess it's like the line is open now. Instead of a wall between us, it's more like a door." She stirs her coffee around and around without taking a sip. "But what scares me is that I don't know if I'm the one with the key."

A spirit with free access to Juniper is a dangerous thing. I know she knows that, even if she's trying to make it sound less serious now. The dead aren't good with boundaries. Failure to control the connection between her and the spirits on the other side means she won't have a moment's peace. Something known to have driven seers mad in the past, according to the old family books.

"We need to break that connection, Junie," I tell her. "Tonight. I'll search through the books. All of them. We'll find a way."

She offers me a smile, but it's a sad one. "Sure, all right."

I grab her hands and force her to meet my eyes. "Listen to me, you're not facing this alone, all right? We're going to figure it out. Together."

Juniper nods, then takes her mug to the sink so she can go get ready for school. I watch as she walks with heavy feet toward the stairs, and the guilt swallows me whole. I may not have wanted her to do that spell, but I didn't stop her, and now she's in danger of being at the mercy of the spirits she's had to work so hard to keep at bay her entire life. And all we got in exchange for her sacrifice were more questions. We're still no closer to figuring out what happened to John Doe or who's been stealing souls.

After Linden and Juniper leave for school, I take a walk around the farm. It's what my body always craves when my mind is racing. Hadrian said he can only tell me the truth now, but has he told me all of it? My feet turn back toward my room, and I take out the final maple key he gave me. I strike a match and set it alight, then watch as the smoke curls out the window.

As soon as it disappears, I wish I could take it back.

CHAPTER TWENTY-TWO

DADDY ARRIVES at the farm just before seven in his best jeans and a freshly pressed button-down shirt. He knocks on the screen door with a bouquet of meadowsweet I know he picked from the big field behind the high school.

"He's here!" Mama calls, nervous excitement coloring her voice. "Where are my shoes?" She bounces around her bedroom, ineffectually looking for the shoes that are sitting on top of her dresser.

Sissy lies draped across Mama's bed, worn out after helping her choose a dress. Or rather, seven dresses that were rejected, one by one, until all that was left was a soft crimson silk the color of a maple leaf with fabric-covered buttons from the neckline to the hem. Linden found it in the attic cupboard where Gran keeps all Zephyrine's things—dresses and gowns, silk robes, boxes of jewelry and hats—shut away since the day she left all those years ago. When we were kids, we would spend hours combing through the treasures and playing dress-up, not realizing the wardrobe was a monument to grief. Even now, Gran's eyes slide over the dress with a palpable sense of loss. I think of the woman I met in the Otherworld, but try as I might, I can't picture her wearing such a thing.

"Land sakes alive, Odette," Gran chides. "You weren't even this het up the first time you dated the man."

"I wouldn't know," Mama tells Gran, treating the loss of her memories rather glibly.

Gran and I exchange a look from across the room. Mama has adjusted surprisingly well to missing all her memories about falling in love with Daddy. Gran says it's because it's hard to miss something you didn't know you had. But maybe it's also because I haven't told her about the corresponding lost piece of her soul yet. I'm determined to fix it before it ever becomes an issue.

Linden helps Mama put on a necklace, this one a simple strand of seed pearls. The only person not crowded into Mama's bedroom is Juniper. She came home from school looking wan as a sheet of loose-leaf paper, then after supper, she fell asleep on the table next to her bowl of sweet potato cobbler.

"Will y'all check in on Juniper tonight while I'm gone?" Mama asks. "I think she might be coming down with something again."

"Just go enjoy yourself, Odette," Gran tells her. "We can handle things here."

I wish I had as much faith that was true.

Mama runs her hands down the sides of her dress in front of the mirror over her dresser, letting out a slow breath and smoothing everything into place one last time.

"Just how long you gonna keep him waiting?" Sissy asks.

"All right," Mama says with a nod. "Don't wait up!" She grabs her shoes on the way out of the room, rushing down the back steps and crashing through the screen door so hard it closes behind her with a decisive slap.

We all rush to the window, watching as Daddy opens the truck door for her and offers his hand to help her climb in. When he walks back around to the driver's side, he spots us, and waves with a smile he just can't seem to turn off lately.

My thoughts of Zephyrine have me reaching for the little leather fairy-tale book that was left in my bag the night I slipped into the Otherworld. I know there must be something about this book I'm not seeing. Why go to all the trouble of getting it to me otherwise?

I press around the outside of the cover, feeling for any sign something has been hidden beneath the leather. There's a tiny pocket at the back where the spine gaps, but it's empty. When I find nothing, I flip through the pages again, looking for clues I might have missed in the poem itself.

"This is the book of poems?" Linden pauses behind me while she dries a casserole dish to read over my shoulder. "If it's really from the Otherworld, I would have thought it would be more . . . gruesome. Maybe even bloodthirsty."

"Not poems," I correct. "Just the one. But I can't figure out what it is I'm not seeing."

"Maybe that's exactly it," Linden suggests slowly, an idea forming as obviously as if a light bulb had appeared above her head.

But I'm not in the mood for any more riddles, and I let the expression on my face tell her so.

"Remember how Aunt Zephyrine hid her notes when she didn't want Gran reading them? If she's the one who put the book in your bag, maybe it's a habit she never outgrew."

I look up, and her eyes are dancing. "Candle magic." We both say it at the same time.

Linden puts the last of the dishes away, then runs upstairs to retrieve the diablerie from its hiding place under her floorboards. When she comes back to the kitchen, we light a long taper candle in the center of the table, then hold the small book overtop it and recite the spell that will reveal any hidden messages.

Slowly, tiny red words appear over the printed black ones on the onionskin paper. They won't stay visible for long, so I read them out loud quickly, page by page, gobbling them up while Linden scribbles them down on a piece of scrap paper. When we reach the end of the book, I blow out the candle, and she reads back her notes.

Druid comes from the word meaning
oak tree and also door.
"A hungry cat, black as night"
—Wampus Cat / cat-sìth?
Awaken the rightful king,
break the connection with Otherworld.

I meet Linden's eyes over the paper. "This is about breaking the connection with the Otherworld. Is Aunt Zephyrine the one trying to destroy the Bone Tree?" I whisper the words, even though everyone else has gone to bed. They feel too unbelievable to speak at full volume.

Linden nods slowly. "It certainly seems that way."

But there's something else. "Read that line again. The one about the Wampus Cat."

" 'A hungry cat, black as night,' " she reads from the paper. " 'Wampus Cat, cat-sìth.' " But she pronounces *sìth* the Gaelic way, *shee*.

"What if the spirit of Lucien Ballard wasn't saying *she*, but *sìth*?"

"You think he was saying the Wampus Cat was responsible for his death?" Linden asks, looking up from where she's studying the old book.

"A Wampus Cat is a woman cursed, and Zephyrine said she couldn't leave the Otherworld as herself, only as a cat."

She nods again. "But if these notes prove that the book belonged to Zephyrine, why would she give us something that points at her as a suspect? And look at this." Linden pulls the note Zephyrine wrote before she was sent to the

Otherworld out of the diablerie where Gran keeps it as a reminder. "The handwriting doesn't quite match."

I lean closer to examine the note, comparing the shape of the words to what I saw of the others before they disappeared once more. "Maybe," I concede. "But she did write this more than twenty years ago and was under duress."

"So what does it all mean?"

"I don't know," I admit, rubbing my eyes in frustration. "Let's get some sleep and pick this up again tomorrow."

Linden heads off to bed, taking the books with her, and I follow not long after. My head is spinning with too many questions and no concrete answers, an annoying state I'm finding myself in more often than not lately. I tug loose the buttons of my shirt as I near my bedroom. Pulling on my pajamas sounds like just this side of heaven right now. But when I step across the threshold, a hand slides over my mouth and someone presses in close behind me.

My body goes stiff, and every self-defense tactic Daddy ever taught us races through my mind. But I know the shape of this body, and instead of fighting him off, all I want to do is lean back and sink in.

"If you scream, you'll ruin all the hard work I did breaking in," Hadrian whispers next to my ear as he closes the door behind us with a gentle kick.

I somehow managed to forget I'd asked him to come.

"Can I take my hand away?" he asks.

I bite him.

Hadrian yanks his palm out from between my teeth, and I spin around to face him.

"Hi, love," he says, shaking out the sting in his hand but smirking at me. "I got your message."

"I told you not to call me that." I pull my lip between my teeth to stop the answering smile I feel starting to turn up at the corners. His eyes drop to my mouth.

"Tell me what happened," he says, and any desire to smile evaporates immediately.

"We tried to contact the spirit of the car accident victim, Lucien Ballard"—I begin—"using the things I found in his truck and a new spell from the diablerie. It worked," I insist when he gives me a disbelieving glare. "But something must have gone wrong at the end."

"What?"

I swallow. "Junie had a nightmare last night, and she wouldn't wake up until we covered the room in fennel and rabbit tobacco. She kept saying something strange in her sleep, *dà shealladh*. Do you know what it means?"

"Spirit echo, a seer of two worlds. It's what Juniper is." Hadrian clenches his jaw for a second, thinking. "That certainly doesn't sound like a twentysomething guy from Florida."

"Are you sure he didn't say anything on the way to the afterlife that could help?"

Hadrian rubs the back of his neck as a curious shade of pink blooms across his cheekbones. "He did seem unusually excited to see me. At one point, he may have said he wished he had his camera, and then he told me that the world deserves to know the truth."

"So he was looking for the Moth-Winged Man," I say, confirming my suspicions. "Lucien Ballard wasn't a poacher at all."

"Show me what you used for the spell."

I cross the room to my dresser, where I tucked away Lucien Ballard's things after we got home from our ill-fated conversation with his spirit, and pull out the cloth-wrapped bundle. Hadrian gestures for me to hurry up and open it, so I roll my eyes and resist the urge to move as slowly as I can. Setting it in the center of my bed, I untie the knot and open the fabric.

He ignores nearly everything, homing in immediately on the smallest item. "This is a bone."

"Yeah, I know. Some people use animal bone fragments for protection charms." I gesture at the rest of the pile. "He seems to have been pretty superstitious. And afraid."

"It's human, Rowan."

I recoil, shifting away from the bed. "Are you sure?"

He gives me a look. "This is sort of my thing."

"Right." I draw out the word, shaking my head in disbelief. "Shit."

"The thing is, I don't think you summoned Lucien Ballard," Hadrian says. "I think you summoned whoever that bone belongs to."

"But he knew things about what happened to Lucien," I insist. "He answered all our questions."

"Are you sure about that?"

I think back to that night in the Forest and the things Juniper asked the spirit we thought was Lucien Ballard. There was nothing in the answers that could verify who spoke them. Some of them didn't even make sense in the context of the question when I really thought about it.

"So, if it wasn't Ballard, who was it?"

Hadrian shrugs. "That's what we need to figure out."

"Can we break the connection between Junie and the spirit without knowing who it is?" I ask, dreading adding another mystery to the long list I already need to untangle.

"Maybe, but I don't think he'll rest now until we return that bone to him." Hadrian lifts his arm to run a frustrated hand through his hair, and I see the tail end of my snake tattoo peeking out from under his sleeve.

I reach for it without thinking, pulling his arm toward me. The adder that slithered from my skin onto his has wrapped itself around another tattoo, a serpent's tongue flower, curling between the leaves and squeezing the stem. The plant—a single, drooping yellow bloom with petals curving backward to reveal a stamen like a forked tongue—appears to be withering, slowly crushed by the weight of the adder.

The tattoo is not one I would have expected of Hadrian—he doesn't seem the floral type. But, if I remember Gran's lessons about the uses of flowers, charms made of serpent's tongue were used to prevent others from talking about you behind your back. I run a finger along the scales of my snake, and Hadrian's arm twitches. "When do I get it back?"

"Soon," Hadrian whispers, so quietly he may not have said it at all.

CHAPTER TWENTY-THREE

THERE IS clarity, somehow, in having everything you thought you knew proven wrong. My thoughts keep returning to Lucien Ballard. Any progress I thought I'd made in solving the mystery of his death is meaningless now, and I'm back to square one. He was a man no one seemed to know.

But if Lucien Ballard was murdered in a town as small as Caball Hollow, someone must know why. All I've been able to discover about him is that he seemed to be both afraid of and drawn to the sorts of monsters that most people don't believe are real. An online search of his name turned up a handful of results, but none of them were him. How does someone live in this day and age and not show up at all on the internet?

One thing I do know for certain is that Sonny Vane must know more than he's letting on. The population of folklore monster hunters in Caball Hollow could comfortably fit at a single table in the Harvest Moon—it isn't a large number—so I find it an impossibility that Sonny Vane didn't know Lucien Ballard, at least in passing. Two people hunting for the Moth-Winged Man must have run into each other a time or two. I suspect Sonny Vane might be the connection between John Doe and Lucien Ballard. I just don't know how.

"There's also the possibility that Ballard's death was truly an accident," Hadrian says when I tell him my thoughts. "Dark, unfamiliar roads late at night, probably with a healthy amount of fear in his veins. Sharp turns, sheer rock. It's a recipe for disaster."

I sigh, tired of chasing my tail and going over and over the same few facts I've managed to gather. "I need to figure out what Lucien was doing leading up to his death and talk to Sonny Vane. He's hiding something, I just don't know what."

"Are you sure your judgment isn't clouded by your obvious dislike of the man?" Hadrian asks. "I know what it's like to be on the receiving end of your mistrust. It's powerful."

"I know he's a liar," I tell him. "And in my experience, that means he's got something to hide. As you might recall."

Sonny Vane has been in Caball Hollow for longer than he's let on, and he didn't say a word after Lucien Ballard's death when the town labeled him a poacher. Maybe Sonny is innocent, but it sure seems like he was intentionally covering up a connection to Ballard. And yet, if the spirit we spoke to wasn't Ballard's, then his death may well be nothing more than the tragic accident it appeared to be.

"When will you speak with Sonny?" Hadrian interrupts my thoughts.

"His whole crew is staying out at that old roadside motel between here and Rawbone. I'll head out that way tomorrow morning and see if I can catch him off guard."

"Let me come with you," Hadrian says. "I know you can take care of yourself," he continues, holding up a hand when I open my mouth to say exactly that. "But the thing is, Rowan, you don't have to do everything yourself all the damn time." His eyes are bright with an intensity I've only seen once before.

When I was panicked with fear for Juniper, he was the only person I thought to call. And he came when I needed him.

"What about you?" I ask softly. "Who do you trust?"

He pushes away from the wall, straightening to his full height. I don't move as he comes closer, watching the line of his throat as he swallows. The truth is, I so badly want to trust him. To let myself feel all the things I've tried so hard to lock away. To let myself want him. I look up to meet his gaze, and my mouth goes dry.

He stills, stopping when there are just inches between his skin and mine. It's like I can feel the electric current of it snapping between us. We've been on a collision course headed straight for each other all along. My fingers find the hem of his soft cotton shirt, and I pull him to me. Sliding my fingers into his hair, I press in closer until all the space is gone.

"Rowan." He speaks my name into my mouth like an incantation. And I burn.

We break apart just long enough for me to pull his shirt over his head before crashing back together. My teeth sink into his bottom lip as his hands slide up my hips, the gentle scratch of his calluses against my skin like sparks. We stumble backward, and I don't care where we go as long as this all-consuming fire never stops.

"Rowan, you still up?" Mama's voice calls softly from the hall with a gentle tap of a knuckle against my door. "I saw your light was on when I came in."

We both freeze. I lost all track of time and space and, judging from the half-drunk look in his eyes, so did Hadrian. I scoop his shirt off the floor where I dropped it and press it into his arms.

"Go." I mouth the word, pushing him gently toward the window.

The last thing I see before I reach for the doorknob is a quick flash of his wicked grin.

"Hey, Mama," I whisper, opening the door just a crack. "How was your date?"

"It was amazing." She smiles, a wistful tilt to the corners of her mouth. "We went out to the drive-in."

"What's wrong?" I ask in alarm as her eyes begin to fill with unshed tears. I step out into the hall and reach for her, wrapping my arm around her shoulders.

"I'm sorry. It's so ridiculous." She dabs at her eyes, embarrassed. "It's just, he gave me the tomato from his burger and took the pickle from mine without even thinking about it. And then, in the middle of the movie, my neck started to pinch, the way it does sometimes from staring up at the screen, and before it had really even registered, he reached over and worked out the knot with his thumb."

"Those don't sound like bad things, Mama," I suggest gently, trying to understand what's made her so upset.

"They're wonderful things," she agrees with a chuckle that sounds like a sob. "He knows all these things about us. All those moments that I've lost. It feels like I've been robbed. We built this entire life that I can't remember. And no matter how much I want to, I'm worried I can't love him the way he deserves."

I stare back at her, wanting to reassure her that everything will be all right. That it will all work out in the end. But I refuse to lie, and I don't know how to get back the piece of her that's missing.

She waves her hands like she's clearing the air before I can even begin to figure out what to say. "I'm sorry, I don't mean to burden you with this. It'll be all right." She tries to give me a reassuring smile, but it wobbles. "Good night, honey." She gives me a quick hug that smells like

Daddy, woody and crisp like the bark of an apple tree, then retreats to her bedroom down the hall.

When I step back inside, Hadrian is gone and the room is freezing, the gauzy curtain fluttering in the mountain air that promises the cold bite of winter.

CHAPTER TWENTY-FOUR

SOMEHOW, IN the hours between yesterday and today, the weather has gone from crisp and cool to downright cutting. A stark reminder that it's the end of October.

Halloween is tomorrow, halfway between the autumn equinox and the winter solstice. It's the one day of the year when the veil between life and death is at its thinnest and the ghosts of the dead are able to move freely among the living. It's always the hardest day of the year for Juniper, and this year will be even harder unless we can break her connection to this spirit for good.

It's barely light out when I creep out of the kitchen with the keys to the old farm truck. I pull the door closed quietly behind me and turn to find Hadrian is already here, leaning against the fence post with two paper coffee cups in his hands.

"Where'd you get those?" I ask, surprised.

"Don't get your hopes up, it's just from the Ick." Hadrian straightens when he sees me, holding out one of the cups. "Gas station's the only thing open this early."

I take the coffee but struggle to meet his eyes without feeling too exposed. "We better get a move on," I mumble, reaching for the door handle as I take a sip. It actually isn't bad.

We pull up to the squat, run-down one-story structure at a little after seven. The Come On Inn was built back when roadside motor lodges were seen as a good investment and has scraped by ever since with a clientele that undoubtedly wouldn't stay here if there were any other choice. One small cement block building contains the office and a longer building, perpendicular to the first, is made up of five rooms that all face the overgrown parking lot. Though it could be argued that a view of white clover, bittercress, and henbit beats one of fresh, gleaming asphalt.

The room on the far end seems slightly larger than the others, so I take a shot in the dark and guess that's the one Sonny Vane would choose for himself, though I'm prepared to knock on each and every door until I find him. But when I pound on the peeling wood door of number five, it's Ona that answers. She smiles when she sees me, even though she's still rubbing sleep from her eyes.

"Rowan, this is a surprise . . ." she begins, only to trail off, her eyes going wide, when she spots Hadrian standing behind me, hands in the pockets of his worn canvas jacket. Ona slams the door in my face.

"You two know each other?" I ask, but Hadrian is already moving past me to put his shoulder to the cheap old door. It pops open like there's no lock at all. He pulls me into the room behind him and pushes the broken door back into place.

Ona is standing across the room, next to the tiny bathroom, staring at him with eyes sharp as knives. "I'm not going back," she insists.

"I'm not here for you," he tells her, and there's a tone to his words that I don't understand.

"You kicked in my door!" Ona gestures behind us to where the door crookedly hangs from its frame.

"Hang on," I cut in. I need a second to rearrange everything I thought I knew. Ona declaring that she isn't going back. Ona, with the familiar-looking eyes and smile. I know why I recognize it now. The golden-eyed charm of Malcolm Spencer, the man who broke Zephyrine's heart and trapped her in the Otherworld. "Who *are* you?"

"Either you tell her, or I will," Hadrian says in a low voice.

Ona shoots him a scathing look, but it softens when she turns to me. "I wanted to tell you earlier, but I couldn't risk it until I knew I could trust you," she begins.

"You're Zephyrine's daughter, aren't you?" I ask, my eyes running over her as if fully seeing her for the first time. It seems so obvious now. She has Gran's nose, and the coffee color of her hair is just like Zephyrine's.

Ona swallows and nods. "She was pregnant with me when she was trapped in the Otherworld. You and I, we're cousins." She gives me a tiny smile.

There's no lie in her words. Yet, even though I've managed to guess the truth, it somehow feels impossible. An entire branch on the family tree that we knew nothing about.

"You have to understand, my mother, she had nothing and no one. She made the only choices she could in order to provide for me." Ona sinks down onto the edge of the bed, hands in her lap.

"That's a bit of an oversimplification," Hadrian chimes in from across the room.

Ona glares at him, then continues. "But she's trapped there, and she did it for me."

"So, what did you do about it?" I ask, stepping closer.

Ona swallows and drops her eyes, taking her time to get the words out. "I stole a book. It was a fairy tale, and not a very good one."

As she speaks, the dominos fall into place in my mind. The book that appeared in my pack after a day of filming with Sonny's crew. The handwriting that didn't quite match Zephyrine's but was hidden using her methods.

"But as I read it, I realized it was more than that. It was the creation story of the Bone Tree and the forbidden prophecy of its end. And that the key to getting my mother out might be the tiny bone that was hidden in the spine."

At this, my eyes fly to Hadrian's, but his face has gone completely neutral like a mask.

"I knew if the bone belonged to who I thought it did, it might be my only chance to break the curse on the Bone Tree, once and for all."

"Wait, tell me whose bone it is," I insist, thinking of Juniper.

"It's the bone of the man whose body was planted to create the Bone Tree," Ona says. "I thought if I could disturb his eternal rest, maybe I could break the curse and free my mother. Like picking a lock. And I knew I was right when I tried it and the Bone Tree spat me out and cracked right down the middle." Ona gestures wildly, like she's reliving the frenzy of that moment. "But I got knocked senseless, and when I woke, I couldn't find the bone anywhere."

I reach into my pocket and pull out the tiny human bone that I found among Lucien Ballard's things. "Is this the bone?"

Ona's eyes gleam when they meet mine. "Where did you find it?"

"First, tell me everything you know about the origin of this bone."

"That poem is really it." Ona shrugs. "There were whispers, but the story of the true king was forbidden."

Hadrian makes a noise that sounds decidedly scoff-like.

Ona shoots him another glare in return. "Does he have to be here? It's like confessing in front of my jailer."

"What does that mean?" I ask, casting a confused glance at Hadrian.

"What does it mean . . . ?" Ona looks momentarily surprised and then a delighted smile spreads across her face. "Oh, of course. You can't tell her." She chuckles darkly. "Poor Hadrian. I do pity you, you know? Which is really saying something."

"And you, Ona." Hadrian stalks closer. "Did you ever once think of all the people you'd put at risk with your plan?"

"People?" Ona surges to her feet, leaning forward like she's ready to fight. "What people? The good folk, all those who couldn't be bothered to show me the slightest bit of kindness my entire childhood? You know what that's like, don't you, Hadrian?"

"Not only the good folk, Ona."

She rolls her eyes. "We all have to choose who and what we value most. For me, that will always be the only person who was ever there for me. You need to decide who it is for you before it's too late."

Hadrian's jaw clenches, but he doesn't say a word.

"Will someone please tell me what the hell is going on?" I insist again, surging to my feet.

Ona looks at Hadrian, dark amusement in her eyes.

He puffs out a breath of frustration and grabs my hand. "Come with me."

Hadrian leads me back across the crumbling parking lot to the farm truck, his long legs eating up the distance so quickly I have to almost jog to keep up. He opens the driver-side door for me without a word, and I climb in, then watch him round the front end to the passenger side. The inside of the truck smells like stale coffee from the two matching cups still sitting in the console. When he gets in, he sighs deeply and stares straight out the windshield.

I want to break the heavy silence, but once I do, we'll move past this moment into whatever comes next, and so I hesitate. Afraid we won't be able to come back from whatever he's about to say. Then it's too late. He's already turning toward me, and my heartbeat speeds up like it knows what's coming.

"I told you about tattoos in the Otherworld," he starts, then clenches his jaw. "About how each of them has to be earned. And every one has a purpose." He leans forward and peels off his jacket. "This one," he says, pointing to the serpent's tongue flower that my adder is wrapped around and slowly suffocating. The yellow petals have fallen, and the leaves are brown around the edges. "This one is given to those who pledge to serve the leader of the Otherworld. It's meant to keep his people loyal, to keep them from spilling any of his secrets. The serpent's tongue is an apt illustration, because if the vow isn't enough to force the wearer to hold their tongue, the poison it releases if they break it ensures they'll never open their mouths again."

He shifts, lowering his head so he can meet my eyes. "There are so many things I want to tell you." He reaches out as if to take my hand, then stops himself. "But I haven't been fully honest with you, Rowan."

A sick realization roils my stomach. "You said what was happening in the Otherworld was connected to what was happening here, but Ona is the one who caused the Bone Tree to fail," I say slowly as I work through the jumble of my thoughts. "And she's not stealing souls. But I know you didn't lie. So what does that mean, Hadrian?"

He looks at me, and I can see the frustration in his eyes, but he clenches his jaw and doesn't answer.

A flash of understanding shoots through me, and I remember the conversation I overheard in the woods between Hadrian and the man called Ciaran Nimh. He hadn't asked Hadrian *who* was stealing souls. He asked if *the James women knew* who was doing it.

Zephyrine had tried to warn me. She said he couldn't be trusted as long as he bore the mark of another. She also said she'd done all she could to protect me from spying eyes, but had to keep her claws covered. I thought she was speaking metaphorically. I let out a disbelieving chuckle. Maybe I'll ask her not to be so gentle the next time she attacks him. No need to spare the teeth and claws.

"You knew who it was all along, didn't you?" I'm getting louder and louder, but I don't care. "You knew who was stealing pieces of souls all over Caball Hollow, including from my *mother*."

"I betrayed him once when he asked me to do something I wouldn't, and he spared me." Hadrian's voice seems to get quieter in contrast to mine. "But I don't know how to stop the Bone Tree from failing. And when it does, you'll be on one side . . ." He trails off, but it doesn't take much effort to guess the words he doesn't say. He'll be on the other.

All the fight drains out of me, and I'm just done. "Get out of the truck," I tell him, my voice flat.

"Rowan." I feel him studying the side of my face, but I stare straight ahead at a crack running through the concrete blocks on the front of the motel. He's quiet for a long moment. "If that's what you want."

I don't turn to look when I hear him grab his jacket or when the truck door closes behind him. I don't look when I'm sure he's made his way across the parking lot. I don't look until I've counted out ten full minutes. Then, when I'm sure he won't see me cry, I give myself another ten minutes to fall apart.

CHAPTER TWENTY-FIVE

HALLOWEEN DAWNS in the hollow like a warning. Fog fills the valley and holds in the smell of moldering leaves and woodsmoke. There is a sharp chill in the air, the kind that turns breath into fluffy white clouds. When I was little, Sorrel convinced me that those clouds were souls leaving their bodies. A pointed reminder of the importance of what we're about to do.

With the sightings of the Wampus Cat, people have gone back to the old ways, leaving saucers of milk out in hopes that she will grant them good fortune and not curse them with bad luck. Knowing what I do now, I'm not sure if I'm more inclined to believe in this custom or less. But there is a weightiness in the anticipation. We might tell ourselves that it's all in good fun, but thrill and trepidation both can make our hearts race and our stomachs drop.

And maybe the costumes we don offer clever camouflage to what we don't want to see. Because tonight the veil is thin and the dead are close.

My toes touch the wooden floorboards next to my bed, and I recoil from the cold that reaches out and leaches the warmth all the way up my leg.

A scream punctures the quiet.

I throw off my quilts and leap for the door. Racing toward the sound, I nearly collide with Sissy scurrying down from her attic room. "Juniper?" she asks, grabbing my arm.

I nod. Halloween has never been easy for Juniper, and there is every reason to expect this one will be the worst yet.

"What's wrong?" I ask as we burst into the room Linden and Juniper share.

But it wasn't Juniper who screamed. It was Linden. She stares back at me wide-eyed, then points. I turn to see their bedroom window frosted over, and on the floor below it, written out in what looks to be every single fennel seed we poured in the keyhole and around Juniper's bed to keep the spirit away, is a single word: AWAKE.

Somehow, Juniper has slept through all of it. Maybe unnaturally so. I rush toward her and press a hand against her cheek.

"Junie?" Her skin is like ice, and her breath is alarmingly shallow. "Junie?" I reach for her wrist to check her pulse. It's slow and sluggish.

I look up to meet Sissy's eyes, my own concern reflected there. Linden crawls into bed beside Juniper and curls around her, rubbing her hand up and down Junie's arm to try and coax some warmth back into her.

"I'm going to get your mom," Sissy says quietly, and she pulls her robe tighter against the nip in the air. "I don't know what's going on, but this seems like a lot more than a normal Halloween reaction."

"It's all right. I know what to do," I tell her.

She looks unconvinced. "Get the salt."

I nod as I push the fennel seeds into a pile with my foot, erasing the message.

She pauses for a moment just outside the door. "Call Sorrel and see what she's got in the apiary."

But I can already hear my phone ringing from across the hall. I'd called her last night and told her everything I'd learned.

"How is she?" Sorrel asks as soon as I answer.

"It's bad," I admit. "I've never seen her like this before. It's almost like he's draining the life from her."

"We need to bury that bone. Now."

Of all the information Ona dropped on me yesterday, the most important right now is that the bone I'd so foolishly given Juniper to summon a spirit was that of the man who was murdered to create the Bone Tree more than two hundred years ago. But at least now we know exactly where the body is buried.

"Tonight at dusk," I confirm. "Anyone out there working to prep for the prescribed burn should be gone by then, but we'll still have enough light to see."

"I'm getting on a bus and heading home right now."

"Sorrel, you don't have to do that. You'll miss classes. Linden and I can handle digging up a two-hundred-year-old grave."

"I know you can, but you don't have to," she says, and I hear a faint announcement from the other end of the line that makes it clear she's already at the station. "In the meantime, there's some juniper honey in my cupboard. Mix it with a little tea of spiceberry, mallow, and lavender. They just called my bus. I'll be there soon."

We say goodbye, and I cross back to Juniper's room. She's awake now, sitting up in bed but looking impossibly small. Her eyes are sunken, and her skin looks nearly translucent.

"How are you feeling?" I ask, even though I can see the answer on her face.

"He's never going to let me go." Her voice is raw like she's been yelling. Or crying. "He's so angry, but it's more than that. He feels betrayed, like something was taken from him. And he has this drive, a purpose . . ." Her voice trails off.

"Juniper," Mama says, voice heavy with concern, as she enters the room. "Sissy told me it was a bad one this year." She shoots a look at Linden and me that says we'll be hearing about that later. "Come on, I ran a bath for you with some of my special salts." Mama helps Juniper climb out of bed and leads her down the hall.

"What do you think Junie meant about a purpose?" Linden asks quietly.

"I don't know, but I definitely don't like the sound of it."

At just after six, when trick-or-treating begins in town, Sorrel, Linden, and I hike out to the Bone Tree to dig up a body. Juniper objected to us going without her, but she barely looks strong enough to hike out to the mailbox.

The sky is the color of a week-old bruise, slightly green and unnatural-looking, and the air is as still as a held breath. The closer we get to the Bone Tree itself, the more evidence there is of the coming burn. Firebreaks have been constructed at the boundary of the planned fire by removing vegetation and exposing bare dirt or sheer rock face. Standing inside that area feels like waiting for a match to strike, even though the burn isn't scheduled to start for another full day.

Tonight, the Bone Tree looks like a man trying to flee across the river, arms outstretched like he's reaching for help.

"How do we know where to dig?" Linden asks.

"He was buried like a seed to create the Bone Tree, so we need to dig as close as we can to the roots," Sorrel tells us.

We only have two shovels, so we take turns, switching out so one person has a break while the other two dig. It's not easy. The cold, clay soil next to the creek is dense and heavy. And bodies are buried deep.

It's nearly three hours before Sorrel's shovel strikes something hard and she calls out from inside the hole. "I got something!" She hands Linden the shovel and kneels to use her hands to clear away the dirt.

After two hundred years underground, the pine box the man was buried in is soft, and the casket has split in places where the roots of the tree have punched through it. Rusted bands of iron hold it together, and other roots have wrapped themselves around the wood like rope.

Sorrel looks up at me. "Do you want to open it?"

"Not really, but I don't think we have a choice," I answer. We switch places and I shove a crowbar into the gap between the lid and the base to pry it open. But it isn't necessary; the soft pine and rusted iron give way immediately. I reach for the lid and pull. Of everything I considered might be waiting for us on the other side, this possibility never occurred to me.

"It's empty?" Linden is the first to voice what we're all thinking.

"How is that possible?" Sorrel asks.

My mind immediately goes to one suspect. Did Ona double-cross us and steal the bones so we can't put the spirit to rest? But, no, the clay around the tree was soft and bare of grass, but certainly there would have been some sign if it had been recently disturbed.

"Look!" Linden calls from above, pointing toward the casket. "There's something on the inside of the lid."

I rub my hands against my jeans to clean off some of the dirt, then pull my phone out of my back pocket and switch on the flashlight while Sorrel holds up the piece of wood. There, on the inside, gouged into the softwood, are what look like claw marks.

"What the hell?" Sorrel runs a finger over the grooves.

"Oh my god." I realize what they are at the same time she does, and we stare at each other in horror. "They buried him alive."

"No wonder his spirit is restless," Linden murmurs.

"There are only marks from nine fingers." I take the tiny bone from my pocket and hold it up to where it would have been if it wasn't cut off before he was buried.

"This gives me a really bad feeling," Linden says. "We can't put the spirit to rest."

Sorrel closes the lid, and we climb out of the hole. We sit side by side along the edge, drooping with exhaustion and coated in a mixture of sweat and mud with fresh blisters across our palms. The sun is well and truly set now, a battery-powered lantern our only light.

I look up at the tree above us and recall the impression I had when we first arrived of a man trying to escape. "So what the hell do we do now?"

November

Mourning Moon

As we prepare to enter the darkest season, remember there is still life all around us, And death, too, is a part of life. It is still growth, even if it happens beneath the surface. In this season of reflection, our deepest desires will come to the surface and force us to identify that which we value most. Dare to take a leap of faith and confidently claim your truest voice. It is a time to let go of past troubles and grief. Dig deeper; burn away reminders of the past. An ideal time for workings of protection, grounding, and familial rituals.

In Season

Garden: Brussels sprouts, cabbage, carrots, garlic, greens, kale, parsnips, potatoes, pumpkins, sweet potatoes, turnips, winter squash

Forage: frost grapes, lion's mane mushrooms, persimmons, turkey tail, shrimp of the woods, wintergreen berries

Fire Cider for What Ails You

Beneath the waning moon, gather the roots of ginseng, ginger, horseradish, and bulbs of garlic. Chop and combine with hot peppers in a glass jar. Cover with apple cider vinegar and let sit through a full cycle of the moon. Sweeten with honey if you must. You'll know it's working when it burns the whole way down.

—Rowan James

CHAPTER TWENTY-SIX

WHEN WE were little, all four of us sisters would sometimes sleep in the same room. We'd curl up two to a bed like little sardines, snuggled in so tight we'd share the same dream. Last night, I dreamt of an adder devouring a magpie. I uncoil my body from next to Juniper on the too-small twin bed, careful not to wake the others. My muscles ache from shoveling clay all night, but morning comes early.

There is only one person I can think of who may have information about the creation of the Bone Tree by the founders of Caball Hollow, and it's the last place I thought I'd be headed right now. But when I climb into the truck, the gas gauge is hovering just above the red. A predictable consequence of driving out to the Forest last night that I didn't notice in my state of exhaustion. I'll have to stop at the Ick on the way home, but first I need to catch Amos

McCoy before he heads into work for his shift at the waste management company.

I have to double-check the address when I pull up on the dirt track out front. The last time I was out here, it looked like it'd been abandoned for decades. Now the vines have been trimmed back, the broken windows replaced, and a new roof put on that somehow makes it seem like the small clapboard house is standing up a little straighter.

When I came with Linden a couple months ago, we learned that Nora McCoy, a former teacher, and Aunt Zephyrine had bonded over their shared interest in the town's history. Nora even descended from one of Caball Hollow's founding families.

Amos and Nora McCoy were also Elam's parents, and the tragedy of his disappearance followed by a cloud of suspicion that Amos had been involved nearly destroyed them both.

I climb out of the truck and head for the front door. Even the rotted boards of the porch have been replaced. I lift my hand to knock, but the door opens before I make contact.

"Thought I heard somebody out here," Amos McCoy says. He looks like he's been fixed up right along with his house. His hair is freshly trimmed, though still unruly, like a white cloud floating above his head. "I'm on my way out, but I can sit a spell. Come on in."

He ushers me into his home, leading me to the kitchen at the rear, where an old enamel table holds the remains of a bowl of oatmeal.

"I hope I'm not disturbing you," I say as he gestures for me to take a seat.

"No, no, not at all." Amos takes the bowl to the sink and wipes off the table. "Hey, listen, I've been meaning to thank your gran."

The statement surprises me, as I haven't heard Gran say a word about Amos McCoy in quite some time. "Is that so?"

"That farmhand of yours has been coming out here fixin' up the place for weeks now," he says with a grin. "I figured she must have sent him. Might take me a while, but I'll pay her back for her kindness."

I swallow hard, knowing Gran wasn't the one to send Hadrian. The lost son who could never really come home.

"Actually, there is something you could do for me that would be really helpful," I tell him. "It's why I came by."

"Name it!" He tucks his thumbs into his pockets and leans back on his heels, happy to help.

"When I was here last, you mentioned that Nora did a lot of research into the history of the town."

"That's right." He gestures to the wall behind me where several old photos hang. "Her family, the Garlands, were one of the first in Caball Hollow."

"But she stopped her genealogy research after she found something distressing?"

"Yeah, Nora was pretty upset and didn't like to talk about it and then, of course, Zephyrine took off not too much later." He shrugs. "Nora never picked up her research again after that."

"Did you happen to keep any of it?" I venture.

"Oh, I was a pretty bad pack rat." He chuckles self-deprecatingly. "But I've mended my ways quite a bit. With the house looking so nice, I wanted to make an effort."

My stomach drops at the thought of being so close to an answer and having it slip through my fingers.

"Which is why I know right where it is." He bustles down a short hall and disappears into a room, only to re-emerge moments later with a large file box. "This old stuff will really help you?" he asks as he passes the box to me.

"Oh, you have no idea." I nod earnestly.

"Well, all right, then. Just bring it back when you're done." He shrugs, and his shoulders droop just the slightest bit. "I'm saving it in case Wyatt ever sparks an interest."

Amos insists on carrying the box out to the truck for me, then I wave as he leaves for work. I don't waste time driving home. I pull the lid off the box right there in the cab of the farm truck. Lucky for me, Nora McCoy was extremely organized, and the final research she did sits at the top of the stack.

A photocopy of an immigration record to the United States from Scotland for someone named James McKeane Darrow, a seventeen-year-old orphan who came into the country alone. Next, a copy of an old property grant for J. M. Darrow, ink faded to nothing in places, with a hand-drawn map of the lot.

It's hard to tell exactly where the plot of land was from this, but something about the location and the layout brings to mind that old chimney standing alone in the middle of the Forest, and an awareness zings through me.

I reach back into the box and pull out a letter from an early Garland ancestor who was writing to express alarm at the rumors of a Wampus Cat stalking the settlement. The beast was said to have first been spotted shortly after the arrival of a strange boy of uncommon beauty who the townspeople believed to be a changeling, a child left by the good folk in the place of a stolen human one. Panic had taken hold at the thought that the cat was prowling to steal souls and there was no graveyard watch to guide them to the Otherworld in this strange new land. Someone back home had sent instructions, delivered in the beak of a bird, on what needed to be done to create one if none were naturally occurring. And the changeling seemed an ideal candidate. At the time of this letter, no decision had been made as to what they would do, but they were clearly desperate.

I put the papers back in the box and notice something has fallen down along the side, pinched between the cardboard and the stack of papers. Squeezing my fingers inside, I pull out the thick card. Just by the feel of it, I can tell it's very old. Black ink calligraphy sprawls across it in careful lines: *J. M. Darrow, aged 15. Portrait commissioned by his mother.*

I flip the card over, and my vision goes white.

John Doe.

John Doe is James McKeane Darrow.

I'm speeding as fast as I dare toward the hospital. I'd thought someone had taken the bones from the grave under the Bone Tree. But I'd never once considered the possibility that James McKeane Darrow had been buried alive. And then stayed that way for more than two hundred years. How could it even be possible? Was the speculation correct and Darrow was one of the good folk?

Deputy Ethan Miranda flies up behind me in his cruiser, sirens wailing. My stomach drops as I slow down to pull over, but he blows right past me. I have a short-lived moment of relief, until I realize he's headed for the hospital, and my stomach drops.

The drive feels even longer than it usually does. The truck sputters and I tap the gas gauge, willing it not to strand me on the side of the road. I'm sweating by the time I reach the parking lot, but force myself to walk slowly through the hospital. There's a strange frenzy in the air before I even make it up to the third floor. When the elevator dings and I step out, I can tell something is very wrong. My steps squeak against the linoleum as I approach John Doe's room. A couple deputies stand in front of the door, talking in low tones.

"What's happened?" I ask as I draw closer.

"He's gone," Deputy Miranda says as he steps out of the hospital room.

My feet stop before I even fully register the words. "He's dead?"

"No, he's *gone*."

I push between the two men to look inside for myself. There are several deputies milling about the room, but the bed is empty. "Vanished without a trace. The staff came in for morning rounds, and the bed was made up with nice, crisp hospital corners and a sprig of lavender left on the pillow."

At the mention of his pillow, I think of the agrimony and mugwort sachet I removed from it. Linden said Gran *wouldn't* make one strong enough to keep someone in a coma, not that she *couldn't*. The instructions in the family book even warn not to overuse, or waking can become difficult. But could the magic really have taken this long to wear off? Whatever the reason, John Doe, or rather, James McKeane Darrow, has managed to disappear just as suddenly as he appeared.

"You're really not supposed to be here," Miranda says.

"Then I'm going to need that emergency gallon of gas in the trunk of your cruiser," I say, turning to face him. "Rolling your eyes isn't very professional, Deputy."

Ethan gives in, pouring just enough gas into the truck's tank to get me to the Ick. Maybe it's lack of sleep, but when I pull into the parking lot, the fluorescent lights seem especially bright. I fill up, then head inside to pay, and freeze. Every letter in the QuickStop sign is lit.

"What happened?" I demand of Dreama Kinnaird without preamble as I shove open the door.

"Isn't it wonderful?" she gushes from her perch on the stool behind the counter. "I came to work the other day, and all the letters were back on! It's a miracle." She pulls the cross on her necklace back and forth on its chain, then twists to point behind her. "And look. When I opened up the store that morning, the missing poster was gone, too. I think it means he's finally at peace." Her eyes well up.

"Not if I have anything to say about it," I mutter under my breath, remembering the last time I was in here with Hadrian and the expression on his face when he looked at that old photo of himself. First, the repairs at Amos McCoy's house and now here. Hadrian is up to something.

"What's that, dear?" Dreama asks. "Oh! Do you know what all the sirens were about? There musta been three, four police cars went flying by here."

"John Doe is gone," I tell her, reaching into my pocket for cash as she rings me up.

A loud crash echoes behind me, and I nearly jump out of my skin. Dreama pushes off her stool, eyes wide. I spin around to see the rack of snack cakes at the end of the far aisle overturned on the floor, with someone collapsed on top of it. Someone in a dark green Forest Service uniform.

It's Vernie, and she's pale as a ghost.

"Call an ambulance," I shout over my shoulder to Dreama as I rush to help.

"What happened?" I kneel on the floor beside Vernie and reach for her wrist to take her pulse.

"It was an accident," she says, her voice weaker than I've ever heard it, but desperate and raw, and I know she's not talking about knocking over Dreama's display.

"What was an accident, Vernie?" I ask, trying my best to keep my voice calm while her heartbeat pounds erratically beneath my fingertips. "Take a breath and start from the beginning."

"I was out checking some of the trails after the storm, and he came out of nowhere, covered in dirt." She grabs on to my arm with her other hand, and her eyes go wide. "He crawled out of the ground, Rowan. But I'd seen him before. Or at least I thought I had. He looked just like the ghost at the same tree all those years before. I didn't think; I just reacted. There was a dropped branch about the width of a bat, and I grabbed it and swung. I think I half expected it to go right through him."

"Who, Vernie?" But I think I already know.

"John Doe," she whispers, and I feel my own heart start to race.

"But how did he get all the way from the Bone Tree to where he was found?"

"I got ahold of myself. I checked his pulse and breathing and was reaching for my radio to call for help, when that girl, the one who works with the video people, showed up. She said she knew him. That they'd been filming something for the show and help was already on the way. She apologized for scaring me. I think I must have still been in a bit of shock, because I didn't question anything she told me. Not until a few hours later when the John Doe report came in."

"Why didn't you say anything?" I ask in confusion. Not taking responsibility for what happened seems so unlike the Vernie I know.

"Because I don't think it was fake, Rowan." Her eyes are so wide, I can see the whites all the way around. "That man crawled out of the *dirt*. That's not natural. But I didn't mean to kill him."

"He's not dead, Vernie," I clarify. "He woke up and disappeared."

Relief washes over her face, and her eyes fall closed.

"Is she all right?" Dreama calls from the front, where she's waiting for the ambulance crew.

"She passed out." I loosen her collar and prop up her legs with a couple boxes of MoonPies. After a few long minutes, her eyes flutter back open.

"They're here!" Dreama calls, holding open the door for the EMTs.

"Rowan," Vernie whispers, and gestures for me to lean in closer. "There's something strange going on out by that tree. Somebody is playing us all for fools."

I watch them wheel her out of the Ick on a stretcher. Of all the suspects I'd considered, Vernie had never entered my mind. But it's the other part of what she told me that really throws me for a loop. I need to get some real answers from my dear cousin, and I bet I know just where to find her.

By the time I pay for the gas and make my way to the Harvest Moon, I'm already hours late for my shift. I push open the back door and step into the kitchen, directly across from where Gran stands at the prep counter.

"Rowan Persephone," she begins with a frustrated shake of her head.

"I'll explain later," I promise, holding up my hands against the look in her eyes. I take my apron off the hook and grab a fresh order pad from the stack under the counter.

"Yes, you will. But right now, we've got a dining room full of hungry customers and only one person taking orders," she snaps. "The special is biscuits and apple cider gravy. And Linden made a sticky sorghum pudding. Get your apron on and get out there."

Mama squeezes my shoulder in silent encouragement as I wash my hands. Then I pull on my apron and push through the swinging door to the dining room. Ona is sitting alone at her usual table, and I head straight for her, ignoring the other customers trying to wave me down. Sissy shoots me a confused look from across the room, but I ignore it.

When I reach Ona, I slam her laptop closed, not caring that she barely manages to pull her fingers out of the way first. "We need to talk."

"We already talked," she disagrees, sliding her chair back from the table.

"I've learned a few things since then." I grab her wrist and pull her outside, not letting go until we round the corner of the building into the small alleyway.

When I'm sure there's no one to overhear us, I whirl to face her. "I just put Vernie in an ambulance. You remember Vernie? She's the one you lied to when your fairy-tale king crawled out of his grave. What was your plan there, cousin?"

She holds up her hands, placating. "I'll admit the poem was not really clear about him being *alive*."

"You're the one who put the book in my bag," I accuse her, shoving my finger in her face. "And was it you who caught me in the binding spell? Why?" I demand.

"I also gave your sisters a nudge to go and look for you," she argues.

And then I realize the answer. "Because your mother would be trapped inside, so you made sure we'd be forced to break it."

"I wanted to destroy the Bone Tree, but when he crawled out of the dirt, I realized I needed to . . . pivot. I couldn't let anyone from the Otherworld find out or they'd just try to put him back in the ground. But I also couldn't drag him out of the Forest alone."

"So you called it in, he was reported as a John Doe, and then you kept him hidden in the hospital in a coma made of mugwort and agrimony."

She shrugs, looking somewhat sheepish. "Waking the rightful king was supposed to destroy the Bone Tree, but Ciaran Nimh keeps patching it back together with stolen bits of souls. I thought you'd figure it out and maybe stop him."

That earns her a dirty look. "Tell me about Ciaran Nimh, Ona."

She looks surprised and suddenly more intrigued. "Ah, so our boy hasn't quite slipped his leash yet, then. Well, cousin, Ciaran Nimh, the false lord of the Otherworld, is known to all those who fear him as the Venomous Dark. If he'll poison his own men for any perceived disloyalty, what do you think he does to his enemies? May you never have the displeasure of crossing his path."

I shake my head, trying to process the sheer amount of information thrown at me today on the minimal amount of sleep I've had.

"The thing I can't figure out," I tell her, "is how you got mixed up with Sonny Vane."

"All right, so I didn't exactly tell you the whole story before." Ona sits on the window ledge behind her. "When I came to after getting thrown from the Otherworld into this one, I couldn't find the bone. I'd gone one way, and it had gone another. I thought my brilliant plan to rescue my mom was over before it even began.

"I went back to search for days with no luck, but then, one day I heard arguing. Sonny and someone else. I don't know who. I never saw the other guy. He'd found the bone. I think he thought it might be evidence of the Moth-Winged Man, or at least he could pretend it was on camera. I looked up the YouTube channel he had stamped on all his stuff and saw that he was hiring." She shrugs. "I thought it was my chance to get the bone back, but I never saw it again. And then, after a couple of weeks, it didn't matter anymore."

"Why didn't you ever come to us for help?" I ask. "We're family."

"I wanted to tell you, I did," she says. "But I was afraid you might try to stop me when you found out what I was doing. My mother told me that she and her sister didn't always see eye to eye on matters of magic."

"I think Gran would do whatever she could to get her sister back," I tell her truthfully. "Family is the most important thing to her."

"The thing is, the plan worked," Ona insists. "The Bone Tree was weakened enough to admit things that weren't meant to come through. But my mother's curse holds her tightly. I need time to figure out how to loosen its hold enough that she can slip out."

"Well, that's one thing we may not have," I tell her, explaining the prescribed burn the Forest Service has scheduled for tomorrow.

"That's it, then. The end." Ona slumps back against the side of the building, eyes bleak. "Unless he releases her from the curse, she'll have no hope of coming home."

"The Bone Tree has stood between life and death, this world and the other, for more than two hundred years. Could fire really destroy it?" I ask.

"Maybe not before, but now, in its weakened state? I think it might," Ona says. "What Hadrian said wasn't wrong. The Bone Tree is what anchors the Otherworld to this place. When it goes, I could search my whole life for another door into the Otherworld and never find one."

My skin prickles as I think about what Hadrian said that day in the truck. When the Bone Tree fails, I'll be on one side of it, and he'll be on the other. Fixing the sign at the Ick to thank Dreama Kinnaird for never forgetting him. Repairing Amos McCoy's house and making it safe to live in again. For weeks now, Hadrian has been saying goodbye.

CHAPTER TWENTY-SEVEN

I CRAWL into bed that night exhausted, but my mind won't quiet enough for sleep. It seems that Juniper's connection to the first Moth-Winged Man, James McKeane Darrow, was severed when he awoke from his magically induced coma. But I won't rest easy until I know for certain that he can no longer haunt her mind.

Lucien Ballard had no way of knowing Darrow, which means there's no proof his death was anything more than what it appeared to be. Perhaps it really was just an accident. But the thing most responsible for keeping me awake tonight is that tomorrow the Bone Tree will burn, and there's no magic I know that can stop a forest fire.

My eyes have barely drifted shut when my phone starts buzzing and dancing across the nightstand. I grab it with a sharp glance over at Sorrel to make sure it didn't wake her.

Blinking at the glowing screen, I realize it's actually very early in the morning. I kick off the blankets and step out into the hallway. The phone number isn't one I recognize, but I swipe to answer it anyway as I head downstairs to the kitchen.

"Hello?" I whisper.

"Rowan?" The voice on the other end sounds far away, and the line crackles.

"I'm sorry, I think we have a bad connection." I lean closer to the window over the sink like somehow that might help. "Who is this?"

"It's . . . Vernie!"

"Vernie?" After closing today, I checked in to see how she was doing. She'd been released from the hospital following treatment for shock and low blood sugar. The staff had instructed her to rest, but instead Vernie went back to work. "What's wrong?"

There's a burst of static that forces me to pull the phone away from my ear.

"What we spoke about at the Ick . . ." Vernie continues. "I *saw* him!" She yells the words as if that will magically clear the line.

"You saw John Doe?" I clarify, and my heartbeat picks up. "Where?"

"Forest . . . near that strange tree . . . where I first saw the ghost . . ."

The line cuts out again, then drops completely.

"Vernie?" I try, just to be sure, but she's gone.

Did she see James McKeane Darrow out in the National Forest? When I learned of his disappearance, I assumed he would get as far away from Caball Hollow as he could. Certainly he'd stay away from the site where he spent more than two hundred years buried alive. But the Bone Tree is also the doorway to the Otherworld, and if Ona's fairy tale is true, he is the rightful king.

I grab a flashlight from the drawer next to the refrigerator and my jacket from the hook by the door, and I race out to the truck. The burn is scheduled to start at daybreak. There isn't much time.

When I reach the Forest, it's still hours from sunrise, and the darkness is deep across the wide expanse of sky, but the moon is nearly full and bright enough for me to hike out to the Bone Tree. I don't want to risk turning on a flashlight and scaring off Darrow. And I've walked this route so many times lately, I could likely do it with my eyes closed, yet it still takes the better part of an hour.

"Vernie?" I call softly when I catch a glimpse of the green of her Forest Service uniform, contrasting against the brightness of the fall leaves even in low light. She doesn't answer, but I don't dare yell any louder.

I push through the branches of the trees and step into the small clearing along the creek. Vernie sits on the ground opposite the Bone Tree, her back to me, leaning against an old oak, like she stopped for a moment to catch her breath.

But there's something off about how she's sitting. It looks uncomfortable, the way she's hunched over, and I immediately worry they let her out of the hospital too soon. Did the strain of thinking she'd killed John Doe weaken her heart? Did she hit her head when she fell?

My steps quicken, eating up the distance between us. When I'm only a few feet away, a heavy feeling steals over me, and I slow.

The air thickens until it feels like water, and each step becomes more difficult. Silently, I will her to turn and notice me. To say she's just been lost woolgathering. Away with the fairies.

"Vernie?" I reach for her shoulder, and at my touch, her head falls forward.

My breath hitches. I press my fingers to her neck, but not even a flutter of a heartbeat pushes back. When I pull my hand away, it's sticky and wet. Blood.

In the moonlight, there is a softness to her face, an emptiness, like a shirt cast aside on a chair, still warm from the brush of skin. It's so different from the way Vernie usually looks, so alive and animated, that I almost can't recognize her. The most real part of her is gone. A sob gets caught in my throat and becomes a gasp for air, and then I can't catch my breath.

I lower her gently to the ground. The shape of her body presses into the marsh grass, surrounding her with a perfect circle like a deer bed. Leaving a trace on the land she loved most before she was forced to leave it behind.

"Rowan." Hadrian's voice is somber, but it still feels too loud.

"No." I reject the idea of what his being here means. That Vernie is truly dead, her life over before her time. And there's no hope of getting her back.

"I'm so sorry, love." I feel him kneel in the grass beside us, but I can't turn away from the woman in front of me, even though I know it's only the least important part of her that's left behind. The real Vernie, all that she was, is gone.

"What do I do?" I whisper as tears spill unchecked, dripping from my chin. "What can I do?"

"Just let her know you're here with her," Hadrian answers softly. "Just be here. That's all you can do. And that's all she needs you to do. Just be here."

"Someone killed her," I admit. The blood on the back of her head. The position of her body, left in the path of a planned burn that will start in just a few hours. It's so obvious I can't ignore it, much as I want to right now.

"I think so, yeah." He hasn't touched me at all since he arrived, but now he curls an arm around my shoulders, pulling me in against his chest. I soak his shirt in tears.

He lets me cry for as long as he can, then pushes me back, forcing me to meet his eyes. "We have to go," he tells me. "I need to help Vernie now, which means I need to cross over to the other side of the veil, but first I need you to hike down to where you can get a signal and call your father, all right? It isn't safe up here."

He's right. My attention has only been on Vernie, but her blood is still warm. Her killer is likely still in these woods. Did Darrow see Vernie and attack her the way she had him?

"Will you tell her that I'll miss her?" I ask, looking up at Hadrian for the first time. He looks tired, like he hasn't been sleeping well. Dark circles smudged beneath his eyes.

He nods, reaching out to slide a hand against my cheek and brush away the tears.

"She doesn't have her jacket," I tell him nonsensically, but my voice cracks at the thought of her body lying alone out here in the cold.

"She'll be all right." Hadrian stands and pulls me to my feet. "Now go, carefully, but quick as you can." He gently shoves me toward the path, and I stumble away, struggling to find my footing through the blur of tears.

I don't look back.

The sky is just beginning to lighten above the mountains when I reach the edge of the Forest. The Ick isn't open yet, but there's a white van I recognize in the parking lot. Sonny Vane must have had a late night of filming to still be out here at this hour. I cross the deserted street and head toward it.

The van's rear doors are open, but there's no one around. I can make out some of the big duffel bags of equipment the YouTube crew is always hauling around, so they must be here somewhere. I move toward the van, and my foot squishes against something soft. It's a small bit of moss on the concrete. A strange thing to find here of all places.

My blood slows, then rushes back. I'd have connected the dots sooner if Vernie's death hadn't thrown me out of my right mind, but everything is clicking into place now. I reach the van and grab the zipper of the closest bag, pulling back just far enough to confirm my suspicions.

Ginseng, wrapped with moss to keep it safe during shipping. The roots are bigger than any I've ever seen, like the ones the old-timers like to talk about from decades ago. I zip up the bag and stumble backward.

But then I think about where Sonny mounted his strange camera that only took grainy stills. Ona said cameras like that didn't need much of a signal at all, and it could even notify him if there was movement. Like a warning system for an illegal poaching operation. And I realize what spot Sonny and his crew must be poaching. The clearing surrounding the Bone Tree, where we've always harvested ingredients for our tinctures and salves because they grow more potent than anywhere else.

"Rowan?" Sonny steps out of the woods, and my stomach drops. I swallow as he jogs toward me. It's too late to run. I'm going to need to put on the best performance of my life.

"Sonny? I thought this was your van. Late night or early morning?" I fold my arms so he can't see my hands shaking.

"What are you doing out here?" His brows draw together, but I'm not sure if he's suspicious or confused.

"I, uh, was hoping to find you, actually. You weren't at the motel, so I thought you might be out here." I lie like

I've never lied before, filling the air with smoke like it'll provide the cover I need to get away.

"Me? What for?" He looks strange in the glow of the security light above the back door of the Ick. Sharper. More dangerous.

"I watched some of your videos. They're pretty good." If there's one thing Sonny loves talking about, it's himself.

He crosses his arms. "I see, so now you're coming crawling back, wanting to be in my videos? You had your chance, and you took off in the middle of filming."

I thought Sonny was out here with his crew, but no one else has followed him out of the Forest. And suddenly I'm feeling a lot more confident. Despite what he says, Sonny Vane is at least an inch shorter than my five foot eight. But I don't know if he has a weapon.

"You're right, it was a bad idea." I take a step backward, slipping my hand into the pocket of my jacket where my cell phone is. "I'll let you get back to it, then."

"Rowan, it's all right. I saw you open the bag."

My blood turns to ice, freezing me where I stand. I'd stopped carrying the pepper spray when my volunteer assignment ended, and the blade of my mushroom knife needs to be unfolded, which pretty much eliminates the element of surprise. Not that it's big enough to do much damage anyhow. I know that, in case of emergency, there's a sequence of buttons to push on my phone that will call for help or set off an alarm or something, but I can't for the life of me think of what that sequence is. I grip the sides anyway, pressing whatever buttons I can find.

"I just needed to keep you busy." He leans forward to emphasize the words, crowding into my space.

"For what?" I demand.

"For me," a gruff voice says from behind me. I spin around and come face-to-face with Ranger Harshbarger.

My mind spirals as Vernie's words from the phone call, and right here at the Ick yesterday, come rushing back. She hadn't been talking about Darrow at all. She was talking about an inside job.

"I'm really sorry you had to see this, kiddo," Harshbarger says, and it's all the more cruel because it's not even a lie.

Before I can take another step or speak a word, something smashes into the back of my head so hard it feels like it is splitting apart. I reach my hand up, expecting to feel bone, but there's too much blood. It's sticky, and my fingers are coated in it. My vision goes dark around the edges.

"That was a sucker punch, asshole," I slur as I crumple to the ground.

My eyes feel like they're filled with sand that scrapes as I try to blink. I turn my head, and a stabbing pain shoots through my brain so hard I'm not sure if I'm about to vomit or pass out again.

"Careful, now," a voice to my right says just quietly enough not to split my skull. "Can you sit up for some water?"

I pry my eyes open and blink at the brightness of the rising sun. Ranger Harshbarger kneels beside me, my head cradled in his arm. I lurch away but realize instantly what a bad idea that was and have to hold my breath until the nausea passes.

"Slow movements might be best," he says. I squeeze my eyes shut against the dizziness that washes over me. "Let's try this again.

"For what it's worth, I am sorry." He slowly helps me into a seated position.

When I'm fully upright, I crack one eye open. We're back at the clearing with the Bone Tree at its center. The shape of Vernie's body, lying in the grass, is just visible from the corner of my eye. But Hadrian is long gone, guiding her spirit to the afterlife.

"It's worth nothing." My voice sounds too loud in my head. I slide my hand into my pocket for my phone, even though I know there's no signal in this part of the Forest, but it's not there and neither is my knife. "You're worse than the other poachers because you know how important the ginseng is for the health of the Forest, but you still took it all just to line your own pockets."

Harshbarger pushes to his feet, anger tensing his jaw. I'm right, and we both know it. "Do you know how little forest rangers make? I've given my *life* to this Forest. I'm nearing retirement, and what do I have to show for it? My compressed spine that aches every night, the arthritis that swells the joints in my hands, hell, the number of punches I've taken from drunk campers. Yet these poachers haul thousands of dollars out of these woods without putting anything into them."

A magpie flies into the clearing, and I watch it land on a branch somewhere overhead. *One for sorrow.* It would have been so easy for him, I realize. Contacts made through a life of catching poachers. Using Sonny's ridiculous monster hunting as cover to smuggle out pounds at a time without raising suspicion.

"And Vernie?" I spit the words at him. "What about her?"

Harshbarger sighs with what seems like genuine regret. "I think she's suspected for a while." He scratches at the stubble on his cheek. "All the years we worked together, I should have known she'd want proof. She knew we'd want to clear out as much as we could before the burn, and I think she wanted to catch me in the act."

The harsh calls of the magpies are like spikes in my head. The sky above them grows gradually lighter.

"I don't know why you're wasting your time," Sonny shouts from somewhere I don't care to try and turn my head to see. "Told ya to just tie her to a tree and be done with it. The fire will take care of the rest."

"Thank you for that valuable insight," Harshbarger tells him, but his gaze doesn't leave mine, like he's searching for absolution. As if by making me understand his reasoning, I'll see it his way. But I'll never understand. And I'll never forgive him.

Sonny Vane scurries closer. There's something about the way he moves through the trees that seems off for some reason I can't quite put my finger on, but I push the thought aside to focus on more urgent matters.

"Come on," he insists. "We need to get out of here before they start the burn."

"You're a damn fool, Sonny Vane," I tell him. "He's clearly framing you for murder."

"No." Sonny shakes his head petulantly. "We're partners. We're helping each other."

I'm so scared that my fear becomes anger, and I turn on Sonny. "Let's just think about how this would play out," I tell him. "If I don't come home today, people are going to start looking. First, they'll find the truck I drove out to the Forest. Then they'll pull the footage from the parking lot camera they installed at the Ick after all the petty thefts these last few months. The one right under that security light. Maybe they got a good shot of your face."

"No," Sonny objects. His eyes go wide, and he looks at Harshbarger as if for confirmation, but the older man remains stoic.

"That's when they'll find my blood. Tell me, Sonny, did you leave whatever you hit me with behind?" I pause. "That dumbfounded look on your face tells me you did, so they'll have your prints and my blood on a potential murder weapon."

"How do you know all this?" Sonny asks, mystified.

"Because my father is the sheriff, you bobbleheaded airbag," I tell him just to see the horrified look on his face.

But I'm only getting warmed up, because I've finally realized why the way Sonny walks looked off to me.

I think I only noticed it now because this is the first time I've seen him in the same type of setting since I watched all those old YouTube videos. Back in the earliest ones, when he wore a mask and only spoke through voice-over, he'd seemed so young and uncomfortable on camera. He moved like a teenager who'd just had a growth spurt and hadn't yet adjusted to the new length of his limbs.

The most recent videos are almost completely the opposite. Since the face reveal, he's appeared on camera in every episode. But always standing still, like when he's interviewing witnesses or presenting information. He doesn't run through the woods anymore. The masked man moved differently, and I think I know why.

"And that's when things will start to get real bad for you, Sonny, because they'll realize you've killed before. Haven't you?"

All the color drains from Sonny's face like someone pulled the plug. "I don't know what you're talking about." He starts to back away, trying to escape what he knows is coming.

"You revealed your identity as the person behind your channel just before you came to Caball Hollow, but that's only partly true, isn't it? The voice-over was you, but the masked man was Lucien Ballard. 'Sunlight on the truth,' right, Sonny? Sun. Light. Sonny and Lucien. You wanted fame, but he never cared about that. He just wanted to find the truth. So when Ranger Harshbarger offered you the chance to get the money you needed to propel your channel to fame and fortune, you jumped at the deal. Lucien refused, but you couldn't risk him going to the authorities."

There are three magpies in the branches above me now, their cries so loud I nearly lose my train of thought. *Three for a funeral.* I swallow and keep going.

"All right, enough of this." Harshbarger tries to stop me, but I'm only getting started.

"It wasn't even that hard to get rid of him, was it, Sonny? We all know how you like bashing people over the head." The pain in my own skull flares at the reminder.

"Then you just had to point his truck at the boulder, sit him in the driver's seat, and weigh down the pedal. Out there in the middle of nowhere, you had plenty of time to remove the weight before the accident was discovered, and no one was ever the wiser."

Sonny looks like a cornered rabbit, but Harshbarger's mouth is a flat line. He knows what Sonny did. It was likely a nice bargaining chip if he ever needed to keep him in line.

The truth is simple. Lies take more words. Like a spell being cast. A web being woven. To dazzle. To confuse. And, worst of all, to agree.

"You can't prove any of it," Sonny says, eyes wild.

"I don't have to, you unsuspecting rube." I throw up my hands. "Do you really think he's going to let you walk out of here after all this?"

Sonny gapes at me in surprise, then looks at Harshbarger. "You did say you wanted to be famous." He shrugs.

Without another word, Sonny turns tail and races off into the Forest, faster than I'd thought he could go. The rapid movement sets off the magpies, and they caw in alarm. They're coming faster now. *Six for hell.*

"Well, that is a shame," Harshbarger sighs. "It'll make this a lot harder."

He steps toward me with purpose, and my heart pounds so hard I can feel it pulsing in my head.

"Please don't do this," I whisper. I don't have a prayer of outrunning him, especially with a concussion. The wind shifts and brings with it the distinct smell of woodsmoke. The fire is coming.

"I am sorry," he says again.

Seven for the devil, his own self.

There's a sound like ripping paper, and Harshbarger freezes. I stare at him in confusion as a trickle of bright red blood escapes from the corner of his mouth.

He drops to his knees, eyes rapidly dulling, then falls forward. The knife in his back glints in the glow of the rising sun.

CHAPTER TWENTY-EIGHT

I LOOK from Harshbarger's body, dead before he even hit the ground, to the other side of the narrow clearing, where Ciaran Niamh stands outlined in the glow of the slowly closing Bone Tree gate.

He's taller than I realized and slim. A beard covers much of his face, but I can see how in his youth he would have resembled James McKeane Darrow. The true king and the usurper. Ona warned me never to meet the lord of the Otherworld.

A handful of men are with him, all with the same serpent's tongue flower tattooed on their forearms. One moves toward me, and I scramble backward. But he stops at Harshbarger's prone form, bracing a foot against his back to pull the blade free. It makes an awful sucking sound as it comes loose. Then the man leans forward and wipes it clean against the green of Harshbarger's Forest Service uniform before sliding it back into his belt. All of them have similar weapons, I realize, and my mouth goes dry.

I look back at Ciaran and find him already watching me. "Rowan James," he says with a smile. "We meet at last."

Slowly, I try to stand. He steps forward to offer his arm, which I pointedly ignore.

"I apologize for the mess." He nods toward Harshbarger. "I had intended for this to be a civil conversation. You don't seem like an unreasonable person, and I'm sure you understand the gravity of the situation."

"What situation?" I ask. My voice echoes painfully inside my skull.

"The Bone Tree is dying." He turns with a sweeping gesture toward the stark white tree.

The smell of burning wood reaches me, and I pause, confused by what in his words could be a lie, before I realize the smoke is real. The fire has already been set, and it's headed straight for us.

"We can't be here," I object, taking several steps to the side, away from Ciaran and his men. "They're burning this part of the Forest."

"That's why we're here, Rowan," he insists, his words strangely accented, like the ghostly voices in the woods. "The Bone Tree won't survive the fire in its weakened state. And if the Bone Tree goes, so does my kingdom."

"That's the prophecy of the true king, right? When the Bone Tree falls, the true king takes his throne."

"Do not call him that," he demands. "He is a boy. An accident of birth. I have ruled for more than two hundred years."

"But James McKeane Darrow is awake, and he's free. Whether the Bone Tree stands or not won't stop him from attacking if that's what he chooses."

"I'm afraid that's where you're wrong." Ciaran paces a small path, hands behind his back. "There are many ways to create a doorway to the Otherworld. Darrow was born of the good folk, and thus hard to kill. But I figured out a way to keep his power trapped inside that tree, and his body trapped beneath the dirt, separated from his soul, both alive and dead. And it barely took any effort to convince the ignorant settlers to do my bidding all while thinking it was their own idea. And as long as the Bone Tree stands, that power is mine."

"I am sorry, but I'm not sure what you expect me to do about it," I tell him, slowly edging closer to the Bone Tree.

"Do you know how I was able to take the throne?" he asks, like a teacher instructing a classroom. "The strongest magic in the Otherworld is tied to two things, Rowan. Blood and name. I was James McKeane Darrow before he was. And the only way to save the Bone Tree is to stabilize it in the same manner it was created."

He steps toward me, and I step away.

"You have the blood and the name of your ancestor. *Caorunn* means 'rowan.' A perfect twist of fate. Caorunn helped create the bridge between our worlds, and now you will save it."

I lunge, racing for the Bone Tree. I manage to slap my still-bloodied palm against the trunk before Ciaran's men overtake me. One grabs me around the waist and pulls me off my feet.

"So, what?" I throw the words at him. "You want to bury me alive like the boy? I saw what they did to him. The gouges in the coffin his fingers made as he tried to claw his way out."

I breathe a silent prayer that there was enough of my blood on my hand when I pressed it against the bark. James blood at the Bone Tree. Future generations may not be able to summon the Moth-Winged Man per our deal with Hadrian, but I still remember how. I only hope he gets the message in time.

"I am sorry it has to be this way," Ciaran says, and the air is clouded with too much real smoke for me to tell if it's a lie. "But the life of one girl to save an entire kingdom is no dilemma at all." He looks at me gravely, and I want to spit in his face. "It will only hurt for a moment, and then it'll be like falling asleep."

He takes a step closer, and I struggle against the iron grasp the other man has around my waist. Then everything happens at once. The Bone Tree gate blows open in a blaze of light and Hadrian bursts out, launching himself at the man behind me and breaking his grip.

"Run!" he yells, shoving me away toward the trees as the clearing erupts into chaos. The other men rush toward him as he fights them off.

I race through the woods I know like my own home, leaping over the exposed roots and ducking the low branches. But the fire is now well underway. And the lick of orange flame draws me up short.

Twigs snap in the distance, and I don't know if it's the fire devouring the Forest around me or Ciaran's men drawing closer. The path that leads toward the exit is already blocked, a wall of heat so strong it pushes me back. The call of a magpie snaps my gaze to the sky, but I can't see anything. My throat aches from the smoke. I turn, habit and instinct leading me higher up the mountain instead. If I can't escape, I need a place to hide.

When I reach the cabin, I collapse against the stairs. The radio antenna rises from the roof like a beacon of hope.

I can call for help.

I stumble to my feet as a magpie lands on the railing above my head with a sharp cry, and I realize too late that they've been tracking me. I spin just as Ciaran and three of his men burst from the trail into the tiny clearing, Hadrian, bloody and bruised, right behind them.

An angry rage twists Ciaran's face. He grabs me by the shirt, yanking me forward. "Enough!" he bellows.

Hadrian freezes, his eyes finding mine. Ten feet and four men separate us, but Ciaran extends his arm and my toes scrabble against the edge of the cliff. Ciaran's men grab Hadrian, holding him by the arms.

"You betrayed your oath," Ciaran shouts, his eyes shooting flames. "Again! For what? Her?" He speaks through gritted teeth and shakes me by the fabric of my shirt.

My feet lose purchase, and my stomach drops.

"You chose your side, and now you'll live with the consequences." Ciaran spits the words. "I may need her blood to hold the gate, but her heart doesn't need to be beating."

He lets go.

Everything slows.

My eyes find Hadrian's, devastation drawn across his face. He bursts into motion, pulling an arm free and yanking the dagger from the belt of one man. He slides the blade between the ribs of the man behind him, then twists, driving a fist into the face of the man who still has ahold of his other arm. As soon as he's free, he runs, closing the distance between us.

We both know he'll never make it.

A dark shape detaches from the shadows and springs at Ciaran.

Then all I can see is the soft blue belly of the sky as a flock of birds cut across it.

The rush of wind pulls a tear from the corner of my eye.

And I fall.

And fall.

And fall.

And then Hadrian fills my vision as he dives off the side of the cliff.

He hurtles toward me, and we slam together in midair. I cling to him, and he locks his arms around me, then wings erupt from his back.

Extending another foot above Hadrian's head, his wings are a beautiful burst of colorful patterns, two sets of two, just like a moth. They unfurl wide, catching the air and slowing us mid-fall.

We land just outside the boundary of the firebreak, and Hadrian presses his mouth against my hair.

"You're all right," he whispers like a prayer. "You're all right, love."

I swallow, my throat gone dry, and reach out a finger to touch the wings that now flow behind him like a cape covered in an array of powdery scales. "I had no idea you could change that fast."

"Neither did I," he admits, pressing his forehead against mine.

"But you jumped off the cliff after me."

He looks down at me, lifting one hand to my cheek, with a look on his face that seems almost reverential. "Where you go, I go," he whispers.

I rise onto my tiptoes and press my mouth against his. His eyes fall closed, and he hauls me against him, kissing me with something like relief, as if he's been starving or drowning and this is the lifeline he never thought he'd see. We grasp at each other with hands and lips and teeth and tongues, and it still isn't enough.

"I really thought I'd lost you this time." Hadrian pulls back to look into my eyes. "Come on," he says, taking my hand.

"Will Zephyrine be all right?" I ask, remembering the shadow that attacked Ciaran.

"She's always been good at landing on her feet," he says, lacing his fingers with mine but not meeting my eyes.

The smell of smoke is thick in the air, and the sky has a yellowish haze. "The fire will reach the Bone Tree soon, if it hasn't already," I say as we start walking.

"When it burns, the stolen bits of souls Ciaran used to hold it together will finally return to the people they were taken from."

"What about you? Will you stay here in Caball Hollow if you can't go back?"

He's quiet for so long I'm sure he's forgotten to answer. I'm about to repeat the question when at last he speaks.

"The magic of the Otherworld is what keeps me alive, or as near as I can be to it. I'm not meant to be in this world long-term. Without a connection to the Otherworld, all I'll be is a skeleton nineteen years in the river."

I jerk to a halt. It feels like being thrown off a cliff again, the ground disappearing beneath me. "If the Otherworld is gone, you're gone," I whisper, staggered. Panic claws up my throat as time runs out. "Let's go back, right now," I demand. "I'll do it. I'll do what Ciaran wanted."

"Rowan, my love, that is something I would never let you do." He shakes his head. "This is the way it has to be, and I've made peace with it."

"There has to be another way," I insist, not ready to give up and just accept things. My mind races, trying to find a solution that doesn't mean someone has to die.

"You know where your bones are buried?"

Hadrian nods. "I found them my first time back in Caball Hollow after becoming the Moth-Winged Man.

The ability to sense death is not the superpower I would have chosen for myself, but it's the one I got."

"What if, instead of saving the old Bone Tree, we could create a new one?" I suggest.

"Rowan." He shakes his head. "It's too late."

"Wait." I pull him to a stop. "It could work."

His eyes fall heavy on mine, and I can see the fear and heartbreak he's struggling not to let show. He's trying to make it easier on me, but I'm not giving up.

"The original was made by the first Moth-Winged Man and the first Rowan James, right? So we'll make our own. And we know where your bones are, so no need to bury anyone alive."

His face slowly changes; maybe he's got some hope. "If the Bone Tree holds long enough to maintain the connection to the Otherworld while we can complete the new one, it could work." He considers for a moment. "Which, to be clear, means we'll be bound to each other to some extent. Forever." He looks at me intently, all traces of humor gone from his eyes.

"How do we do it?"

"Rowan," Hadrian insists. "This is an important decision."

"Yeah," I agree. "But it isn't a hard one. I'm not saying that I know at eighteen that you and I will be in love forever. I'm saying that even if we hate each other again tomorrow, I'd still want you to live."

A smile cracks the dark clouds in his face and sunlight breaks through. "You love me?"

"Shut up." I turn to walk away, my cheeks gone hot, even though I have no idea where I'm supposed to be going.

Hadrian catches my hand and tugs, pulling me back into him. "Rowan, every time I've called you my love, has it ever been a lie?"

I stop short, thinking back to the very first time he said it in the tent we were forced to share. It had been a joke, or so I thought, but it was never a lie. It was true from the very beginning.

I look up into his face, and his eyes shift from teasing to something like awe. "I love you, too, *mo chridhe*."

"Then let's go save your life," I whisper.

Elam McCoy's body has been in the Teays River, caught beneath the surface in some underwater pocket, for the last nineteen years.

Hadrian takes out the knife that he used to steal my snake tattoo and repeats the process. But this time, as the snake comes to life beneath his skin, it splits down the middle, becoming two identical snakes. The serpent's tongue flower has completely disappeared, and in its place is a rowan branch. Hadrian slices his arm and makes a small corresponding cut on my hip, then presses them together. One of the snakes sheds its skin, just like it did before, then slithers onto my hip. When everything has settled, the tattoo has changed. Instead of one snake biting its own tail, it's a snake and shed snakeskin, each biting the other's tail and wrapped around the rowan branch in a figure eight. The symbol for infinity.

"Names have power," Hadrian murmurs to himself with a dark chuckle.

"What do you mean?"

"Elam means 'eternal tree.'" He smiles at me, sad but hopeful. "In ten minutes, you need to start walking into the river. I'm going to do the same from the Otherworld side and, if this works, eventually we'll meet."

"You can't go to the Otherworld, Hadrian. The Bone Tree is burning." I catch him by the shirt like I can hold him here.

"I don't have a choice, Rowan. It's only a bridge when someone crosses it, remember?" He leans down to press a too-quick kiss to my lips, then unfurls his wings and leaps.

When he's about twenty feet up, his wings flicker and vanish in midair. He starts to plummet like a stone, straight for the earth, until his wings burst back into place. "Holy shit," I whisper, and keep watch until I can't see him anymore like I can will him to stay in the sky. I know what this means. The Bone Tree must already be on fire, the connection to the Otherworld barely holding on, and he's going to walk right into it.

All my life, I've rushed headlong at everything. Jumping into action, often without thinking it through first. So it feels especially cruel that the most important thing I've ever done requires me to stand still. The seconds tick by impossibly slowly, and I count them out loud just so I can feel like I'm doing something.

When ten minutes is over at last, I take my first step into the freezing water. The slick riverbed threatens to pull my feet out from under me, and the current tugs at my ankles and then, as I walk deeper and deeper, my thighs. There's still no sign of him.

My vision goes blurry before I even realize I'm crying. How could we go through all of this and make it so far for none of it to matter? To lose him anyway? He can't die. I won't allow it.

Something hard hits the water in front of me, and then a large shape moves in my direction. I rub my eyes, and Hadrian is there, rushing toward me, covered in ash and missing most of his shirt, but alive. We crash into each other and hold tight.

I half drag Hadrian back to shore as the ground beneath our feet shakes and rolls like thunder. Then, right before my eyes, a tree breaks the surface of the water, stretching for the shore. Smaller than the last, but white as bone.

CHAPTER TWENTY-NINE

FRANCES VERNON was laid to rest beneath a bright blue autumn sky. Caball Hollow had never seen such a crowd, with forest rangers attending from all across the country and a procession that brought Main Street to a standstill for a full hour.

But I think maybe the moment Vernie would have liked best was when an osprey, *Pandion haliaetus*, soared overhead, its wings spread wide, right as her funeral drew to a close. Working to help reintroduce ospreys to West Virginia was one of her proudest accomplishments. She was one of a kind, our Vernie.

I pat the letter of recommendation in my pocket as I kneel beside her grave. In only a week, the grass has already grown back as if it had never been disturbed. I came to tell her that I submitted my application on the Forest Service website today. I think she'd be proud of that, too.

It took me a while after her death to be able to open the letter and read what she'd written. It was somehow like having her back and losing her again all at the same time. But I want to be that person she saw in me.

I make my way back to the front of the cemetery, where Hadrian waits for me in the old truck. He's back working at the farm part-time now, when he's not busy with his other job.

"Hey, love." He reaches over to brush away the tear beneath my eye. "Ready to go home?"

I'm tasked with hanging a birthday banner across the kitchen wall while Linden puts the finishing touches on a spiced walnut persimmon cake, Gran's favorite. I stretch to tack down the top corner, and the chair wobbles beneath me. I topple backward, but Hadrian catches me before my stomach even drops, setting me on my feet but keeping his arm around my waist. His thumb brushes against the snake on my hip.

It's unseasonably warm for mid-November, the last gasp, I'm sure, before the cold really sets in. All the windows are open to counteract the heat of the big, old oven that dominates the kitchen.

"Should we check?" Juniper asks, holding up a persimmon seed.

Old folk wisdom says that cutting open the seed of a ripe persimmon can predict what sort of winter you'll have. If the seed contains the shape of a spoon, expect a lot of snow. If it's a fork, you'll enjoy a mild season, and if it's a knife, get ready for frigid, cutting cold.

Juniper carefully takes a paring knife to one of the seeds. She hasn't felt the presence of James McKeane Darrow since the Bone Tree burned to ash, and she finally seems back to her old self. But there's something unsettling in knowing he's still out there, somewhere.

"What is it?" Linden asks.

Juniper holds it out to show us. "Knife."

"Uh-oh," Sorrel says. She took the early bus home from school this morning to be here for the party. "Guess we better enjoy this sun while we can."

The crunch of gravel out back announces an arrival, and moments later, Daddy and Ethan Miranda walk through the door. Sonny Vane is still at large, but there have been a few sightings up in Ohio. It's only a matter of time until he's caught. I'm sure of it.

"Mama just texted," Sorrel calls. "Gran will be here any second. Everybody hide."

"Look who we found outside," Daddy says, ushering Cole into the kitchen. Linden sets down her spatula and throws herself into Cole's arms. He's back in town for good now, or at least until they start at Georgetown next year.

"Quiet, everyone, I think they're here!" Sorrel drops the curtains back into place and ducks behind the table. "Ethan, get the lights."

Hadrian pulls me into the alcove under the stairs with him, and I have to hold a hand over my mouth so I don't laugh.

"You know I don't like a fuss," Gran is saying over her shoulder to Mama as she opens the door. "It's just a birthday."

"Kind of a big one," Mama counters, switching on the light.

"Happy birthday!" we all shout at once, jumping out from everywhere to surprise her.

"Land sakes alive!" Gran clutches dramatically at her chest. "Likely to be my last one with all this stuff and nonsense. Whose idea was it to scare the daylights out of an elderly woman?" But she's grinning from ear to ear.

Mama laughs, reaching up to rub her thumb across the engraved swan of the shiny gold locket she wears. Missing items have been reappearing all over town lately, much to everyone's confusion. Word is, the newly elected mayor will be spearheading an investigation into a possible gas leak at the old abandoned coal mine. No one else has an explanation for the strange rash of lost memories and missing items, or their equally sudden return.

Daddy steps closer to Mama, and his expression softens at the sight of the necklace. Quietly, he slips his hand into hers and gives it a squeeze. They're taking things slow and figuring out what a new relationship could look like.

By the time Gran blows out her candles after supper, we've finished the cinnamon tea and Sissy has broken into Gran's stash of apple pie moonshine. She pours a measure into my teacup with a wink.

"I have some good news," Daddy announces. "We got a confession for the vandalism at the Harvest Moon." Everyone starts to talk at once, and Daddy holds up his hands to quiet us. "Parker Hammond, one of the assistant coaches at the high school, and Bryson Ivers, along with a couple of their friends from over in Rawbone."

"I bet those were the guys Hammond was with when he hassled me out at the Ick this summer," Linden says, her voice hot with anger.

"Why'd they confess now?" Cole asks from beside her.

"They won't say, but they all seemed pretty convinced that something worse would happen to them if they didn't."

"Know anything about that?" I whisper to Hadrian.

He winks at me, and his eyes flash red. "After I helped fix up the McCoy place, and the sign at the Ick, I may have taken care of some other unfinished business."

I look around at the kitchen full of all the people I love. Gran once told me that I was not a sin eater—that the lies of others didn't define me. But that's exactly what I was doing. And I was letting my anger shape the way I saw the world. I spent so much time focused on the lies that I started to expect them even before they were told. Trust is something we have to learn how to do, like anything else, with a little practice.

"Did you make a wish?" Linden asks.

Gran smiles at her wistfully. "I always do."

A clatter from the front room has us all turning to look down the hall when a woman's voice calls out.

"Apollonia? I'm home!"

ACKNOWLEDGMENTS

STORIES DEVELOP in lots of different ways, like catching a glimpse of something out of the corner of your mind's eye or hearing a snippet of conversation follow you as you wake from a dream. This one started with a spark.

But, perhaps unsurprisingly for Rowan's story, it was a bit stubborn. Second books are notoriously difficult, and this was no exception. Coaxing that initial spark into what became *Lies on the Serpent's Tongue* was a huge growth experience for me as a writer. In the end, stronger than the pressure of creating on a timeline or even the fear of failure is my immense gratitude for those who have invested their efforts, time, and expertise into this book and me as an author.

First, thank you. Yes, *you*, the one holding this book in your hands, or your mind, or your heart. The messages I've received telling me how much these characters and their stories mean to readers have made me so happy (and also a bit terrified—see above). It's because of you that I get to keep doing this thing I love, and I am profoundly grateful.

Pete Knapp, my brilliant agent, thank you for your unerring counsel and keen understanding of the publishing industry. I honestly don't know how you do all that you do, but I'm so grateful to have you in my corner.

Thank you to my editor, Polo Orozco. Your gentle encouragement and thoughtful insight helped me keep going, especially in the moments I wasn't sure if I could. You make me a better writer, full stop.

Thank you to James Akinaka, Brady Emerson, Danielle Presley, Shannon Span, Felicity Vallence, Liz Vaughan, and everyone at the Penguin Young Readers and G. P. Putnam's Sons Books for Young Readers publicity, sales, audio, and marketing teams who helped this story reach its readers. I feel so incredibly lucky to work with some of the very best, most creative, and hardworking people in the industry.

My heartfelt gratitude to Jessica Jenkins for designing another stunningly gorgeous cover and to Imogen Oh for bringing the concept to life better than I could have ever dreamed.

Thank you to the extraordinary team at Park & Fine Literary and Media, especially Stuti Telidevara, Kathryn Toolan, and Ben Kaslow-Zieve. And to everyone on #TeamPete, thank you for being such a supportive and caring group.

To the incredibly supportive bookstore staff and librarians. It is because of your efforts that my books have found their way into the hands of readers, and I appreciate you so very much. An extra heaping scoop of gratitude to my favorite childhood bookstores, Between the Covers in Harbor Springs, Michigan, and McLean & Eakin in Petoskey, Michigan, for the full-circle moment of signing my debut novel among the shelves where my dream began.

To Sasha Peyton Smith and Ginny Myers Sain, who took time out of their very busy schedules to read *Bittersweet in the Hollow* and then wrote such beautiful things about it.

To Andrea Hannah and Rebecca Mix for being the best launch-day conversation partners on top of being incredibly talented and generous writers and the most supportive and kindest of friends.

To Erika Vecchio, Jessica Holmgren, Nick Katsarelas, Julie Bitely, and Amy Kukla Duwe for being the best sort of friends anyone could ever have. Thank you for always cheering on my dreams as if they were your own.

To my sister Josie, who has always been the first to read anything I write (and the only one to read some of it), thank you for being my very first friend and still my very best one. To Ava and Ellie, my favorites of all the Gorls, you're the best part of everything. And David, for keeping us all fed when I was away with the magpies.

And to my family, with all my love. This past year has been full of some of the highest highs and lowest lows, but your love and support is like the warm glow of the light above the kitchen sink that always stays on.